Shepherd's Run

Prodigal Recovery Series #2

Wanda L. Dyson

Last Will and Testament for Rosswell Shepherd

To my son Steven James Shepherd: I leave my Mustang—you always did feel more comfortable in the fast lane. I leave my war medal—never forget what really matters in life: honor, justice, and mercy. And I leave you one-third of Prodigal Fugitive Recovery Agency—use all your talents to make the lives around you easier, fuller, and richer. You have the ability; don't waste it.

Prologue

Why did judges think they could trust the word of a pathological liar, repeat offender, and all around low-life when he promised to show up for court while facing years in prison?

Corey Burns, arrested for sexual assault on a minor, had jumped bail and was on the run, *literally*, on the run. With bounty hunter Steven Shepherd little more than twenty yards behind him, Corey was running as hard as he could, determined to elude Steven's attempts to take him to jail. Ignoring the stitch in his side as he chased Corey down Prospect Street, Steven was forced to jump over trash cans and sidestep the bottles, trash can lids, and flower pots that Corey tossed out to block him.

Brick townhouses over a hundred years old lined the street and the uneven sidewalk merely added to the charm of overflowing flower boxes and brightly painted doors. But it made for perilous running.

"Steven?" His brother's voice came over the mic.

He didn't bother slowing down as he breathlessly answered Nick. "Prospect . . . near Median Court . . . heading west."

"Push him forward. If he turns right on Lorey, Rafe will cut him off. If he turns left, Conner has him."

"And . . . if he goes . . . straight?" Steven asked between heaving breaths.

He heard Nick laugh. "I hope he does."

Steven couldn't help smiling in spite of the effort to stay right on Corey's heels, but fatigue kept the smile from lasting very long. The chase had gone on for the better part of four blocks and he was feeling every step of it. His legs were heavy with the burn of muscles objecting to the strenuous workout. His heart pounded. His lungs heaved. And he was soaked from perspiration.

Wiping the sweat from his face, he pushed himself a little harder. He really wanted to put the cuffs on Corey himself. Rafe, Conner, and Nick always seemed to be the ones to actually bring down the fugitive, and usually, that was just fine with Steven, but Corey had knocked him down a flight of stairs in his attempt to escape and now Steven wanted to make Corey regret that move. Needed to.

Nick and Steven Shepherd owned Prodigal Recovery Agency. Rafe and Conner worked for them. The third Shepherd sibling, sister, Marti, ran the bail bond division of the company.

Up ahead, there was a small bicycle with training wheels sitting at the foot of the stairs leading to one of the townhouses. Corey grabbed it as he ran past and tossed it back at Steven. It missed Steven, but he had to jump over it.

As he landed, his badge, hanging around his neck, flew up to hit him in the face and his foot hit an uneven spot in the pavement. The sharp stab of pain shot up his ankle. Ignoring it, he shoved his badge inside his shirt and kept running, trying hard not to give in to the urge to limp.

A little blue car pulled up to the intersection just as Corey ran past. Steven rolled over the hood of the car, ignoring the honk of the horn by the driver. He stumbled as he came off the car, but regained his footing in two or three steps.

Corey tripped over something and it was the break Steven needed. He jumped forward, snagging Corey by the back of the shirt as the man came up on his feet and the two went down, rolling across the sidewalk.

Grabbing one of Corey's arms, Steven struggled to pull it behind his back so he could cuff him. Pushing one knee in the center of Corey's back, he ignored the grunt of pain as they wrestled on the sidewalk.

Steven felt something slam against his head, knocking him sideways. He lost his hold on Corey as he heard a woman scream, "Get off that boy!"

A young woman stood over him, eyes flashing, lips tight with pure outrage, and her purse slung back and ready to whack him again. Corey jumped to his feet and before Steven could roll out of the way, slammed his steel-toed booted foot down on Steven's knee.

He heard himself howl as the sharp, hot, stabbing pain racked up his leg. Corey took off up the street, laughing, Steven looked up at the woman. "That was no boy. He was a sexual predator that jumped bail."

She took a step back, throwing her hand over her mouth as her eyes went as wide as the handbag she was carried. She must have everything in there but her car. And he wasn't sure about the car. "I'm sorry. I didn't know. He looked so young."

Easing up into a sitting position, Steven hit his mic. "Corey's coming your way. I'm down."

He heard Rafe reply, but couldn't make out the words as the pain grabbed his attention. The woman knelt down. "I really am sorry. I didn't know you were the police. You weren't wearing a badge or anything."

She had brown hair that tinted with red in the bright sun and hazel-green eyes that made him forget all about his pain. He reached inside his shirt and pulled his badge out.

"Oh. I really do apologize."

"That purse should be registered as a lethal weapon."

She smiled and he felt the world tilt a little. Or maybe that was the pain. He couldn't say for sure.

One of the Prodigal Recovery SUV's came screeching to a halt at the curb and Nick jumped out. "Are you okay? What happened?"

The woman slowly stood up. "I'm really sorry. I hit him."

Chapter 1

Three months later
ATF Task Force Office
Baltimore, Md

Alcohol, Tobacco and Firearms Agent Peter Chamberland had done his fair share of undercover work over the years and sometimes, he preferred the stress of maintaining his cover and the constant danger to the boring hours doing paperwork and dealing with the local law enforcement.

His parents had divorced when he was eight. Both had remarried and started new families, leaving him to feel as the odd child out. As soon as he turned eighteen, he joined the military, then went to college, and eventually joined the

ATF. He hadn't spoken to his parents or half-siblings in years. And he didn't miss them. He wasn't one to get sentimental about anyone: he didn't buy birthday gifts or anniversary cards for friends or family. At Christmas, the people closest to him were lucky to even hear a *Happy Holidays* coming from him.

His ex-wife once told him he was the coldest, most detached person she'd ever met. She admitted that it attracted her to him in the beginning because she truly thought she could make a difference in his life. She'd been wrong. And leaving the courthouse after their divorce, she told him she was glad they never made the mistake of bringing children into the world.

He never really liked being married—too many emotional demands he didn't know how to deal with. But he did regret never having children. Maybe he wouldn't have been the best father in the world—heaven knows he had been a lousy husband—but it did bother him from time to time.

So he kept his attachments to a bare minimum. His boss, Benedict, and his team—the closest thing to family he had.

Here it was, late on a Friday night, and Chip and Lisa were still here, working on every lead they could muster up. The rest of the task force were either out on the streets, home with their families, or across the street at the diner getting a late dinner.

"Peter?" Lisa slapped some papers down in front of him. "Guess what?"

Lisa Somers was thirty-four, stood six-foot-one in her bare feet, and was as stunning as any model on a runway. More so, in Peter's opinion, because she actually had meat on her bones. She wore her dark hair long and usually just pulled it back in a ponytail and preferred fatigues and combat boots over a dresses and frills any day of the week.

In a pair of slim jeans and an oversized sweatshirt, she still managed to look like classy as those long legs of hers ate up the distance of the room.

Peter slipped off his reading glasses and rubbed his eyes. "Please don't make me think. I'm not sure, but I think my head will explode."

"We raised some of the serial numbers off the guns we confiscated."

"Good work."

"Oh, it gets better." Lisa edged a hip on to the corner of his desk. "These guns were destroyed. They don't exist."

Peter tossed his glasses down and leaned back in his chair. "Explain that."

"Six months ago, four counties in North Carolina ran a gun exchange program. Bring in a gun and get a free ticket to one of three concerts. They took in about four hundred guns ranging from a .22 all the way up to two TEC-9's and one fully automatic assault rifle. There were also two sawed-off shotguns, and a pellet gun. I guess some kid thought a gun was a gun. Anyway, the guns were combined into one shipment and sent out to a contractor to be destroyed."

She handed him another sheet of paper. "The contractor signed off as receiving the shipment and then sent this back a week later stating that the weapons had all been destroyed and billing the state for his fee."

Peter glanced at her and then looked down at the document in his hand. "So, you're telling me that some of the guns that were supposedly destroyed ended up in this warehouse in Baltimore?"

She shook her head. "No. I'm telling you the *entire shipment* of guns supposedly destroyed ended up here. Look at the total number of guns in that shipment. Four hundred and four. Take out the pellet gun and what did we confiscate? Four hundred and three. Including two TEC-9's and one full automatic assault rifle."

"I want someone to talk to this contractor in Wilmington. Find out how those guns jumped out of the furnace and hitchhiked to Baltimore."

Lisa slid off the desk. "Already on it. I called Raleigh and they have a couple of our guys checking it out. They'll call me as soon as they get something."

"What's Chip working on?"

Newton "Chip" Averton had ten years with the agency and was as sharp as an eagle's beak and had the eyes to go with it. He was thirty-two and married with three young boys, but he looked more like some college football player in search of a frat party somewhere.

"Wonder boy is tracking down shipments from Wilmington to Baltimore, hoping to step on something that smells like a gun shipment." She yawned, covering her mouth. "Boats, trucking lines, rail—he's on them all."

"If there's something to find, he'll find it. Why don't you go home and get some rest. We're not going to crack this tonight."

Lisa rolled her neck, stretching. "I think I will. I didn't get much sleep last night. Call me if anything breaks."

"Foregone conclusion."

"You heading out any time soon?"

"In a few, yeah. Why? Need a ride home?" Her Jeep had gone in for service and she was still waiting for it to be fixed.

"No, the dealer finally gave me a loaner. I threatened them ever so politely."

Peter couldn't help smiling at the thought of Lisa talking to a mechanic with her hand resting on her weapon the entire time. "Remind me to call you in the next time the cleaner loses one of my suit jackets."

Lisa laughed as she gave him a little finger wave and strolled away.

Peter picked up the list of guns on the destruction list. Who took the guns before they went into the furnace? The owner of the business? One of his managers? It had to be someone that had the power to move the shipment out of the warehouse without anyone saying anything or noticing anything, and then sign off that they were destroyed.

He leaned back, rubbing his chin. How many other shipments had been given the same treatment? Did North Carolina always use this same contractor? Were there any other states that used him? And if this wasn't the first time—and Peter was ready to bet his next six months of pay on it—how come this hadn't been caught before? And why had it been caught now?

"Lisa?" Peter called out as he looked up and then realized she was gone.

Chip swung around in his chair. "Did you need something?"

"How is it that we caught this?"

"Great detective work?" Chip grinned as he kicked his feet up to rest on the corner of Lisa's desk.

Peter ignored the sarcasm. "This can't have been the first time they've done this."

"Usually, when the guns are destroyed, a clerk goes in and removes all the serial numbers from the database. The clerk in question, a Mrs. Thelma Hosteller, was called away for her sister's funeral and didn't get it done as quickly as she usually would have. So, when we caught the shipment and ran the serial numbers, bingo…they were still in the system."

Peter thought for a moment. "Is there a list of all the guns destroyed in the last, say, three years?"

"Sure."

"Get it. And then run the serial numbers against all the guns we've confiscated in the same time period. See if we get any hits."

"On it." Chip dropped his feet and swung around in his chair.

Peter slipped his glasses back on and studied the report Lisa had given him. For nearly three years, he and his team had been working on the guns making their way into the hands of the gangs up and down the I-95 corridor, from Washington to Philadelphia. Every time they thought they had the head of the snake—like the Carver brothers last year—they found another snake entirely.

His phone rang and without taking his eyes off the report he was reading, he lifted the receiver. "Chamberlain."

"It's Benedict. I have a lead for you. There's a sale about to happen."

Peter grabbed a pen and shoved papers off his notebook. "Talk to me."

Chapter 2

Monday, 1:10 pm
Prodigal Fugitive Recovery Offices, Baltimore, Md

"Come on, Killer. Put a move on it."

With the little dog trotting along behind him, Steven carried the bags into his brother's office and set them on the coffee table. The warm, oily smell of steak and cheese subs and fries, mixed with the pungent odor of the onion rings had been assaulting him ever since he'd picked them up and it was all he could do not to snatch a few before he got back to the office. But the crew was waiting. And hungry.

Rafe reacted first, pulling his feet off the coffee table and taking in a deep breath. "Oh man, that smells good." Standing about five-eleven in his socks, Rafael Constanza was a forty-year-old former police officer with black hair and dark brown eyes. After a shootout at a robbery where Rafe was shot in the face, Nick lured him over to Prodigal. He loved being a fugitive recovery agent almost as much as he loved women. Even with a nasty scar across his face, he had that whole Latin-come-hither thing going on that Antonio Banderas would envy.

Conner smacked Rafe's hand when he tried to steal an onion ring. "You ordered fries." A former professional wrestler, Matt Conner was the brawn of the team. Bald with hazel eyes and an earring in his ear, he stood about six-six—100% pure muscle. He could intimidate most fugitives with just a look at his beefy hands and arms the size of telephone poles. Steven got a kick out of telling some of the fugitives that Conner was really Vin Deisel, picking up extra money between movies. Surprising how many actually believed the tale.

Rafe grabbed a couple of onion rings anyway, ignoring Conner's rebuke. "Didn't your mom ever tell you to share?"

"Sure. Let me have some of your sandwich."

"Dream on, big guy. But I'll let you have some of my ketchup packets."

Nick picked up a sub and took it back to his desk. He peeled back the paper with a smile similar to the one he used when his wife, Jessica, flirted with him. Anticipation. "Okay, while we're stuffing our faces with all this artery-clogging food we are going to deny to our wives we even ate—"

Rafe tossed a balled-up napkin at Nick. "Excuse me. I don't have a wife to lie to, thank you very much. Just because you and Conner are in marital denial, don't include Steven and me. I can eat this stuff all I want and the only person that I have to lie to is my doctor."

Steven glanced over at Conner. He had to envy the man. Ria was a more than just a wife to Conner. She was his partner in life. Not the least bit intimidated by him, she would go nose to nose with him when she thought he was wrong, and give him all the support in the world when she knew he was right. She worked when money was tight and stayed home to take care of home and hearth when it wasn't. And if she heard someone talking trash about her man, well . . . lookout . . . she wasn't afraid of confrontations and could be as scary as Conner in her own way.

A partner. That's what he wanted. So why couldn't he find her?

Marti appeared in the doorway. "You threw a party and didn't invite me?" She reached over and snatched one of Conner's onion rings. "Nick, I need a ride over to Intake."

"What's wrong with your car?"

She eyed Conner's food again. Conner pulled it all into his lap and shifted his body. She laughed. "Like that would stop me." Then she turned back to Nick. "I have a couple of bonds to write and one of them asked me to give them a ride home and I agreed."

"Why?" Nick popped the top on his Mountain Dew. "You know better than that."

"Look, don't go all big brother on me, okay? He was picked up for writing bad checks, not rape and murder, but I would still feel better having one of the guys with me. Can I have Conner?"

Conner snorted. "I'm going to tell Ria you said that."

"Like I'm afraid of your wife."

Rafe picked up the second half of his sub. "*I'm* afraid of his wife."

"That's because she isn't bamboozled by your slick attempts at being charming. She knows you're just a lonely boy looking for a mommy."

"Hey! That's low. Really low. And I was going to share my fries with you."

Nick pointed at Steven. "You take Marti. You're almost done eating."

"Why me?" Steven shoved a fry in his mouth.

"Why not you? Afraid some woman will hit you with her purse?" Nick laughed as he dumped his trash and reached for his coat. "Reminder. I'm out the rest of the day. Rafe is in charge. Any problems, get him to solve them and don't bother me with it."

Steven jerked to his feet, brushing crumbs from his shirt. "Let's go, Marti."

"Hey, what's your problem?" Nick asked as Steven headed for the door.

Steven glanced back at his brother. "You."

Marti came running out of the building, juggling her coat, purse, and stack of files. "There's no point in you going if I'm not with you."

He yanked the SUV's door open and climbed in behind the wheel without a word. By the time Marti climbed in, he had the engine started, his seatbelt clipped, and was slipping his sunglasses on.

"You want to tell me what set you off?" she asked. "And don't say *nothing*."

"Last time I checked, I was a full partner in this business."

"Yes. So?"

"So, I'm tired of Nick treating me like some hired gopher."

"Oh, come on, Steven. It's not like that." She grabbed the door as he slammed to a stop at a red light.

"It's exactly like that. I'm expected to run for coffee, go get lunch, play driver, make calls, take messages and next week, he'll probably have me doing all the filing."

"I don't think Jenna will allow that. She has a fairly tight grip on her position as office manager."

"She'll do what Nick tells her just like everyone else around there."

"He just doesn't see you as bounty hunter material. Come on, Steven. You were never cut out for this business. You were a professional student, collecting degrees."

"Dad left me a third of this business. He trusted me to take my place here. It's Nick who doesn't want me around."

"Be real, brother mine. If you hadn't inherited a third of Prodigal, you wouldn't be here. So tell me, if Dad were still alive, where would you be right now?"

"I don't know but I bet I wouldn't be an errand boy."

Chapter 3

Tuesday, 5:30 pm
First-Rate U-Store Facility, South Baltimore, Md

Andrea drove her car just beyond unit four-twenty-seven and parked. She didn't exactly like the look of the men she was supposed to meet, but she didn't plan on staying long enough to get to know them. Picking up the key to the storage unit lock from the console, she climbed out of the car.

The street lights were just coming on, having very little effect on that twilight mood between early evening and night. There was a slight chill in the air that promised spring was about to hit with all the warmth and beauty it had been withholding for months. Andrea hunched down in her jacket and wished she was wearing a heavier coat.

A young man in torn jeans and a down jacket leaned against the door of a dark panel van. His olive complexion was so light, she wasn't sure if he was Latin or Italian, but he had an attitude that dared anyone to ask. His partner was shorter and stockier, with a face that looked as if he practiced being mean and nasty in front of a mirror every night, but still hadn't quite mastered the art.

As she approached, the one in the torn jeans straightened, giving her a look that sent chills down her spine and asked, "Where's Paul?"

"He couldn't make it." She held the key out to him. "He asked me to give you this."

The man took it and tossed it to his partner. Then he reached down and picked up a metal briefcase sitting between his feet and handed it to her. "Tell Paul that if I'm happy, we'll do business again."

She wanted to ask him what business, but he turned and walked toward the rear of the truck, so she returned to her car, opened the door and tossed the case into the back seat. It didn't make any sense at all. Paul said this was his cousin, here to pick up a dresser he had in storage. So what was this about business?

Whatever it was, she was suddenly quite sure she didn't want to know. Climbing quickly into the car, she put the car in drive and hit the gas.

And almost hit a big black Expedition as it came around the corner and stopped right in front of her. She would have yelled at the driver, but the flashing lights and sirens froze her in place. Men in black jumped out, guns drawn, screaming at her to get out of the car, but she couldn't wrap her mind around what was happening. One of the men stood in front of the car, feet apart, aiming a gun straight at her face. Another yanked the car door open and pulled her out, slamming her face first to the pavement.

"Please. Why are you doing this?"

She started crying as her cheek was ground into the concrete, biting into her flesh and the officer pressed his knee into the small of her back as he pulled her arms hard enough to make them feel as though they were breaking. "What are you doing? Stop it! You're hurting me!"

Two officers hauled her to her feet. She lifted her head and looked straight into the eyes of a man wearing an

ATF jacket. He had the metal briefcase open on the hood of her car and glared at her with pale eyes like shards of ice. "Quite a haul."

She glanced over at the briefcase and gasped at the stacks of money. "That's not mine."

"Yeah and I'm the Easter Bunny." He snapped the case shut and picked it up. "Take her in."

Chapter 4

Wednesday, 12:47 pm
Baltimore Central Booking and Intake Center

"I am *not* selling stolen guns! This is all a big mistake." Andrea Morrow twisted her hands in her lap, hoping the two men across the scarred table would believe her. The alternative was unthinkable. "I don't know the first thing about guns."

The interrogation room—no, wait, they call it an *interview* room now—was fairly new and freshly painted. Someone, somewhere, decided the word interrogation sounded too harsh, so now they used the word interview. Well, it didn't feel like an interview and they could call a pig sty a mud puddle all day long and it would still smell like a pig sty.

"Miss Morrow, you were recorded taking a briefcase full of money from known gun dealers and giving them the keys to a storage unit that contained a large quantity of stolen weapons. Now, what part of that recording is false?"

Perspiration beaded on her forehead and upper lip. It was all happening again. And once again, no one would believe her. Feeling light-headed, she looked up at Agent Chamberland, or The Ice Man, as she was started to think of him with his white blond hair and cool blue eyes. He never showed any emotion at all—just stared at her with those pale-as-glass eyes as if he couldn't wait to step on her and crush her like a bug.

"All of it," she insisted. "Maybe that's what you see, but there's an explanation. I didn't know what was in that storage unit. I *swear*."

Agent Chamberland stood there, arms folded across his chest, an immovable force that seemed determined to crush her. "You're a kindergarten teacher, is that right?"

"Yes," she said, leaning forward. "At Millway. I've been there five years."

She a ran a finger over a deep scratch in the Formica tabletop and thought about the small tables, perfect for the four and five-year-olds, in her bright classroom. The pictures of baby animals on the bulletin board that the children had collected and hung with such pride. Would everything she worked for crumble into dust? She swallowed back the scream.

"And your boyfriend called you and asked you to do him a favor?"

She nodded at Chamberland. "We were supposed to have dinner. I was home when he called and said he had to work late." She pushed her hair back behind her ears. "Look, I've explained this at least twenty times already. Why don't you just call Paul. He'll explain what happened."

"We've tried to call him, Miss Morrow." Chamberland scratched his chin with his thumb. "The number you gave us went to a prepaid cell phone. No one is answering and we can't trace it. We went to the address you gave as his employment. There is no such company as Forton and Conrad in that building. And no Paul Roush works for *any* company in that building. So, let's try this again."

What? She knew he was there. She clasped her hands together as if it would keep her from shattering into pieces. "Paul asked me to come by his office and pick up a set of keys to give his cousin who needed something out of Paul's storage unit. He met me out in front of the building and gave me the keys and the address. Please go ask around the building again. Maybe you just missed him the first time."

"Do you have a picture of Paul?" the other agent asked.

She thought for a moment and then her heart sank. "No. We haven't been dating that long. I can't think of any pictures he'd be in. Maybe one of the people at the party where we met at might know him well enough to have a picture."

"That's convenient. Another rabbit trail." Chamberland glared at her and if his eyes were cold enough to freeze water before, they were enough to give her frostbite now. "I'm getting a little tired of the dead ends, Miss Morrow. As we can't find any legitimate information on a Paul Roush matching your details, I suggest you start telling us the truth."

Andrea stared at Chamberland and then at the agent sitting across from her. Realization began to emerge through the confusion and the fear. She had only met Paul six weeks ago. How well did she really know him? He said he worked on North Seventh and she'd picked him up there once when his car broke down, in front of the building. She never questioned anything he'd told her. Why would she? He was nice-looking, funny, thoughtful in ways a lot of men aren't, and had never pressured her for anything. In fact, he'd never even kissed her. He claimed he had been swept away the first time he saw her. If he lied about where he worked, what else was a lie?

Everything?

Dropping her head, she closed her eyes. Her heartbeat echoed and her breathing filled her ears, muffling everything except the nagging fear that her life as she knew it was over.

Finally, she looked up at Chamberland as the tears welled up in her eyes. "I've been set up, haven't I?"

*

Wednesday, 2:25 pm
Baltimore Central Booking and Intake Center

"Prodigal Recovery," Steven said, slapping the paperwork for Turner down on the counter in front of an officer. "Bringing in a prisoner."

The officer took the paperwork and paged through it. "You'll have a little wait. I'll have an officer take him down to holding until we're ready."

Surprising. A few years ago, the wait was expected. The old booking center had been nicknamed—and not so affectionately—as Baltimore's Abu Ghraib. Holding cells meant to hold eight prisoners were holding up to eighteen. Prisoners were forced to lie in vomit, and not always their own. A third of those arrested and brought in were held and released without being charged because they had been held too long without a hearing. Most took it in stride, but when a burglary suspect with seventeen prior convictions was released because he didn't receive his required hearing within twenty-four hours, the city was outraged. The city finally filed charges against the Department of Public Safety and Correctional Services and a new Central Booking and Intake Center was built. And it was state of the art.

Now, when someone was arrested, they were no longer taken to the nearest police station. Everyone went straight to Central Booking. Here they were interviewed, photographed, given a bar-coded wristband that enabled computers and cameras to track his every movement, fingerprinted with the new electronic fingerprint scanner, and then placed in one of the holding cells. A Court Commissioner would look over the charges and decide on bail. Then the person would appear by video-telephone before a local judge, who would review the charges and the amount of bail and approve or deny it. If bail was denied or if the person was unable to make bail, they'd be moved from a holding cell to a prison cell.

Fast, efficient, and far more law enforcement friendly.

The desk officer stood up and stretched, looking over at the leash Steven held, then down at his dog. "You can't have him in here."

"Know somewhere I can leave him?"

The officer tilted his head in disbelief. Steven shrugged. "I know, I know—but my ride just left and I'm stuck." They had been just a block from Intake when Rafe informed Steven that he had an errand to run. And that he wasn't going to take the little Bichon with him. If he'd told Steven before they headed over to Intake, he could have had

Nick take Killer back to the office and Marti would have watched him until Steven returned. Now—

"Not my problem, Shepherd. Get the dog out of here."

Steven handed his fugitive over to a guard and walked Killer outside. "What am I going to do with you?"

Nick had found the little dog—cold, wet, and hungry—abandoned in a parking lot one day and unable to leave him to his fate, turned him over to Jenna to take to Animal Control. Steven took a liking to the little guy and kept him. Of course, not knowing the first thing about owning a dog, he had allowed the canine to take over his life. Now, the dog suffered from separation anxiety and if Steven left him alone too long, he tore up everything he could find. After losing the leg to one of his kitchen chairs, he decided it was just easier to take the dog everywhere with him.

The dog yipped and jumped up on Steven's leg. Leaning down, Steven picked him up. "Now, cut that out. No licking. My reputation is taking one already, you being here."

When his cell phone rang, he pulled it out and answered it without even looking at the screen. "Yah-lo"

"Steven?"

Brace yourself. The only time his ex-fiancé, ever called was when she was in some scrape or another and needed either money, assistance, or both. Inevitably, Brandy called at least twice a year every year since they broke up some eight years ago. When he'd first met her, she was a secretary who adored animals, camping, action movies, and jazz. Steven found her to be smart, beautiful, and fun-loving. Until the night he realized money was missing from his wallet. He asked her about it. She denied any wrong doing. And the melodrama began. Her boss was harassing her. Her ex-boyfriend was stalking her. Her neighbor was imposing on her. Her car broke down. Her landlord was threatening to evict her. She couldn't afford to go to the doctor. When he finally put his foot down, two of his credit cards disappeared from his dresser and within days had been maxed out to the tune of nearly fifteen thousand dollars. And he felt obligated to pay it off since he'd been stupid enough to leave the credit cards in a place where she could find them. Not that he expected her to search his bedroom, but a thief is a thief.

"Steven, darling. Are you there?"

"I'm here but working. Can we talk another time?"

Immediately, her calm tone flew out the window and the sobbing began. "I'm so sorry. I hate to call you like this."

Yeah, right. But you didn't know where else to turn.

"I just didn't know who else to turn to."

"Brandy, stop the theatrics and hear me. I told you the last two times we went through this—no. No money. None. Nada. Not a dollar. You still owe me for the credit cards."

"I never took those credit cards," she sobbed heavier into the phone. "I can't believe you'd leave me in jail like this."

"Jail? Why are you in jail?" He knelt down, placing the dog on the sidewalk and encouraged him to walk as Steven paced.

"Some guy lied and told the police I stole his checkbook and wrote a bunch of checks."

Which is what he should have done, but couldn't bring himself to put a woman in jail. Sap.

She sobbed heavier. "Please come help me. Please. I don't know anyone who can help me the way you can."

Interpretation: I've called everyone I know and they're all fed up with me and won't help me and I figure you always say no but then you always come through, so you will this time, too.

"Where are you now?"

It was amazing how fast her sobbing stopped when she thought she'd gotten what she wanted. "I'm in Laurel."

"If I can get away, I'll see what I can do."

It only took her a split second to hear the stipulation and the sobbing started all over again. "But, Steven. You can't just leave me here! There are criminals in this place. I don't belong here."

And at that moment, Steven reached his limit. "You know what, Brandy? Stealing from friends and acquaintances makes you just as much a criminal as the ones that steal from strangers. It's still stealing."

"But I didn't," she whined.

"Considering the fact that you stole from me, I find it hard to believe you didn't do this." But doubt began to nag at him. What if she *was* innocent? What if she really was being blamed for something she didn't do?

"You mean you aren't going to come get me out of here? You're going to make me stay here?"

"Maybe if someone had left you there the first time someone pressed charges you wouldn't be there now."

"You know what? I was really sorry that I borrowed money from you, but now I wouldn't pay you back if you were the last man on earth!"

Click.

The rage in her voice lingered long after she was gone. Wow. She actually admitted to taking the money. Of course, she called it borrowing rather that stealing. Maybe he should call Marti and just let her know about Brandy. Let her make the call. Then again, he'd have to warn his sister that Brandy wasn't exactly known for keeping her word.

He was mulling over his choices when he heard a familiar voice behind him. "You guys at Prodigal don't have anything better to do than hang around here like it's a dog park?"

Steven turned to face ATF Agent Peter Chamberland. As always, the arrogance that wrapped around his cool ruthlessness had Steven taking a step back. "What are you doing here in the trenches? I figured you'd be briefing the President on your outstanding job with Carver by now."

Chamberland's lips curled in what could only be identified as an amused smile. "Cute." He reached over and scratched the dog behind his ears. "And I'm not surprised Nick demoted you to dog catcher."

It was a direct hit but Steven didn't want Chamberland to know how deep that hurt went. "Seriously, Baltimore is a little out of your usual stomping grounds, isn't it?"

"We go anywhere, anytime." Chamberland glanced around. "Why are you standing out here?"

"I just turned in a fugitive, but they made me take Killer here out of the building."

"Killer?" Chamberland smiled with near-warmth as he scratched at the Bichon's chin. Then he glanced over at the Expedition parked at the curb and jerked his head. In response, a young man climbed out from behind the wheel and hurried over.

"Sir?"

"Watch this dog. Mr. Shepherd and I need to talk."

The young agent stared up at Chamberland as if he couldn't quite wrap his mind around the fact that he'd just gone from ATF agent to dog sitter.

"You have a problem following orders, Nebel?"

"No, sir."

Steven set the dog down and handed Agent Nebel the leash. "Be careful. He thinks he's a Rottweiler."

The agent shot Steven a look and then walked Killer down the street.

Chamberland led Steven back into the building. "We've been tracking shipments of illegal guns. We know that at least three shipments have come in through the Baltimore ports. If we know of three, there are more."

Steven glanced up as two young men, handcuffed and cursing, were being led into the fingerprint room. "What does this have to do with me?"

"We caught some of those involved."

"But not the ringleader?"

Chamberland frowned and shifted his gaze to look down the hall. "I wish. I think he suspected we were on to him." Chamberland turned back to Steven. "We caught one young woman that we think was being used."

"By?"

"We don't know for sure. She claims she was just asked by her boyfriend to drop off keys and got swept up in all this. Thing is—we can't find any trace of this so-called boyfriend."

Steven stopped at the vending machines and fished down in his pockets for a wad of singles. Chamberland waved him off. "It's on me."

"You're making me nervous, being so nice and all."

Chamberland didn't even smile as he fed a couple of singles into the machine and punched his selection, then nodded for Steven to make his choice. "I don't know whether she's an innocent being framed, or just a very good actress."

"So what does this have to do with me?" Steven punched for a bottle of water and then dug it out of the chute.

"If she is innocent, she's going to need some help. I just figured you could bail her out."

Steven tipped his head back and drank some of the water, taking his time while he weighed Chamberland's words. After the way the ATF agent handled Krystal's abduction last spring, Steven wasn't inclined to trust him. "Just playing good Samaritan, is that it?"

"Not exactly, but I don't want to see an innocent kindergarten teacher go to prison simply because she didn't have good taste in men."

Steven studied the man for a few minutes. Those pale blue eyes gave away nothing. Or maybe there was nothing there to find. He had a hard time telling the difference. Give him a company's yearly report and he'd have dissected in minutes, but people weren't nearly as easy to understand as numbers.

"Well, it won't hurt anything to talk to her. Where is she?" Steven twisted the cap on his water.

"Follow me."

Chamberland led Steven to interview room three where he could see her through a two-way mirror. The room was dim and it took a second for Steven's eyes to adjust. The only light in the room was coming through the two-way mirror from the room next door. He stepped up to the mirror.

The woman could have been in her early twenties or early thirties, it was hard to tell. She sat alone at a table, hands in her lap, her light brown hair tousled from hours of running her hands through it, dressed in an understated brown tweed jacket over a tan sweater and brown slacks.

This was not what he expected. Not that he was exactly sure *what* he thought he was going to see, but this unassuming young woman wasn't it. When she lifted her head, he hoped to see some subtle sign of menace or malice. Her make-up was smeared from crying, and her nose red from the rough, low-grade tissues. When he looked into her eyes, he felt a jolt. *No way. Not her.*

Steven grabbed the agent by the arm. "This is a joke, right?"

"What are you talking about?"

"That woman is as involved in criminal activities as I am!"

Chamberland looked amused as he folded his arms across his chest. "And you know that from what? Two seconds of evaluation? Wow, Shepherd…I want you on my team. We could cut interrogations down to minutes instead of hours."

"How could you even arrest her?" Steven didn't have much respect for Chamberland before. He had even less now.

"I know you don't think the little schoolteacher fits the mold of a hardened criminal, but remember, we have the evidence. So if you believe she was framed, play the hero and help her out."

"If you know she was framed, why are you even bothering to charge her? Why not just cut her loose?"

Chamberland tightened his jaw and glared through the ice blue eyes until his stern expression softened. He let out a sigh and tapped a finger on Steven's chest. "I repeat, I have the evidence. But I asked you to help her, didn't I? I could have just tossed her into the system and let it eat her alive."

"Yeah, yeah. You're just a peach of a guy." Steven knew something didn't feel right, but he couldn't say for sure exactly what was bothering him. On one hand, he didn't trust Chamberland's apparent benevolence. On the other hand, the schoolteacher *had* been dating a criminal. And experience had taught him that women saw the words *Use Me* written across his forehead. He needed someone to step in and make the right call.

He pulled out his cell phone and dialed the office. "Jenna? Is Marti around? I have a bail that needs to be written."

"Sorry, Steven. She had to go down to Prince George County to write two bails and then she was heading over to Montgomery County. I don't expect her back for a couple of hours."

"Okay. Never mind." Well, that didn't work. He needed some serious help. He scrolled through the address book and dialed a number. "Is Liz there? I need a favor."

Less than a minute later, he heard a click and then she came on the line. "Let me get this straight. You take me out to dinner, say you'll call, and it's been what? Three months?"

Steven cringed. He'd met Liz at a birthday party for a friend and after talking to her for fifteen minutes, had asked her out. Two nights later, they went out to dinner and then to a jazz club. Had it really been three months? Okay, he owed the woman some flowers. "I'm sorry."

"Well, if you're calling to ask me out again, the answer is no."

Glancing at the ATF agent, Steven ducked his head and strolled further down the hall. "I'm really, really sorry, Liz. I had a good time, honest, I did. It's just that, well, uhm—"

He heard her laugh, which only confused him. "Steven, Steven, Steven. Honey, I didn't feel any more of a spark than you did. I'm just having a little fun at your expense. Sorry about that. Now, what did you call for?"

Taking a deep breath, Steven glanced back over at Chamberland then stared down at the floor and lowered his voice. "I have a young woman here at Intake that needs a really good attorney, so I'm calling you."

Checking to make sure Chamberland was still at a distance, Steven casually strolled another few feet away. "I know this sounds complicated, but you should meet her. I know I'm not the best judge of people, but I think she's innocent. Even the ATF doesn't think she's guilty but they're not dropping the charges and they asked me to bail her out and—"

"Whoa, slow down. The ATF? What has she been charged with?"

"They're saying she was selling stolen weapons and they have her on tape making the deal and everything."

"But they don't think she's guilty?"

"No. So they asked me to bail her out."

"The ATF came to you and asked you to bail out someone they're charging?"

"Yep."

"Something smells funny and it isn't my lunch. I'll be there in ten."

"Thanks, Liz." But she had already hung up. Steven closed his phone and stuck it back in the belt holster.

"Who did you just call?" Agent Chamberland asked when Steven strolled back over.

"A friend of mine. An attorney."

Chamberland's lips thinned out as he folded his arms across his chest. "I didn't ask you to call an attorney. I asked you to bail her out. The state will provide her with an attorney."

The agent's reaction sent little tremors up Steven's personal judgment radar. "Is there something you're not telling me, Agent?"

"No." The agent unfolded his arms and took a sip from his drink. "I just don't want to be tied up here any longer than I have to be."

"Then what's the big deal?"

"No big deal, Shepherd. I just don't feel like having some attorney complicating what should be a simple enough deal. You bail her out and before she has to appear in court, I find the man that set her up and she's in the clear."

It sounded simple enough but Steven still felt a little uneasy. "I doubt Liz is going to complicate your life."

"She better not."

"All she's going to do is make sure the system doesn't railroad this woman."

"Railroad?" Chamberland sputtered out a quick laugh. "You read too many novels, Shepherd. I'm out here asking you to help this woman, not in some dark hallway paying off a judge to convict her of some trumped-up crime."

"Then what's the big deal? Liz goes in and pleads her innocent. Your people claim she's guilty. The judge sets bail. I bail her out. Done deal. You'll be out of here in under ten."

"You better hope I am, because last time I checked, I still have custody of your dog." Chamberland peeled back his lips in a sorry excuse for a smile and smacked Steven on the back in what appeared to be a friendly attempt at camaraderie.

As he watched the agent stroll off down the hall, Steven couldn't shake the feeling that he'd just been played.

Chapter 5

Wednesday, 2:55 pm
Holding Cell- Baltimore Booking and Intake Center

Andrea was tired of pacing the small cell, but she couldn't sit still. She hated the smell of ammonia trying to mask the urine and vomit, the starkness of the room, the lack of privacy, and the endless noise—the slamming of cell doors, the officers yelling at inmates, and the vulgar screaming, pleading, and threats from the cells.

And she hated not knowing what was happening. Her entire life had been shoved aside for this one moment in time and it terrified her that she had no control over anything. She was being charged for a crime she didn't commit. She was locked up in a cell she hated. She was without friends, family, or a kind face.

And she was exhausted.

Those agents had kept going at her all evening, all night, and into the early morning hours. After a two hour break, they'd started up again. When one would stand up to leave, giving her the impression they were done with her, another would come in and start the questioning all over again. Her brain was now mush and every bone in her body ached.

Still, she couldn't stop the jitters that kept her pacing.

The door opened and she turned, not even sure what to expect anymore. Had they come to take her before a judge? But it was Chamberland again. Ignoring him, she went back to pacing.

"How long have you known Marco?"

"I've never heard of a Marco." She reached the wall and turned, packing back the tiny length of the cell.

"Where did you first meet him?"

"I've never met him."

"You were selling guns to his people. Of course you know him."

Andrea turned to face him, folding her arms, clenching her fists. "What part of *I-don't-know-him* don't you get? I never met him. I've never heard of him. And I wasn't selling anything to him. And I sure hope your career isn't hinging on this case or you might find yourself flipping hamburgers at McDonalds."

Chamberland's eyes widened. "So, she has a little backbone after all. I was wondering how long you could keep up the mousy little schoolmarm act."

Andrea desperately wanted to lunge out at him, scratch his face, smack that supercilious smile off his face, crush those black sunglasses under her heel, but she'd never been that tough or that strong. Just once she'd like to strike back at a tormentor. Just once, she'd like to give as good as she was getting. "If I had any real backbone, you wouldn't keep pecking at me like a chicken on a corn cob."

"What would you do? If you were a tough chick?" Chamberland folded his arms and leaned his shoulder against the wall. "I'm just curious."

"Why are you doing this? Is your life so small and lonely that the only time you can feel anything is when you're bullying someone smaller and weaker? Did you get bullied a lot in grade school?"

She saw the muscle in his jaw twitch and knew she'd hit her target. Unfortunately, it didn't give her nearly as much satisfaction as she thought it would.

Chamberland pushed off the wall and moved toward her, forcing her to back away. "I'm going to give you one more chance to come clean with me. Where is Marco?"

"I don't *know* any Marco. I never sold any guns. I'm not a criminal." She hated the fact that tears pooled in her eyes, but there was nothing left in her to hold them back. "Please leave me alone."

Chamberland reached for the door and then stilled. He glanced over his shoulder at her. "Fair warning. You'll make bail and be released, but this is just starting. Not only will I be watching every move you make, but I can guarantee you, there are some nasty men out there that are going to want to make sure you continue to keep your mouth shut."

Wednesday, 3:10 pm
Baltimore Central Booking and Intake Center

Steven felt a hand on his shoulder and expecting it to be Liz, whirled around with a smile on his face.

"Wow. I've never known you to be so happy to see me."

It wasn't Liz.

"Rafe. Thought you were someone else. Here to pick me up?"

Rafe dug a roll of mints out of pocket. "Yeah. Ready?"

"No." Steven glanced at his watch. Where was Liz? He wanted her to have time to meet with her new client for a few minutes before going in. She'd said ten minutes and it had been nearly forty. "Hold on a minute." Pulling out his phone, he called her office.

"I'm sorry, Mr. Shepherd. I don't think she expected it to take this long. But she's on her way."

"Okay, thanks." He closed his phone as the hearing room door opened and people began to file in. "I called an attorney for someone."

"An attorney? For who?"

Steven quickly explained about Andrea Morrell and Chamberland. Rafe started laughing. "You mean the same woman that clocked you that day with her purse and allowed Corey to bust up your ankle and put you a brace for six weeks? And now she's in trouble and you're all in a tizzy to help her out? Steven, listen to me. There are some women—and quite a few of them at that—that have the word *trouble* written across their lives. Why do you always feel you have to save them?"

His words stung a little. "She needs an attorney and I called one. It's no big deal."

"Just checking." He nodded toward the hearing room. "They've opened the doors. We have to get in there."

Steven hesitated a second. "Go on in. I'll be there in a sec."

"Make it quick."

"If my guy comes up and I'm not in there, you can handle it."

With a nod, Rafe left.

And then, as if in answer to prayer, she came striding around the corner like a general heading into battle. She stopped in front of him, tilted her head, and looked him over. "It's a different look for you, but I like it. How are you, Steven?"

She was a tiny little thing—barely standing five-foot-nothing—but she had about seven feet of attitude in her big blue eyes. Her auburn hair was pulled back in a simple ponytail that still managed to look elegant, or maybe it was the black power suit and white silk blouse that screamed expensive. She wasn't what he would call beautiful in the classic sense, but she had nice overall features—beautiful eyes, wide mouth, thin nose, high cheekbones—that came together in a pleasing enough manner that could draw a person in. She was successful, she was ambitious, and she was a good person. So why couldn't he have fallen for her?

"Good to see you, Liz."

"I need to see my client." Short, sweet and to the point. Talk about the proverbial what-you-see-is-what-you-get.

As soon as he introduced her to Chamberland, they dismissed Steven and headed to the holding cell area. As Steven sat down in the back of the hearing room with Rafe, he stretched out his legs and folded his arms across his chest, keeping his gaze on the monitors in the front of the room.

Rafe slouched down in his chair, getting comfortable. "So what's the deal between you and this woman?"

"Who, Liz? I took her out once, but nothing really clicked."

"Not the lawyer. The client."

"Nothing. I just felt sorry for her. Rafe? Am I sucker when it comes to women and sob stories?"

Rafe held out his hand and started ticking off his fingers. "Madelyn, Brandy, Raye, Deeanne, Susanne. Need I go on? If it's female and in trouble, you rush in where most men would know better than to tread."

"Point taken."

Rafe's grin just grew wider. "That's okay. Steven Shepherd, super-hero, is here to save the day."

"And you're trying to tell me that if you were in my shoes, you wouldn't do everything in your power to help her?"

With a little nudge on the shoulder, Rafe sat up a little straighter. "Of course I would. I'm just jealous I didn't see her first."

"I'm telling your girlfriend you said that."

"You do and you'll never see that little dog of yours again."

"Killer! I have to go get him." Steven held out his hand. "Give me the keys to the SUV. I'll put him in there until we're done."

"You are not putting that dog in my SUV. Last time you left him in there, he chewed the armrest." But he handed over the keys anyway.

By the time Steven found the agent walking his dog, put the Bichon in the Prodigal SUV and rushed back in, Rafe was in the hallway. He held up some papers as Steven came jogging up. "We're done."

"Thanks. Has Andrea been charged yet?"

Rafe folded the papers and shoved them down his back pocket. "Andrea, is it? Wow. First names already."

"Miss Morrow. Whatever."

"No. Not yet. I gather we're waiting."

Steven didn't even bother answering as he brushed past Rafe.

"Yes, we're waiting," Rafe mimicked as he followed Steven back into the hearing room. "I hope you don't mind, Rafe. You didn't have anything planned, did you, Rafe?"

Steven shot Rafe a look. "It won't take long. Relax."

"Steven?"

"What?"

"What's with this woman?"

"She hit me to protect what she thought was an innocent boy." Steven turned to look over at Rafe. "Now, does that sound like the kind of woman that would be brokering stolen guns?"

Andrea couldn't stop shaking. Not even when her lawyer reached over and squeezed her hand. It was all happening—she could see it, hear it, understand it—but it was like walking through a bad dream and not being able to find your way out.

When they asked her if she was going to plead guilty or not guilty, it was easy to say not guilty, but when the judge set bail at a hundred thousand dollars, she felt like the world had come to an end.

And all because she'd broken her rule and dated a man she didn't really know. Didn't know at all, as it turns out.

Andrea and her attorney were taken to an interview room and left alone. There were three chairs around a metal table and a video camera mounted up in the corner. "I don't have a hundred thousand dollars. I don't even know how I'm going to pay you."

Liz just patted her on the hand. "Don't concern yourself about that right now. Your bail bondsman is already here and ready to take care of the bail. As for my fee, it's pro bono."

The woman's kindness brought a new wave of tears. "Thank you. One of these days, I'll pay you. Maybe a little at a time."

There was a knock on the door and a man stuck his head in. She watched her attorney greet him, taking in the wavy brown hair, the lean frame, and the quick smile. He stood there in a brown leather jacket, blue denim shirt, with his hands tucked in the pockets of his jeans. Since he had a badge hanging around his neck, she dismissed him as another police officer. But then her attorney brought him over and introduced him as Steven Shepherd from Prodigal Fugitive Recovery. Recognition sparked.

"Wait. I know you." Andrea gently pulled her hand from his. "You're that man. The bounty hunter."

He smiled gently and pulled out some papers from inside his jacket. "We also have a bail bond division. Why don't we have a seat and fill these out so we can get you out of here."

"I'm really am sorry about that day."

"Don't worry about it. I'm all healed."

Liz raised an eyebrow. "Sounds like a story I'd enjoy hearing."

Steven laughed. "I'll tell you later. Right now, let's get Miss Morrow fixed up."

"I didn't do this," she explained as she slowly sank down in the cold metal chair. "It's all a mistake."

"I believe you." He clicked his pen and started asking her questions. Full name, address, place of employment, birth date, nearest relative, names and phone numbers of two close friends.

She answered all the questions, but her mind was still stuck on her place of employment. "They wouldn't let me call in this morning to let the principal know I wouldn't be there. I don't know if I still have a job."

Steven looked up from the paperwork. "When did they bring you in?"

"About six last night."

He looked over at Liz and then back to her. "You mean to tell me they've had you here almost twenty-four hours and never allowed you a phone call?"

Liz started pacing. "When I get through with them, they'll be lucky if they aren't asking you to write bail bonds for their own sorry selves."

"I wouldn't bail Chamberland out of juvenile detention." Steven went back to writing. "Okay, bail is set for one hundred thousand, which means you're going to have to come up with ten thousand."

"Dollars?" Andrea felt that bubble of panic again. "I don't have ten thousand dollars!"

"What about your parents? A friend?"

She shook her head as the tears started spilling over again. "I don't know anyone with that kind of money."

Steven sat back in his chair and stared at her for a few minutes. "Okay, never mind that for now. We'll figure something out."

"What do you mean, never mind for now?" Liz placed both hands on the table and leaned forward. "If she doesn't have it, she doesn't have it. And I want her out of here."

He looked at Andrea—her eyes filled with tears, pleading for someone to help her. Then at Liz—her eyes filled with fury and pleading for him to help. He was trapped and he knew it. And he'd more than likely live to regret it. "Okay, okay. I'll cover it for now. My sister will more than likely have my head for this."

Chapter 6

Wednesday, 5:32 pm
Prodigal Fugitive Recovery Offices, Baltimore

"You did what?" Marti slammed a file folder down on her desk as she came up out of her chair. "Bad enough that you wrote a bail bond without consulting me, but you put ten grand of our money on the line? What in the world were you thinking?"

Fifteen years ago, his little sister, Marti, had simply walked out the door one day and disappeared. Six months ago, she had shown up at Steven's house, determined to help Nick get his daughter back safe and sound.

Amazingly, she was still here. Nick had given her the job of overseeing all the bail bonding in the company and it was a job she took very seriously. They all knew it was Nick's way of trying to keep Marti from running away again, but it was one of those things no one ever spoke out loud. Still, there was nothing that said he couldn't write a bail if he wanted to. He was licensed, same as she was.

Steven picked up his dog, who when the yelling started, began clawing at Steven's leg. Obviously he didn't like the yelling any more than Steven did. "I was thinking that I own as much of this company as you and Nick and I have as much right to make a decision as the two of you. I am not some child that needs your permission to breathe."

"Ten thousand dollars, Steven!"

"I know how much it was. You should have seen her, Marti. It was like seeing a baby lamb circled by a pack of wolves. Was I just supposed to leave her there?"

"You were supposed to get her bail. The woman is a school teacher. She's lived here for five years. Are you trying to tell me that she doesn't have any assets at all? No friends or family to help her out? What about calling her parents? They probably own their own home."

"She says her mother can't afford to help and she doesn't know anyone that can. She'll pay what she can when she can. Give it a rest, will you?" Steven tried to head down to his office, but Marti blocked his path.

"Give it a rest? The three of us sat right there in Nick's office and made the decision to expand this company from strictly bounty hunting to also writing bail bonds and that the bails would be my territory. When did you and Nick have a meeting and decide to change things?"

"When did I do what?" Nick stepped out of his office, a scowl on his face and a cell phone at his ear.

"Steven took it upon himself to write a bail today for a hundred thousand dollars and didn't bother to get the ten percent assurance."

"You did what?" Nick took a deep breath and turned his attention back to his phone call. "Honey, let me call you back. I have to fix something."

He ended the call and stepped back. "In my office. Both of you."

Steven followed Marti into his brother's office. It was like being called into the principal's office for an infraction at recess. Only Nick could be way worse than a school principal. "Look, I called Marti in on this, but she was down in PG County and wasn't expected back for hours. I had a decision to make and I made it. It's on me if something goes wrong."

"The decision for any bail is mine. You are a bounty hunter. I am the bail bonds agent." Marti's hands were flying as fast as her words. "What part of that do you not understand?"

"I understand it all perfectly. Contrary to popular belief around here, I am not a child."

She poked him with her finger. "Then what possessed you to cover a hundred thousand dollar bond without getting our assurance? Do you have any idea how bad this could hurt us?"

A sharp whistle cut through the argument and the room fell silent. Steven looked over at Nick who was just pulling his hand from his mouth. "Do I have your attention now?"

Marti dropped down in the nearest chair, glaring at Steven with a self-satisfied smirk. But it didn't last long.

"Marti, I understand your concern, but haven't you been out on a take-down with us?" Nick circled his desk and settled down in his chair, leaning back and folding his hands over his trim stomach.

"Well, yes, but—"

"Then why is it okay for you to be a bounty hunter when we need you, but Steven can't write a bail when he feels the need to?"

Marti eased forward in her chair, perching on the edge. "A hundred thousand, Nick, and he didn't get a dime from this woman!"

"I understand. We'll handle it. But weren't you on your way somewhere?"

Marti slapped the arms of the chair as she stood up. With a parting glare in Steven's direction, she left the office, slamming the door behind her.

Nick rotated his chair to face Steven. "What were you thinking?"

"That I was making the right decision at the right time for the right reason. This woman is not a criminal and she'll pay us."

"Explain it to me."

So Steven did. When he mentioned Chamberland's name, Nick's eyes narrowed a bit, but other than that, there was no reaction at all as he went over the entire story.

"Do me a favor," Nick replied when he was finished. "Try to get some kind of collateral. It might cool Marti off."

"What's with her, anyway? I knew she wouldn't be happy with me, but I didn't expect her to go off like that."

Shaking his head, Nick rocked back in his chair. "She's been a little off all day. I asked her about it, but she won't tell me anything. I thought maybe you could get something out of her, but I guess that's out of the question now."

Steven rubbed his forehead as the headache he'd been keeping at bay for hours hit him full force. "Well, now that the next world war is over, can I go home?"

"Just do me a personal favor. Make sure she calls in as scheduled. She misses one check-in and you know Marti will yank her bail faster than your dog can get into trouble, so be warned."

"I gave her the number to the machine and made it clear she has to call in every Wednesday, from her house phone, before six p.m. or bail is revoked. She'll call."

All bail recipients were required to check in once a week to make sure they hadn't skipped out of town. To verify that they weren't calling from some pay phone in Topeka, they had to call in from their home phone. Rather than bothering to take every call that came in on Wednesday, they had a machine and a caller ID hooked up to that number. At the end of the day, Marti went down the checklist with the caller ID and made sure every number was accounted for. If any number was missing, their file was turned over to Nick and assigned to one of the bounty hunters to find the person and take them back to jail. Bail revoked.

"I hope she does." Nick picked up the phone, a clear indication the storm was over. "For your sake."

Wednesday, 5:40 pm
Maryland Correctional Facility, Hagerstown, Md

Norman Rotterbach clenched the phone and lowered his voice to something just above a low growl. "I trusted you to make the exchange and you blew it. Don't go blaming no sniffling girl for your screw-up. So, I'm out what, almost two hundred grand and all you can say is sorry?"

Norman noticed he was starting to draw the attention of some of the inmates waiting to use the phones and turned his shoulder, ducking his head. "I knew I couldn't trust you to handle something like this. I never told you to get her involved, did I? No. That's on you. Stupid is as stupid does. Maybe she's smarter than you, is that it? You tellin' me some sissy girl is smarter than you?"

"No!" Paul's voice had a little shake in it that pleased Norman. "I heard that the Feds were on to us. I was just trying to keep from getting caught, okay? If the Feds hadn't been there, it all would have gone down without a hitch. The Feds were there, man. Nothing I could do about that."

"That's where you're wrong." If Paul had been standing there, Norman would have slapped the boy into next week. "And that's why you will never be anything more than a loser. If you heard the Feds were on to us, you should have called me and I would have told you to cancel the buy. If you hadn't shown up and Marco's people hadn't shown up, then the Feds would have been wasting their time. I'd have my guns and Marco would have his money, and we wouldn't be having this discussion, now would we?"

"But—"

Norman hissed with frustration as he ran a hand over his bald head. The boy showed promise sometimes, and other times, like now, was nothing more than a complete idiot. "But, nothing. Marco is furious. As he should be. Now, you make it right. You hear me?"

Norman hung up the phone and headed back to his cell. It grated on him that he had to depend on other people to run his operation while he stayed locked up, but for now, there was nothing he could do about it. Paul had begged him for a chance. He swore he could be trusted. Relied on. Norman snorted as he made his way back to the recreation room. Just like a woman to step in and mess everything up. Ungrateful dogs, that's what they were. Take and take and take and do nothing but whine the rest of the time. Oh, but the minute they find out he's leaving prison with a huge stash of money, they'd be lapping at his boot tops to get his attention.

"Hey, Rotterbach! You got a visitor!"

Norman lifted an eyebrow at the guard as he changed directions and followed the guard to the visitor's area. What were the chances that his stupid wife had finally decided to show up, acting all remorseful? He smiled to himself. Well, he wasn't going to let her get away with it. Not much he could do here with the guards to step in, but when he got home, she had a beating coming to her she'd never forget.

But it wasn't his wife waiting for him. Two men sat there, hands clasped on the table in front of them. Wallace and Shiff. Officer's Walrus and Whiff, as Norman liked to think of them. He slid down on the stool across the table from them. "What do you want now?"

"A little information, Norman."

Norman looked around and then settled his gaze on the older of the two. He set his elbows on the table and leaned forward. "I don't talk to cops, haven't you heard?"

"Cut the act, Norman. We know you've heard about the Feds busting some of Marco's men trying to buy stolen weapons."

Norman shrugged. "Might a heard something about it. So what?"

"Just curious. Marco just lost a lot of weapons. Seems he might be looking around, if he can still afford to."

Norman leaned back in his chair and studied the two men. He hated cops, but as cops went, these two weren't the worst he'd ever dealt with. So far, they'd never lied to him. That had to count for something."

"What's in it for me?"

"Maybe you want to stay out when you get out."

"Maybe doesn't do much for me, fellas. But thanks for stopping by." Norman went to stand up when the younger officer reached across the table and grabbed him by the arm. The two had a staring contest for a few seconds and then Norman slowly sat back down. It was a game they played. Sometimes it worked, sometimes it didn't.

He let the two officers sit there for a long moment before he finally spoke. Just another power play. One more way to feel as if he was still in control of his life. "Marco has his lawyers working on it. His men will be out in a few hours. Just a bleep on his radar, as it were."

Officer Wallace stared down at his hands. "He just lost a boatload of money. Is he going to try again?"

Norman shrugged. "Marco wants guns and he'll get guns. Feds won't be much more than a speed bump in his ride."

"You hear about any more guns coming in?"

Norman rolled his neck as he let the question hang in the air. "I hear things. Nothing I can hang my hat on. Maybe a couple of weeks. Maybe less. Something about some nice automatics coming in. Russian made. Nothing on how many. But Marco will want them. Especially now with the Mexicans buying up all the guys they can get."

"If you get the chance," Wallace stood up. "Let Marco know the Feds aren't done with him, yet."

Norman snorted as he rocked back in his chair and watched the two cops head for the door. "Like you think he don't know that? He ain't worried about the Feds. They bother him again, he'll put them down like dogs."

Wallace looked back as he reached the door. "Chamberland is worse than any mad dog. He gets the scent on Marco, he won't let go until Marco is behind bars."

Wallace didn't bother waiting for Norman to respond, pulling the door closed. The guard nudged Norman to his feet and returned him to his cell.

Wednesday, 6:15 pm
Timonium, Md.

The sun was low in the sky, casting a pink aura around the gray clouds that streaked across the horizon. A light breeze had kicked up, hinting at the possibility of rain before sunrise.

Steven pulled his car into his driveway, as always, eyeing the lawn to make sure that everything was neat and tidy. He walked down to the curb and pulled the garbage can and recycling bin back up to the house.

He felt like stewing in his sister's dressing-down, but he couldn't keep his mind on the resentment. It kept drifting back to a certain schoolmarm with big brown eyes. He couldn't even remember the last time a woman made enough of an impression for him to remember her name. Andrea Morrow. Yep. He remembered this one's name. And the fact that she had looked so vulnerable. So wounded. A big change from the day she stood over him with a loaded purse and righteous fury.

And that was a puzzle in itself.

The woman he saw in jail today had practically folded in on herself.

He retrieved the mail from the mailbox and tucked it under his arm as he unlocked the front door and shoved it open.

The last thing he needed in his life was to get too involved. He'd bailed her out. Done deal. From here on in, she was on her own. He didn't need to get any more personal than that. Especially with a woman who was in trouble with the law. It had taken him a long time to realize that he had some kind of hero complex, running out to rescue the damsel in distress, except that he usually found damsels that were faking the distress in order to get what they wanted and then they moved on.

He swore never again. Next time he fell for a woman, she would have a good job, good credit, and was comfortably settled in her life. She'd be looking for a man to partner with, not bail her out of a mess and pay off her debts.

As soon as he hung up his coat, he turned on his television, then let Killer out into the backyard.

That didn't mean he wouldn't still help women in trouble. There were four women he was currently helping. Four single mothers who needed the boost out of the trap of poverty. Maybe it was something in his DNA or something, but he enjoyed that part of his life. He just wasn't going to be stupid enough to get romantically involved with one of them.

He opened the freezer to see what he could find for dinner. Just as he pulled out a Boston Market frozen dinner, he heard a familiar voice on the television.

"We did recover a stash of weapons in a storage unit near Glen Burnie."

Dropping the frozen dinner on the counter, Steven hurried to the living room. Sure enough, it was Chamberland's sidekick, adjusting his sunglasses as he stared out into the hoard of cameras. "We had been expecting the buy to go down and had cameras in place, so we have the entire deal on tape. Six men were arrested at the scene and the woman who sold the weapons was picked up later by our agents. The money has not yet been recovered. We estimate that she had nearly a quarter million dollars in that case. So far, she had refused to tell us where she hid it."

Obviously, being demoted to dog walker for an hour had affected his memory. "If anyone has any information, please call us at the number on the screen. Thank you."

"That dirty, low-down rat!" Steven spun around and headed back into the kitchen. "It was a set-up. He set her up."

Chapter 7

Wednesday, 7:10 pm
Sykesville, Md

Andrea tried calling her principal at home, but only got his voice mail. She left a tearful message, half-way explaining why she hadn't shown up for school that morning and promised to show up the next day.

As soon as she got home, she'd taken a shower, threw her dirty clothes in the trash and made herself a cup of hot chocolate. Comfort food.

It didn't help.

She could still feel the horror of that little interrogation room, could still feel the condemnation in those icy eyes of that ATF agent, the disapproval from the judge, the distain from the District Attorney.

And the kindness of Liz and Steven did little to erase the terror that she may go to prison for something she didn't do.

How could she have been so stupid? She'd trusted a man she barely knew. Were there signs she missed? Was there something in her that couldn't see bad things in people until it was too late? How long had she adored and loved her father until one day she realized that he was a bad man that liked to beat up on her mother and drink most nights until he was mad enough to come home and terrorize the family?

She should have stuck to her promise to never fall in love. This just confirmed she was right all along. She was no judge of character and she could easily marry a man that would beat her, humiliate her, and destroy her just the way her father had beaten down her mother.

When the phone rang, she picked it up. "Hello?"

Nothing.

"Hello?" She repeated.

"Where's the money?"

"What? Who is this?"

"All you need to know is that I don't like being double-crossed. Now where is my money?"

"I have no idea what you're talking about." Why did it suddenly feel as if the nightmare was only just beginning?

"If you don't turn that money over to me real quick, you're going to find out just how much you miscalculated. No one cheats me, do you get that?"

There was a bite to the steel in his voice that reminded her of her father when he was on one of his binges. "I don't have any money, do you get that? The police took it."

"They said on television that you got away with the money and that when they arrested you, you'd stashed it somewhere."

"That's crazy!"

"Crazy or not, I'll believe the ATF before I'd believe a woman with two hundred thousand dollars of my money. You better have every dime of my money. You hear me, girl?"

Shaking, she tried to think. Act. React. But the man wasn't the least bit interested in what she had to say. She slammed the phone down as a rush of desperate memories swamped her mind, yanking her back to a time she only wanted to forget. In an instant, she was no longer a grown woman in charge of her own life. With just a few choice words, she was forced to suffer the torment of her childhood once again.

Foolish of her to think that she'd overcome the scars. Or that she was no longer susceptible to the same crippling symptoms. *You hear me, girl? You'll be sorry.* How many times had she heard those words and bore the brunt of what they represented? How many times had they come just moments before a fist? Or a slap? Or a belt?

Slowly, she sank to the floor, wrapping her arms around herself, trying to remind herself that she wasn't eight years old any more. That she wasn't a helpless child. Rocking, she kept talking to herself. *I am strong. I am strong. No one is going to beat me. No one is going to punish me for breathing. For living. My daddy is gone. He can't find me. He can't hurt me. I'm okay.*

She reached out and picked up the pink squirrel off the floor. If her precious Chaos was here, he'd lean against her, whine softly, lick her hand, anything to let her know that he was there and that he cared. But he was at the Vet's office.

Hugging the squirrel, she tried to calm down. At ten tomorrow morning, she had to be in her classroom. If she didn't show up for work, she'd be fired for sure. And if she didn't meet this man, he would come after her.

Why did he think she had his money? He said he heard on the television? She picked up the remote and flipped through several channels before realizing that she wouldn't hear anything now until the eleven o'clock news. She left it on an old black and white movie and muted the sound.

How in the world had this happened? One day, she's in her classroom, helping Peter clean up his finger paint and showing Kristen how to apply paste to her cutouts and the next day, she's being grilled by the ATF and charged with brokering stolen weapons. It was surreal. If she didn't feel so overwhelmed, she'd think she was dreaming and due to wake up any minute now.

Her attorney told her that the charges were all just a formality, but would be dropped as soon as the truth came out. But what if the truth didn't come out? How many times had she heard about people going to jail for crimes they didn't commit? She could lose everything she'd worked so hard for.

And her mother would be devastated.

Her mother! Andrea grabbed her cell phone and made the call. "Mom? It's me."

"Andi! How are you, baby? How's work?"

"Okay. Look, Mom. I have something I need to tell you."

"Hold on a sec. Let me turn down the television. Okay, sweetheart. Talk to me."

Tucking her feet under her, Andrea slowly went through the entire story and then listened to the silence on the other side. "Mom? Are you there?"

"I'm here. What can I do to help you?"

"Nothing." She wiped away the tears. "I have an attorney and she said she'll take the case pro bono, so I won't have to worry about that."

"I wish I could be there for you."

Andrea knew if there was one person who understood the stress of dealing with the legal system, it was her mother. How many times had her mother gone back to court because Dad had ignored the restraining orders? And how many times had they slapped him on the wrist and let him go? It had been a long, drawn-out battle of restraining orders, broken time and again, only to have more arrests, more charges, more promises and those broken time and again. Finally, her father had grown so angry he'd gone to her mom's work and attacked her there. When a co-worker tried to help her mom, her dad had hurt him so severely, he was hospitalized for nearly four months. That was that. Her dad was arrested and charged and sent to jail.

Before he got out, her mother divorced him, changed her and Andrea's names, and moved to another state, starting their lives over. But neither Andrea nor her mother had ever really moved beyond the pain.

"What about the bail?"

"The bail bondsman is letting me pay it off as I can."

"How much was it?"

"Ten thousand dollars."

"And out of the kindness of his heart, he just decided to trust you for the money? There's a catch, honey. You know how this works. Men do not hand out ten thousand dollars to a woman they don't know and not expect something in return."

"I was just anxious to get out of that place. I didn't even stop to think."

"That's exactly how they operate, baby girl. They target vulnerable women who are desperate for a knight on white horse. They show up with a little hay and some grain and pretend the horse is just outside."

Andrea closed her eyes and rubbed her forehead. "I don't know what to do, Momma. Everything is so crazy.

How can they think I'd do this kind of thing? I've never even had a speeding ticket."

"It doesn't matter. We'll find a way out. Maybe I can take a few days and come out there. Help you through this."

"And lose your job? Mom, you can't." Her mother had just taken a new job as a secretary for a doctor and had been there less than two weeks. This was not the time for her to take time off.

"I can't stand the thought of you going through this alone."

"I'll call you every day and keep you updated. That way you will go through it with me."

"It's not the same."

No, it wasn't, but it was the only option. After years of scraping by, her mom had finally managed to work her way up to getting a really decent job with good pay. For the first time in her life, she would be able to get a nice apartment in a nice part of town and afford to trade in that old Chevy for a newer more reliable car. Andrea wasn't about to take any of that away from her.

"If things get too bad, we can talk about you coming out here, okay? But for now, my attorney says not to worry."

Andrea looked up at the television and saw footage of herself and Liz leaving the courthouse with Steven. "Mom, I have to go. I'll call you tomorrow. I promise."

She picked up the remote and turned up the volume.

"Okay, baby. Sleep well. Love you."

"You, too, Mom."

She set the phone down as she listened to one of the ATF agents recap the events of the day before. How could he lie like that? No wonder someone thought she had the money. That ATF agent was practically guaranteeing it. She heard her phone ringing, but it took a few rings before she could bring herself to answer it.

"Hello?"

"Andrea? It's Liz. Have you seen the news?"

"I'm watching it now. How can he lie like that? He knows I didn't take anything! This whole scenario is a lie!"

"I know. I have a call in to his supervisor."

"Someone called me. He thinks I have the money. His money. He wants me to give it to him. What am I going to do, Liz? I don't have this money!"

"A man called you?"

"Yes. Earlier. Said he heard on the news that I had hidden the money from the cops and now he wants it."

"Do you have somewhere to go? Somewhere this guy can't find you?"

"Like where?"

"A friend. What about your mom? Can you go visit her for a few days?"

Andrea slowly sank down on the sofa as what her lawyer wasn't saying cut through the conversation. "I'm in danger, aren't I?"

"Yes, Andrea. You are. If this guy thinks you have his money and you aren't turning over to him, there's no telling what he'll do to get it. I've seen men murder for less."

"Thank you for that image."

"I'm sorry. I'm very concerned. I don't know why Chamberland did this and when I get my hands on him, he's going to be very sorry that he did, but in the meantime, I want you to get out of that apartment. Go somewhere. Stay out of sight."

"I can't, Liz. I have a job. I have to go in tomorrow or they could fire me."

There was a long stretch of silence that pulled at Andrea's thoughts. Finally, she started to see the big picture. "You think they've already fired me."

"You're under indictment for brokering stolen weapons. Right now, as far as anyone can see, there will be a trial and you could go to prison for a very long time. Yes, the minute they get word of this, and they probably already have, they will have no choice but to let you go. They have to answer to the parents of those children you teach."

Andrea felt as if someone had punched her. She hadn't thought anything could get worse, but it just had. "No."

"I'm sorry, Andrea."

The sympathy in Liz's voice was hard to take. Fresh tears welled and spilled. "This is so not fair. I didn't do anything wrong. Now my life is destroyed. It's not fair, Liz. It's just not fair."

"I know. And the sad thing is it happens to people all the time."

"What ever happened to innocent until proven guilty?"

"It put you at home tonight rather than a jail cell."

It didn't make Andrea feel one bit better. Her job, her life, her future. It was all spiraling away from her and for what? Because she trusted a man. Hadn't her mother told her to never, ever trust a man?

"Andrea, I want you to go somewhere safe and don't worry. I'm on this. I'm all over this. Please trust me."

"I do. It's just so hard to understand how this could have happened to me. How do I get my life back?"

"One day at a time."

Wednesday, 11:50 pm
Timonium, Md

Steven tied the garbage bag and lifted it out of the kitchen trash can. As he opened the back door to take it out, he heard the door bell. Setting the bag down at the back door, he headed for the front door. The bell rang again and then pounding on the door.

"I'm coming. Have a little patience." He looked out the window and then pulled the door open. His sister came barging in.

"About time. I didn't wake you, did I?"

"You know better than that. But I was just taking out the garbage. What brings you by so late?" He headed back to the kitchen, letting her follow him.

"I saw the news. Did you know she got away with almost a quarter million dollars? And you let her slide on the ten grand?"

"It's a lie." He picked up the trash bag and pushed the storm door open to the back deck. It didn't surprise him that his sister followed him right on outside. "I don't know why Chamberland is doing this, but it's a lie. I was there. He told me he arrested her on the spot and he showed me the video. She didn't go anywhere with anything. It's a set-up."

"A set-up?"

After making sure the lid on the garbage can was secure so that Killer wouldn't be tempted to try his luck at getting in it, Steven headed back in the house. "Yes. I haven't figured it all out yet, but he lied to the press."

"The only reason he'd do that is if he's trying to lure someone out of hiding."

"Exactly. But that puts Andrea is a world of danger." He locked the back door and turned off the porch light. "Would he do that?"

"He did it to our niece, if you recall."

Steven wandered back into the living room and plopped down on the sofa. His sister sat down across from him in a chair. She slipped her coat off and let it stay tucked behind her. "Steven, if she's in danger, we could lose our money."

"Is that all that matters to you? The money?"

Marti dropped her head then slowly lifted it again. "I'm sorry. That sounded pretty cruel. It's not just about the money, although I admit that is one of my concerns. We could take a serious hit on this, Steven. At the same time, this woman needs to watch her back. We both know that Chamberland is only out for himself. He doesn't care who gets in his way or who gets hurt."

"He did protect Krystal."

"He never should have had her there in the first place. She could have been killed by a stray bullet."

"True." Steven leaned back, stretched out his legs. "But in the end, he kept her safe. Right now, I'm concerned about Andrea. How does he plan on keeping her safe? Someone is going to come looking for their money."

"And when they do and she doesn't have it, she's in a world of hurt." Marti tipped her head. "There's nothing you can do, Steven."

"I know," he replied wearily. "I know."

But after seeing his sister out the door and locking up, he promised himself that he was going to check up on the school teacher the next day. And if Chamberland wasn't protecting her, Steven was going to call a press conference of his own.

Marti eased the Corvette out of her brother's driveway and shifted into drive. She would never admit this to Nick, but she got a kick out of driving this car—loved the feel of the machine on the road, the sound of the engine rumbling like the low, throaty growl of a lion, and the power. Oh, the power.

And the satisfaction of knowing that she now owned it while its former owner sat in jail. Smiling as she thought of Michael in a jail cell, she headed home. Thoughts of Michael fled when her cell phone rang a few blocks from home.

"Hello?"

"Miss Shepherd? I'm not calling too late, am I? I can never keep track of time differences between the West coast and the East."

She quickly pulled over to the curb and shifted the car into park. "No, it's fine, Jack. What do you need?"

"I have a picture I want you to look at. I'm going to fax it to your office. Is that okay?"

"Sure. I'll head right over there and take a look. You think it's him?"

"I don't know, honestly. You look and tell me if he looks familiar. But he's living on the McConnell Air Force Base in Wichita, Kansas. And he was at Andrews during the time frame you gave me."

Marti stepped down on any hope she had that Jack was on the right track. She'd hit too many dead-ends to be allow herself to be optimistic now. No point in it. If they found him, then she'd give herself permission to feel something. Until then, stick to the business of tracking down one of the most elusive prey she'd ever come across.

"I'll let you know when I see his picture. Until then, keep looking."

"You got it."

Marti swung a U-turn at the next intersection and headed back to the office.

Chapter 6

Friday, 1:10 pm
Prodigal Offices, Baltimore

Steven hummed a jaunty tune as he studied the screen on his laptop. Scrolling down, he looked at the line graph and then leaned back in his chair, smiling. Up again today. That was three straight quarters of growth. He was right. This was going to make him a nice chunk of change.

"What are you smiling at?"

Steven leaned back and looked over his shoulder at Jenna, the office manager. "Nothing. What do you need?"

"Just dropping off this file. Nick wanted you to start making some calls, see if you can find out where this guy is."

Steven grunted as he swung around and took the file from her. "More like he wants me to get the guy on the phone and convince him to just drop on by the office and turn himself in."

Jenna's lips curved up as her eyes tracked beyond him to his laptop. "You could be right about that. What is that? One of those stock trading websites?"

Steven reached over and closed the lid. "Just curious about them."

"Well, don't get too carried away with that stuff. It'll rob you blind if you don't know what you're doing."

Jenna was what Steven considered a true organizational diva. She was a widow of five years with a son in college, worked full time at Prodigal, mothered everyone in the office, always made sure there was coffee made and lunch delivered on those rare occasions when it was necessary, and could out organize anyone, any time, anywhere. Prodigal would fall apart without her. The fact that she was a good looking woman was something she tried to hide with over-sized clothes, baggy jeans, sneakers, and no makeup. She may have convinced herself that men didn't notice her with that prim and proper mother act, but she was wrong. If anything, it made men want to break through her walls. "You know I don't get carried away by anything."

"Except learning. Never met a man that loved school the way you did. It's a shame you quit. You were so close to your doctorate."

Steven swallowed the disappointment that reminder brought up. "Maybe one of these days, I'll get around to that writing that thesis and graduate."

"I'm not sure why you needed all those degrees to become an accountant, but whatever rocks your boat."

She left his cubicle with a little smile, leaving him to his work. He stared at the doorway. No door. It rankled him sometimes that his brother has the office and he was relegated to a cubicle like Rafe and Conner. He owned as much of this company as Nick did, but you wouldn't know it by the way he was treated. Oh, sure, it's not like there was actually room to build a second office just to soothe his ego, but that wasn't really the point.

Steven opened the first file folder and read over the particulars. Willy Plodder. Two counts of receiving stolen goods. Three counts of selling stolen goods. Drug possession. Possession of a deadly weapon. Just a real nice guy, from the looks of it.

He read down the list of contacts and decided to start with the girlfriend first. Of course, he couldn't come right out and tell her he was a bounty hunter looking to take her boyfriend back to jail, but there were ways to get the information. He just had to hit on the right one.

"Is Willy there?" he half whispered when she answered the phone.

"No. Who is this?"

"Joey. I got some goods to move and thought he might be interested. Know where I could find him?"

"What kind of goods?"

"Never mind. If he isn't looking to make a few bucks, I'll find someone that is."

He waited a few seconds to see what she would do and smiled when she jumped at it. "Wait. Who did you say you were?"

"Joey. Look, I don't have time to play, ya know? Time is money. Here's my number." He rattled off the number to a cell phone Prodigal used strictly for making contact with fugitives. "If he's interested, he can call me. Soon."

Steven hung up and jotted down a note in the file that he'd made contact and what lure he'd used. His phone intercom buzzed and Jenna's voice piped through. "Steven? Agent Chamberland returning your call on line two."

"Thanks, Jenna. I got it." He punched the line. "Chamberland? What in the world do you think you're doing?"

"Waiting for a double bacon cheeseburger and fries, why?"

"I'm not amused."

"And I'm not a mind reader. What do you want, Shepherd?"

"I want to know why you set Andrea Morrow up like that? Why did you have your men lie to the press? Do you know the danger you've put her in?"

"I know exactly what I'm doing and I don't need you interfering in my investigation. Mind your own business, bounty hunter."

Steven clenched and unclenched his fist. "It is my business, Chamberland. That's my investment you're putting at risk. Anything happens to her and I'm out ten grand."

"Cry me a river. You're not going to lose your so-called investment. I've got her under so much surveillance that she won't be able to sneeze without one of my men handing her a tissue."

"You better hope nothing happens to her."

"You do your job and let me do mine. You have a nice day now, ya hear?"

Chamberland disconnected and Steven slammed the phone down.

"Don't let the man get to you."

Steven whirled around to see Rafe standing in the doorway with his gear bag in hand. "He set her up."

"Well, you can worry about that later, right now Nick needs our help. Let's roll."

Steven grabbed his gear bag from the corner and followed Rafe out. But he couldn't shift his thoughts off Chamberland. It went against everything in him to know that someone in law enforcement would be so unethical. Would outright lie. Sure, Nick told him that police officers had to lie sometimes to get a criminal to confess, but that was a criminal. Andrea Morrow was no criminal.

He'd bet his mutual funds on it.

Rafe leaned across the hood of the Prodigal SUV. "You with me here?"

"Yes." Steven tossed his gear in the back and climbed in the front seat. "If that woman gets hurt, so help me, I'm going to break Chamberland in half."

Rafe laughed as he buckled his seat belt and started the engine. "Steven! You're starting to sound like your brother."

"It's not right."

"I didn't say it was. But I don't think I've ever heard you be so . . . violent." Rafe pretended to shudder. "It's just so aggressive of you."

"Shut up, Rafe."

Laughing, Rafe backed out of the parking space. Then, as he shifted into drive, he sobered. "Look, if she gets hurt, I'll help you break Chamberland in half, okay? But for now, let's concentrate on not getting hurt bringing in our fugitive. Priorities, Steven. Priorities."

Friday, 2:00 PM
Meadowbrook Veterinarian Clinic, Sykesville

Andrea walked up to the receptionist and leaned forward. "Hi, Mary."

Mary had been with Dr. Habak from the beginning of time. She was easily on the back side of sixty-five, had short white hair, bright blue eyes, and a smile for everyone that came and went. "How are you doing, Andrea?"

"Good, I guess. Is Chaos ready to go home?"

"Probably is. I just wasn't expecting you until after work." She reached over and grabbed Andrea's file.

Andrea didn't bother to reply. She didn't want to admit that she'd lost her job—well, placed on administrative leave until further notice—or that she'd been driving around, trying to avoid a man that was threatening her.

Andrea paid the bill for the dog's two day stint with the vet after swallowing the squeaker in one of his toys. Dr. Habak had assured her that he'd eventually eliminate it without any damage, but Andrea had been overly-concerned and insisted that Chaos stay with the Vet until the squeaker was gone. Looking back, it was another one of life's little lessons about God's provision. If Chaos hadn't swallowed that gadget, he wouldn't have gone to the vet. If he hadn't been at the vet's, he would have been stuck in that apartment for nearly twenty-four hours without being walked and without food. And that would have driven her to confess to anything if they'd agree to let her go home and take care of her dog.

As she led Chaos out to the car, he danced around her as if they'd been separated for years. She'd bought Chaos after seeing him a pet store window as a twelve-week-old German Shepherd puppy. The sign in the window with his price had been reduced twice and it seemed they were desperate to get rid of him. As soon as he'd dropped his front end down and barked at her, she'd fallen in love. Now, four years later, he was a ninety-five pound bundle of devotion and love.

And would protect her with his life.

She opened the car door. "I missed you, too, now get in and let's go for a ride."

Chaos jumped in and then immediately hopped into the backseat where he settled down with his head between the seats. Andrea fastened her seat belt then reached back and scratched her dog behind the ears. She sniffed back the tears that welled up as she started the engine and pulled out of the parking lot.

She didn't want to go home and she didn't have any other place to be. When she looked up and saw the sign for Frederick and Hagerstown, she decided to head west. What better on a day like today than a nice drive in the country? Not that she believed for a second that it would make all her troubles go away, but with any luck, the man that called her wouldn't be able to find her and would give up. Okay, so he probably wouldn't give up that easy, but she didn't know what else to do and at least driving made her feel relatively safe.

Chaos nudged her shoulder and that drew a tiny smile from her. "I know you probably want to go home, but it's a long and complicated story. You remember Paul? You remember how you growled at him the first time he came to the apartment to pick me up? Well, you were right and I should have listened to you. He's a really bad man and now he's gotten me into big trouble and I have no idea how to get out of it. Would you believe I was arrested?"

Chaos whined low as if commiserating.

"I know. It's hard for me to believe, too. And now some guy is looking for me and I don't have what he wants and I don't know what to do."

Andrea saw the Mt. Airy exit and signs for McDonalds, Taco Bell, KFC, and Subway. Her stomach growled, reminding her that she hadn't eaten a thing all day. She eased across the lanes and hit the exit. "What's it going to be, Chaos? Hamburgers or Tacos? I know you're not into subs."

When she reached the bottom of the exit ramp, she could see McDonalds straight across the intersection. She also noticed a blue sedan that had been following her down I-70 was still behind her. Was he following her? Or was she just being paranoid?

The light changed and Andrea drove straight through and up the hill to the McDonalds. The blue sedan stayed behind her, turning when she did onto Ridge Drive and then right into the McDonalds parking lot. Her heart started to race as she slowly drove around the building.

The sedan pulled into a parking space and middle-aged man in a suit climbed out and strode across the parking lot, talking on his cell phone. Heaving a sigh of relief, Andrea circled the building again and pulled in the drive-thru lane.

After picking up her food at the window, she pulled forward to unwrap a hamburger for Chaos when she noticed that the man in the blue sedan was standing inside the building, talking on a cell phone, and staring at her through the window. Was it just coincidence? Or was he watching her?

She quickly pulled out of the parking lot and made her way back to I-70. The blue sedan was nowhere in sight, but as soon as she pulled out of the McDonalds, a silver Buick pulled away from the curb and was now right behind her.

"This is crazy." There was no way they were following her. But just to be safe, she drove to the next exit, pulled off and turned left. The silver sedan hung back, but there was no doubt he was coming down the exit right behind her. She sped up and ignoring the red light, cut across to the ramp back on to I-70 heading back to Baltimore.

Her left knee was shaking and her hands gripped the steering wheel like a python around his dinner. Glancing into her rearview mirror, she saw the silver sedan dart across oncoming traffic, horns blaring at him as he sped to catch up to her.

Chaos whimpered.

She felt like whimpering along with him. Where was a policeman when you needed one?

Friday 4:10 pm
Baltimore, Md

Baltimore City Police Detective Harold Wallace stared out the picture window of the diner.

"What are you looking at?" his partner asked as the waitress set two club sandwiches down in front of them.

"Those two over there. In the black hoodies. Up to no good. I think I've arrested both of them five or six times. You'd think that would at least slow them down."

"Don't tell me about it. I'm starving and I'm going to be very upset if I have to leave my meal to arrest a couple of punks that will be back out here on the streets in a couple of hours." Randy stared at Harold for a few seconds and then leaned forward. "We're doing everything we can, Harry. Every day, we're out there, putting our lives on the line for a city that doesn't care and a room full of bureaucrats that are more concerned with the next election that doing the job they were elected to do."

Harold snorted as he picked up his sandwich. "Like that so-called stimulus package. They gave us what? Three or four officers? Like that was going to make a difference? You want to create jobs? I have a few thousand for them. More officers on the street, support personnel, larger prisons, more prison guards, better equipment for the officers that are out there every day, fighting impossible odds. And how about more judges to hand down sentences a little stronger than a slap on the wrist."

Randy just grunted in agreement while he chewed. "What did you think of Chamberland's claim we're close to finding the source of the illegal guns?"

Baltimore had instituted Project Exile, a joint agreement between state and federal prosecutors to seek heavy sentences against illegal firearm possession offenders. The task force consisted of one lieutenant, one sergeant, and four detectives from both the Baltimore City and Maryland State Police Department, a detective from the Baltimore County Police Department, and the ATF.

As detectives, both Harold and Randy had been recruited to serve on the Project Exile Task Force.

Harold just shook his head. "Rhetoric. I've heard it a thousand times before. The Feds come in, talk up a good game, arrest a couple of people we've already been watching, and then walk around with their chests puffed out like they've really accomplished something. Then they're gone and things go back to the way they were."

"So you don't think they're close at all?"

"To the real source of those guns? No way. Who did they get? A couple of low-level flunkies who know better than to talk. They're already out on bail. What does that tell you? And have they even once tried to talk to Rotterbach? Not once. And everyone knows nothing goes down in this city involving illegal weapons and explosives that he doesn't know about."

Harold tossed his sandwich down on his plate as he jerked to his feet. "They just mugged a woman. Go! I'll pay the bill and be right behind you."

Randy turned and bounced out of his seat with all the energy and agility of his twenty-nine years. It just made Harold feel every second of his fifty-three. He should have retired years ago, but what else did he have to do with his time? Tossing money down on the table, he hurried out after Randy.

From the time he knew what a police officer was, he wanted to grow up and join the force. And he'd loved every minute of it—even being a rookie and no one actually enjoyed being a rookie. But he had. It was all part of the life of a cop. But everything had changed when his Thelma died three years ago. His daughter was married and living in Oregon. His son was on his second marriage and living in Minnesota. And he was lucky if they came home once every three years. All he had were pictures on the refrigerator of his grandkids. What kind of life was that? Eating alone. Sleeping alone. Living alone.

So, there was the force and while he still loved it, he hated the feeling that he was just a pawn in some politician's game—all show, all illusion, no substance, no real change.

Randy had one of the young men face-down on the sidewalk when Harold caught up with him. He was cuffing him, sweating profusely, and breathing hard. "The other one got away, Harry. Sorry."

"It's okay. We'll get him." Harold reached down and hauled the young man to his feet and shoved him forward. "Let's go down to lock-up and see what he has to say for himself."

Friday 6:15 pm
Connecticut Avenue, Washington D.C.

Pouring a double shot of bourbon into a glass, Kevin Fitz paced around the room as his wife, Sara, calmly—and quietly—packed his suitcase. Too calm. And too quiet. "Sara, please talk to me."

"I think I've said all I had to say." She shook out a folded shirt, balled it up and tossed it into the suitcase. Then she straightened and held up a hand. "No. Wait. I take that back. I *know* that I've said all I had to say."

Desperation clawed at him as she turned her back on him. He'd gone too far. "If I could take it all back, I would."

He'd always thought of his wife as sweet, gentle, almost fragile. Rail thin with finely sculpted features and big green eyes, she always looked like a lost waif, a trait that captured his heart the first time he saw her walking across the campus at the college. Truth was, Steven Shepherd saw her first and was immediately intrigued enough to want to meet her. He'd hauled Kevin around for twenty minutes before he finally managed to "accidentally" run into her. She was sweet, gentle, almost fragile, and even Steven couldn't find it in him to be upset when she admitted she was falling for Kevin. At the moment, however, there was nothing fragile or gentle, or even sweet about her.

She was furious.

He'd gone on a business trip to Austin, met a waitress and well, the affair had lasted nearly six months before he was finally overcome with enough guilt to break it off and confess to his wife. But he had confessed and that should count for something. "I love you, Sara."

Her lip practically curled in derision as she turned and walked back into the closet.

Swigging back the last bit in the glass, he walked back over the window and stared out at the evening's rush hour traffic. Cars, busses, and cyclists jockeyed for a position one second closer to getting home. Pedestrians on the sidewalk huddled under umbrellas as they rushed from crosswalk to crosswalk. Lights were coming on. Buildings were emptying out.

His life was emptying out. With every minute that passed. He had to get himself out of the jam he was in. Running a hand through his hair, Kevin resisted the urge to hurl something through the window. "Sara, I don't want to lose you. I want you to forgive me and let's just go on with our marriage."

"Until the next time? Or the time after that?" She stood in the closet door with an armful of clothes. "At what point am I allowed to say enough and end this farce? You tell me, Kevin. When will you allow me to feel what I'm feeling without regard for what you're feeling?"

"I understand you're mad at me."

Kevin didn't think it was possible for her eyes to get any bigger, but they did. And then they narrowed and he saw a muscle twitch in her jaw. "Mad at you? Is that what you think? That I'm *mad* at you? The first time you cheated on me, I let it go. I forgave you. I told myself that it's human nature to fail. The second time you cheated, I didn't even tell you that I found out. I just nursed my hurt in silence. But this time? This time has crossed the line from mad to devastation. Do you understand the word devastation? It means it's all gone. Blown up. Leveled. There is nothing left here for you, Kevin. No love, no compassion, no forgiveness. Nothing. It's all gone. And now . . . I want you gone."

Devastation.

He choked back a laugh as he headed back for the bourbon. *There has to be a way out. There has to be a way to change her mind.* Staring at the bottle on the table, he tried to remind himself that if he got drunk, he wouldn't be able to think clearly and he needed every brain cell he could muster up just to figure a way out of this mess. Then again, being drunk would give him a blessed little block of time where he just wouldn't care.

"I don't want to lose you." Kevin set his glass down on the dresser. "I love you too much. I can't live without you."

It was the simple truth. He couldn't imagine his life without Sara. Sweet, funny Sara. The woman that always seemed to know exactly how to comfort him when he had a bad day. Who could make him laugh at the oddest times. Who held all his secrets in the palm of her hand. And now she was going to just toss him out? End their marriage? How was that possible?

Sara zipped the suitcase closed and folded her arms across her chest. "I've packed everything you need to survive for a week. I'll make sure the rest of your things are ready for you to pickup before the week is up. Tomorrow, I'm going to see an attorney and file for divorce. The more you fight this, the harder I will make this for you. Now, get out."

"I can't leave you," Kevin told her. And it was the truth.

"You should have thought of that when you decided to break our vows with Alice and with Yolanda, and now with this waitress."

"Wendy."

"Whatever. I no longer care enough about you to care who she is. You killed all that when you betrayed me. Without trust, there is no love. And no marriage."

He followed her out of the bedroom and into the kitchen where she put water in the kettle and put it on the stove. "I know what I've done seems terrible, but I swear those girls meant nothing to me. It was just—"

She whirled on him, pointing a knife in at him. "Don't even go there. Don't give me that old it-didn't-mean-anything speech. You did want you wanted. Now I'm doing what I want. I want you out of here and out of my life."

"I hurt you. I get that now. But I never meant to, I swear."

"No, all you get right now is that I'm ending this and you don't want that. It's all about you. That's the way it's always been. What Kevin wants. What Kevin feels. And Sara just has to go along like the good little wife. Well, now it's about what Sara wants." She turned around and started slicing the lemon on the cutting board.

"I understand. I do. And I'm sorry."

"Sorry you got caught. But if I give you another chance, you'll just do it again."

"I won't. I promise." He reached out to touch her shoulder, but she stepped back, raising the knife again.

"I've heard that before, too. Get out."

"You're my life, Sara."

"No, you just don't like change. You don't like people to rock your little boat. Well, I'm not rocking it. I'm sinking it. Now, are you going to leave or do I have to call the police and scream about you hitting me and then you get arrested on top of everything else?"

Kevin swallowed hard. She meant it this time. He couldn't find any wavering in her at all. She really would call the police on him. She wasn't going to let him stay. Maybe after sleeping a night without him she'd change her mind.

He retrieved his suitcase from the bedroom and then walked back in the kitchen. She was dunking the teabag in the steaming water. "If you need me. If you want to talk, call me."

"Don't hold your breath." Staring out the window, she lifted the cup to her lips and took a sip.

Chapter 8

Friday, 7:20 pm
Dennys Restaurant, Baltimore, Md

Steven set his laptop down on the table, hung his coat on the back of his chair, and smiled at the three ladies sitting there waiting patiently on him. "I'm sorry I'm late."

Eva waved a french fry she was nibbling on. "Work comes first, we all understand that." Eva was the oldest of the three women. Born in Venezuela, she had come to this country with her husband when she was just a young bride. Within ten years, her husband had abandoned her with four children. With a pile of debt, no job, and limited English skills, she struggled to raise her kids, teach herself English, and work two jobs to keep a roof over their heads. Now, at the age of forty-seven, her children were grown and gone, and she wanted more for herself than to work as a hotel maid until the day she died. Steven had met her when her daughter's boyfriend jumped bail and Steven had shown up with Conner to find him. Of course, she wasn't hiding the boy she didn't consider good enough for her daughter (and had been proved right) but while Conner searched the house, Eva had been watching Neil Cavuto on Fox News and Steven asked her if she played the stock market. "No, but I want to learn this. It seems a smart way to make much money. Yes?"

Steven had given a quick lesson in how it could also be a quick way to lose money. She asked for his help. The rest was history.

Next to Eva was Shaina. She had her first child at sixteen and her second at eighteen. Now, at twenty-four, she was attending night school three nights a week, working full time, and hoping to be off welfare within the year. Her dream was to own her own boutique someday. She and Eva worked at the same hotel together.

The third woman was a thirty-three year-old red-head named Leesa. She had been married with two children when her husband was killed in a drive-by shooting on his way home from work. He had been an innocent victim, driving down a street at the moment a gang war was erupting. Struggling to keep her two boys away from the gangs, she was determined to move them out to the suburbs. Eva had brought Leesa to one of their meetings and she'd been with them ever since.

And so, once a month, for the past four years, the three women would meet with Steven and he would help them go over their finances, their meager savings, and the investments he was making for them. None of them had ever imagined a day when they could say they had stock portfolios and just having it, small as it was, was enough to give them the confidence to step out of their circumstances, dream for more, and work hard to achieve it.

Leesa slid an envelope across the table to Steven. "I worked some overtime the last month. I want you to invest it all."

"Are you sure? We agreed to half your overtime."

"I'm okay. The new budget is working out just fine, so invest this for me."

Steven set the envelope aside. "Okay. If you change your mind, let me know." He opened his laptop and fired it up. "Let's look at the portfolios."

The ladies scooted their chairs closer together as a waitress took Steven's order. Then Steven spent the next hour explaining how each stock was doing, which ones he thought they should hold on to and which ones to sell. They looked at the prospectus for a couple of new ventures that Steven thought showed promise and together, discussed the pros and cons of each one.

Alone, none of the women would have raised enough money to start investing, but Steven showed them how together they pool their resources and build a portfolio. Each woman invested what they could and each month, Steven's computer would calculate how much each woman had contributed and what percentage of the entire portfolio she owned. Steven never told them that if he hadn't contributed the major part of the initial investment, none of them would be here. It didn't matter to him. And as he watched each woman's self-esteem grow, the less he wanted it to matter.

But tonight, his mind wasn't fully on stock portfolios and percentages. It wasn't on the three women across from him, trusting him with their future. It was on a brown-eyed school teacher.

Friday, 9:12 pm
Sykesville, Md

Andrea sat in her apartment, curled up in the corner of the sofa with Chaos next to her. All the lights were out. Her fingers were clutched deep into the dog's fur. And she couldn't stop shaking. It wasn't about what was happening. Nothing was happening. The sedan she thought was following her turned out to be an unmarked police car who blazed by her with lights flashing, on its way to somewhere. She and Chaos had driven around for hours until she was tired of driving, tired of hiding, tired of trying to run from some faceless, nameless threat.

She returned home assuming it was the worst thing she could do, but what alternative did she have? She couldn't just drive around the beltway for the next twenty years.

There had been only two messages on her answering machine. Both from the same man. The first one simply said that she had one more chance to make it right before he was sending someone to *talk* to her. A shiver had gone down her spine when she heard the way he emphasized that word. The second message was far less cordial. "I'm coming for my money and I'm going to have to teach you a lesson. You know all about teaching and lessons, don't you?"

It was all about the waiting now. Letting the fear build until she was almost hysterical with it. Her stomach was clenching, her head was pounding, and she could almost smell the sweat beading her face. Jumping at every shadow. Every noise. Every footstep in the hall was death coming for her. Every voice on the street was a killer warning her he was close and getting closer.

She clung to Chaos, taking small comfort from his warmth, his heart beating beneath her fingers, the little pants between sighs as he allowed her to keep him close.

And she prayed. Harder than she'd ever prayed in her life. She begged for forgiveness for every sin she'd ever committed in her life, even the time she stole a pack of bubble gum when she was six. Sure, she'd been taught that all her sins were forgiven when she became a Christian, but at hour like this, it didn't hurt to make sure. If she was going to die, she wanted to make sure she was going to heaven. And maybe, just maybe, if she prayed hard enough, God would send some small miracle and save her life.

She didn't want to die.

She didn't want to be tortured. And they would torture her. They'd want her to tell them where the money was and she couldn't tell them what they wanted to hear.

Suddenly, Chaos stiffened. Slowly he lifted his head and then his shoulders. A low growl rumbled up from his chest.

Andrea pressed herself deeper into the sofa. If she could just make herself disappear.

A knock on the door and Andrea had to slap her hand over her mouth to keep from screaming. Chaos was off the sofa and across the room before Andrea could stop him. He barked furiously at the door, a ferocious warning to whoever was on the other side.

But they knocked again, obviously undeterred by the sound of a dog threatening to tear them apart.

"Miss Morrow? It's Steven Shepherd. Prodigal Recovery and Bonds."

It took almost a full two minutes before the fear abated enough for her to understand that it was not a killer outside a door. She jumped up off the sofa and ran to the door. "Peace, Chaos."

The dog immediately stopped barking and sat down. Andrea unchained and unlocked the door and eased it open. "I'm sorry for taking so long. I wasn't expecting you."

Steven stood there, concerned etched across his brow. "It looks like you expecting trouble. Are you okay?"

She stepped back and waved him in, locking the door behind him. "I'm not okay, but I have no idea what to do about it."

"You look like you haven't slept in days."

"Not since I was arrested. And now it's worse."

"I heard what Chamberland put out on the news, but he says he has men watching you." He knelt down and held his hand on to Chaos.

The relief that washed over her nearly made her knees buckle. "He has men out there watching over me?"

"So he says. Great dog. Very well behaved."

"His name is Chaos and he should be. I put him through enough training."

"And you're concerned about someone harming you? With a dog like this?" Steven stood up. "Most men would think twice before crossing him."

"He'll take down a man and hold him by the throat until I tell him to let go, but he can't stop a bullet." She tugged the cuffs over her sweater down over hands and clenched her fists. "I don't think I could stand to lose him."

"Good point. Look, I didn't mean to stop by without an invitation, but I was a little concerned and I was out and about anyway, so I thought I'd just stop by and make sure you were okay."

"I've been terrified." She brushed a lock of hair back. "I wish I'd known that there were police out there." But now that she did know and the fear was abating, she just wanted to curl up in bed and sleep for about twenty-four hours. Let the police worry about the bad men. She'd just wake up when it was all over.

He pulled a card from the pocket of his jacket and handed it to her. "If you need anything, call me. This has my office and cell. If you call at three in the morning and I don't answer, it's probably because I'm in the middle of chasing some fugitive and can't answer. Leave a message and I'll call you back."

"When do you sleep?"

"While I'm on stakeouts," he laughed, zipping his jacket and moving back toward the door. "I need to go. Get some rest and like I said, if you have any questions, give me a call. I'll help if I can."

"I appreciate that."

She locked up after he left, double-checked the windows, and then staggered into bed, not even bothering to change. The last thing she remembered doing was calling Chaos up onto the bed and telling him to "guard."

Chapter 9

Saturday, 8:15 am
Sykesville, Md

Paul sat slouched down in the van, parked across the street from her apartment. Word was, the ATF had her under surveillance, but so far, he hadn't seen any sign of them. That didn't mean they weren't there, of course.

So, he'd wait and watch and catch her when she was the most vulnerable. He wasn't sure when and where that would be, but the moment would come and he would take advantage of it.

He still couldn't believe she'd double-crossed him the way she had. She'd completely fooled him and that…well, that was just a mistake she was going to truly regret. Acting all innocent and stupid and then taking off with all that money. He wouldn't be fooled again. She was going to hand over every dime of that money and then pay for taking it in the first place. And pay dearly.

Paul shifted in his seat, stretching out stiff muscles. He glanced over at his coffee cup and wrinkled his nose. Ice cold and what he wouldn't give for a cup of hot coffee, freshly brewed, and doctored with a bit of cream and sugar. Dunkin Donuts, 7-11, Highs. He didn't care where it came from as long as it wasn't some fancy brew with some stupid name like double latte Colombian espresso with non-fat something or other.

The nearest Dunkin Donuts was just three blocks away. Maybe he could drive over there and be back before Andrea came out for her morning run.

He reached for the ignition. And then pulled his hand away. With his luck, she'd come out one minute after he left and he'd miss her. That's just the way his life was going these days.

Sure enough, he glanced over at the front of her building and she came bouncing out the door as if she didn't have a care in the world. He felt the bubble of rage and made a fist. He was going to enjoy hurting her.

Andrea zipped up her jacket and stepped out into the chilly morning. The sun was playing hide and seek with fast moving clouds across a pale blue sky, but the brisk wind dispelled any warmth the sun could administer.

Holding the leash in a loose grip, she took a deep breath and glanced furtively around the parking lot. Nothing seemed out of the ordinary, but nothing was the same. Somewhere out there, she knew that people were watching. The good guys watching for the bad guys. The bad guys watching for her.

With one last look and still not seeing anyone, she started jogging down the sidewalk, Chaos panting happily at her side. This was his favorite time of the day, when they would run down to the park and then they'd play ball for a little while before walking home.

She'd slept hard and deep the night before, but she still felt groggy and a half-step out of sync with the rest of the world. Everyone around her was going about their typical Saturday morning routine. They had no idea that there were evil men just around the corner, planning evil things. Why would they? She didn't have a clue either until she'd been unceremoniously placed in handcuffs and hauled off to jail and educated in short order just what lurked in the shadows.

She stopped at the corner and looked both ways before jogging across. Her running shoes slapped the pavement. As her muscles settled into a familiar rhythm, she could feel her spirits lifting a little and the fear slowly lifting. It didn't matter what had happened yesterday or the day before. She was alive today. She was breathing and running and feeling the cold on her cheeks.

They reached the park and she let Chaos off the leash. Pulling the tennis ball out of her pocket, she tossed it as far as she could. The dog took off after it. Another jogger ran by. A couple wandered by, walking two dogs.

Mid-March in Baltimore could be winter one day and spring the next. Nights could drop into the thirties or barely drop below fifty. It was a struggle to know how to dress from day to day. The weatherman claimed that today would climb into the high sixties. She doubted it would even hit fifty-nine.

Chaos returned with the ball, dropping it at her feet and sitting down to wait for her to throw it again.

She threw the ball. Chaos took off after it.

"Hello, Andi. Miss me?"

Andrea whirled around. It took a moment to see him through the hat, sunglasses, and fake mustache. But when she did, every bit of peace she'd been feeling evaporated and it felt as if the sun sank behind the clouds. "Paul. What are you doing here? Do you know what you've done to my life?"

"Where is the money?"

"I don't have it. I never did. The ATF just put that out to lure you into coming out of hiding. Seems it worked." She glanced beyond him, expecting the ATF to come running from all directions, ready to put Paul in handcuffs.

Paul took a step backwards. "They won't watch forever, Andi. And when they give up, I'll be back. And when I come back, you better have every dime of my money. Don't even think of double-crossing me again."

He left, walking quickly.

Chaos dropped the ball at her feet. She continued to stare at Paul as he crossed the street and disappeared around the corner. Why hadn't the police arrested him? He was right here and no one touched him.

Andrea quickly attached the dog's leash and headed home as fast as she could. An icy fear crept over her raising goosebumps on her skin. Moisture popped out on her forehead as vivid, frightening images expanded from the corners of her mind. She no longer felt safe. She no longer felt protected. There was no surveillance team. There was no ATF. No police. She was at the mercy of Paul and his anger. He was going to hurt her and hurt her bad.

And there was no where to turn. No one to help her.

That bounty hunter. Steven. He'd lied to her. He was in on it with all the other police and ATF agents. He was one of them and she had forgotten that. She'd been so anxious to be released from that prison of fear that she'd jumped on his white horse of lies and look what happened.

Paul could have killed her right then and there and no one would have cared.

She was just the bait in their hunt for a bigger catch. The little fish they cut and toss out there to lure in the sharks. Her mother had warned her, but had she listened? No.

From the time she was just a little girl, she had known the ways of men and women. Men controlled and women were little more than possessions with about as much worth as any other possession—a car, a tractor, a horse, a cow and maybe even a good hunting dog, although she always thought that her grandfather thought more of his hunting dogs than he did his own wife. And when she died, he buried her without so much as a tear and then married the widow Marvin down the road less than three months later.

And hadn't her own father told her the way of things? Women are mindless, emotional creatures and that's why God set it that they are only here to serve their men and be subservient in all things.

Not that Andrea believed for a second that she was a mindless creature. Emotional? Sure. But she had a good mind and knew how to use it. She'd gone to college, earned a degree, and obtained a good job. Of course, all that was destroyed now. By men, of course, who didn't think her life worth respect or consideration.

Andrea had her keys out and in her hand before she started up the stairs and as soon as she was inside her apartment, the door was slammed shut and locked with every lock she had.

Chaos whined softly and she realized that she still had a death grip on his leash. She reached down and unclipped it. "Sorry, boy."

He didn't seem to hold a grudge and trotted off to his water bowl. Andrea crossed the room and quickly closed all the curtains and blinds. No point in making this easy for them.

Saturday, 12:30 am
Prodigal Office, Baltimore, Md

Marti Shepherd leaned forward and double-checked her hair and makeup in the little mirror she had propped up on her desk. Her hair had been teased up into a windblown mess and the black eyeliner was a little too thick. She looked like a cheap hooker with a hangover.

Perfect.

Conner was kneeling down a few feet away, tucking his cammo pants into the tops of combat boots and then tightening the laces. When he stood up, he stretched and flexed, looking a little like a six-foot-six inch version The Rock. Well, why not? Conner used to be in the ring himself, going up against some of the best wrestlers in the business.

"Conner."

Rafe tossed a can of mace to Conner. He snagged the can mid-air and secured it to his thigh. Rafe, a former cop, was only about five-foot-ten, so next to Conner, he could almost be mistaken for a teenager. Until you looked him in the eye. Saw the keen intelligence. The tiny lines around his mouth. And the disfiguring scar down the side of his face from a bullet wound.

Marti glanced over at Jenna, the Prodigal Office Manager, who was putting fresh batteries in all the radios. The woman was putting on a good act of being totally oblivious to Rafe but Marti could practically see the sparks arcing between the two of them. She was surprised the room didn't go up in flames. If Jenna could just accept that Rafe honestly loved her, or if Rafe could somehow break through Jenna's self-imposed walls.

"You ready, Marti?" her brother, Nick, asked as he came out of his office and tossed his gear bag on a chair near the door.

"As ready as I'll ever be."

It was rare for Nick to be working on a Saturday these days, but his wife, Jessica, was planning to spend the day taking their daughter shopping for clothes. Nick opted to hand over the credit cards, give them his blessing, and head straight for work. And as soon as he found out that Conner had tracked down Ollie Burch and was planning to go after him, Nick had been grinning ear to ear. Not hard to tell how much the man loved his job.

"Okay." Nick braced both hands behind him on Jenna's desk and leaned back. "Let's go over this one more time. Ollie Burch—"

The front door swung open and Steven rushed in, gear bag in hand. "Sorry I'm late."

"We're used to it," Nick replied dryly. "As I was saying, Ollie Burch is expected to be at his grandmother's ninetieth birthday party tonight at six. Before he shows up to be the darling, devoted grandson, he's expected to spend the afternoon at his favorite house of pleasure with any two or three girls of his choice. According to our informant, he's expected to meet our guy there around three."

Conner was leaning against the wall, massive arms folded across his equally massive chest. "So, Marti goes in, confirms our man is in there, maybe tries to get his attention and hopefully gets him off in a room alone."

"Correct. The less we have to deal with the other clientele, the better. I'd like to go in, grab him, cuff him, and haul him out with very little muss and fuss. Steven will cover the back. As soon as we have Marti's signal, Conner, Rafe, and I will go in the front. While Rafe holds everyone from interfering, Conner and I will go up and get good 'ole Ollie. Any questions?"

"And if Marti isn't Ollie's type?" Rafe asked, winking at Marti.

"I am every man's type," Marti replied, pouting out an air kiss back at him. "But just in case the man is brain dead as well as stupid, I will follow Ollie and make sure the women he chooses don't decide to help him out." She was packing a pistol, strapped to her thigh, under her skirt.

Steven, still struggling to catch up, was strapping into his Kevlar vest.

Jenna finished with the radios and handed them out. As the team hooked them to their belts and connected them to the headpieces, Marti took a moment just to breathe it all in. She'd missed so much of their lives and soon, she'd be gone again and she'd miss so much more. Conner, faithful and loyal, the solid rock of Nick's life and of Prodigal. He would step in front of any danger to protect those he loved. His wife, his kids, Nick, Rafe, Steven. Maybe even her. Hard to say. Then there was Rafe, the light and laughter, the charm and steadfastness. He cared deeply but rarely let it show. Jenna, the glue and the sanity. The love. Jenna was the type of woman that loved deeply. Even though she was barely a couple years older than the men, she treated them like sons.

And Steven. Precious, confused, Steven. The brainiac. When they were in school, she and Nick would spend hours and hours of studying for tests and Steven would just breeze through and ace everything. She and Nick were lucky to pull B's and C's. Steven? Straight A's. And never broke a sweat doing it. And he's a bounty hunter? What a waste. All those years in college earning degree after degree and he gives it all up to do something he doesn't even enjoy. It made no sense to her at all.

"Okay, team," Nick moved away from the desk. "Let's go get our man."

When they arrived at the brothel, Marti went in first, swaggering with an arrogance not far removed from her normal attitude of get-in-my-way-and-I'll-mow-you-down. It had been an attitude born of necessity over the years and had saved her life more than once.

The brothel was housed in a rundown neighborhood, in the middle of a residential area. While the outside of the house was as nondescript and depressing as the rest of the houses on the street, the inside was a surprise. There wasn't so much as a handprint or a scuff mark on the walls, the carpet was spotlessly clean and freshly vacuumed, and the furniture was dust-free. The air smelled faintly of air freshener and roses.

Talk about putting silk on a sow, but if they wanted to pretend they were some high class joint, that was their deception to live with.

Ollie hadn't arrived yet, but her immediate problem was the other women in the house. They didn't take kindly to a new face in the crowd. Competition ran deep in these circles, where every dollar could be the difference in the game of survival.

"What we have here?" A big black woman with hair dyed as close to white blond as she could get it, claw-like nails painted blood red, and a black leotard that showed every curve sauntered over. She looked Marti up and down with enough derision to make a lesser woman curl up and crawl away. "You looking for something, sugar?"

Marti made an equal show of looking the woman over and then curled her lip. "It ain't you, honey."

As Marti went to stroll past her, the woman grabbed Marti's arm. Marti stopped, looked at the woman's hand and then looked into her face. "Remove it or lose it."

The woman cackled. "Ain't you the tough one."

Marti made one quick move to the left, swept her foot out and the woman's eyes went wide with shock as she hit the floor. Marti looked down at her, sprawled on the floor. "Tough don't begin to cover it. *Sugar.*"

The test was over. The other women all stepped back and let her by. She had taken down the biggest and toughest of them. No one else would challenge her.

Being a bounty hunter was about taking certain calculated risks based on solid information. And sometimes, you had to be ready to go with your instincts and change the plan at a moment's notice.

Marti stopped in front of a heavy-set woman sitting in an arm chair in the corner. She had a small table at her right hand. A glass, a bottle, and an ashtray were all it held. All the creature comforts the woman wanted. She was close to sixty by Marti's best guess and the hard years were barely covered by the heavy make-up and garish red lipstick.

"I take it this place is yours."

"You take it right. The name is Rose. What do you want?"

"I need to talk to you. Alone."

The woman stared at Marti for a long moment and then nodded to the other girls. As they left the room, Marti took the time to scope out the layout. The house was a simple two story colonial. The living room had little to offer except three sofas, a bar on wheels in the corner, and a television mounted on the wall. Dark drapes covered every window. There was an entry way on the far wall that led to what was probably meant to be a dining room but with a desk and filing cabinet, must be the madam's office. Everything was immaculate.

Rose lifted her chin. "Okay, we're alone. Talk."

"In a few minutes, a man named Ollie is going to be coming through that door."

Rose reached over and poured herself a drink. She didn't offer Marti one. "He's expected."

"And he's leaving here with me."

The woman took a deep swallow and then holding the glass with both hands, tilted her head. "And why is that?"

"Because right now, this house is surrounded by bounty hunters. They are all armed and they are looking for trouble. This can be easy for you or this could be a nightmare. You play nice with us, we take our man and you go on with your day as if nothing happened. You try to warn Ollie we're here and we call our friends down at Vice and tell them all about you."

Rose smiled as she took another drink. "Ollie is bad news, honey. I sure hope you're prepared for that. He ain't gonna be as easy to knock down as Gigi was. Last time he was here, he beat two of my girls so bad they couldn't work for days."

"Trust me. Ollie isn't bad enough for what's coming."

The madam reached down in her pocket and fished out a pack of cigarettes. As she tapped one out, she said, "I don't want my place tore up, ya hear me? You break it, you pay for it."

Marti smiled. "Fair enough."

Knowing that her entire conversation was being heard by the team, she expected Nick and Conner to be coming through the door within about two minutes. She was wrong. They were in the door before Rose had her cigarette lit. Rafe came as far as the door and hung back, probably keeping watch for Ollie.

When Rose saw Conner, she coughed and laughed at the same time. "Well, ain't you the big 'un."

Conner smiled at her. "I get the job done."

"I just bet you do, sweet thing. I just bet you do."

Nick thanked the woman for her cooperation and then asked which room she would most like send Ollie into."

"Third door on the right. He likes that room 'cause he can see up and down the street from there."

"Good enough." Nick turned to Rafe. "Stay back there in Rose's office out of sight. Let us know when he's on his way up. Conner and I will be up in the bedroom. As soon as he comes in, we'll take him."

Nick turned to Marti. "We don't need you to lure him up if you don't want to do this."

Marti rolled her eyes. "Oh please. Don't go playing big brother now. I'll bring him up. I don't want any of the other girls getting hurt just in case Ollie gets rough."

Rafe disappeared back in Rose's office. Conner and Nick headed upstairs.

Ten minutes later, Ollie came through the door, bellowing for Rose to pour him a drink. Marti made a quick study. Even though she'd seen his picture, she knew that photographs could never tell her as much as seeing them move, talk, act and react. Ollie was about six feet and most of his two hundred and twenty pounds seemed to be centered around his gut. Belligerent, tough, half-drunk and mean as a cornered grizzly. He had big beefy hands and small, narrowly spaced eyes with a habit of squinting. More than likely, he was a bit near-sighted and too stubborn to get glasses.

Marti rolled her shoulders and then sauntered over. The other girls had already been told by Rose to let Marti have Ollie unless the man flat out refused her. As Ollie picked up the drink Rose had poured for him, Marti sidled up next to him and ran her hand down his arm.

"Hi, there. I bet you could be a real good time."

Ollie glanced down at her and shot her a wide grin. "And I bet you know how to treat a man."

"Oh, my yes. I sure do. And I think I know exactly what I want to do to you."

Ollie's grin only got wider as he dropped an arm over her shoulder. "I like a couple girls."

Marti ran her hand up his shirt. "Honey, if I can't get you so wrapped up you can't move within a few minutes, I'll personally come back down here and get three more of the girls to come up there and make sure you have the time of your life and I'll even pay for it."

He seemed to think on it for a minute and then nodded toward the stairs. "Let's go. Let's see if you can give as good as you talk."

"Oh, trust me. You have no idea."

Marti led the way up the stairs and up to the bedroom door. Then she stepped back and let him open it and step through first, but he held back. "You first, girl."

Marti flashed him a flirtatious smile over her shoulder and sauntered into the room, hoping he had his attention centered on her hips and not the room itself.

As soon as he made it through the door, Marti turned around. "Ollie, you missed your court date. Hands behind your back."

Ollie bellowed and grabbed for Marti. She danced back out of his way. Conner elbowed him in the face as Nick kicked out and hit Ollie on the side of his leg, hoping to knock the man to the ground. But Ollie was like an enraged bull. He swung out, clipping Nick on the chin, sending him staggering back a couple of steps. Conner took advantage of the moment to dive on him and the weight of Conner's body and all that muscle took him face down on the carpet. Nick grabbed an arm and tried to pry it back to cuff it, but Ollie wasn't going to let it happen that easy.

Rafe appeared in the doorway, ready to step in and yet unable to as the three men wrestled around on the floor. He drew his gun and started yelling for Ollie to yield, but

Ollie was beyond hearing anyone or anything as he tried his best to get away from Nick and Conner.

As Nick knelt over Ollie, trying to bend his arm back, Marti carefully reached out and pulled Nick's tazer from his utility belt. She made sure it was charged and then waited for her opportunity.

Rafe looked over at Marti. "Get ready."

"Born ready," she quipped with more confidence than she was feeling. If she missed, Ollie would be charging her like a runaway train.

A minute or two later, Ollie caught Nick in the chest, knocking the wind out of him. As Nick rolled back, Marti yelled, "Clear!"

Conner released Ollie, moving back. Ollie came up on his knees, his face contorted with rage. As he looked up at Marti, she smiled down at him. "Night-night."

The tazer hit him full in the chest. He racked back, screaming as the electric volts shot through him. He collapsed back on the floor, clutching his chest.

Conner moved fast for a man his size, taking advantage of the fact that Ollie had both hands gripping his chest and cuffed him quick. They would have preferred to have him cuffed behind his back, but sometimes, people just didn't cooperate.

Marti reached down and pulled the tazer barbs from Ollie's chest. "Next time, just put your hands behind your back and do what you're told to do."

"Next time, I'll kill you."

Conner shook his head as he helped Rafe lift Ollie to his feet. "Let's try this again, Ollie. Prodigal Recovery Agents. You missed your court date, violating the terms of your bail bond. Bail is hereby revoked. You're going back to jail."

Ollie started crying. "I'm sorry, I'm sorry. Please don't do this. It's my grandma's birthday. I have to go see her."

Marti rolled her eyes. How many times had she seen this? They act all hard and tough and mean as spit until the cuffs click shut and then they have a total meltdown.

Conner fastened the leg shackles. "Your grandmother will have to do without you this year, Ollie."

"No," the big man whined. "You don't understand. I'm her favorite."

"I wouldn't count on that lasting much longer," Marti quipped as she followed them out the door and down the hall. "If she's smart, she'll find someone that can keep his nose clean."

"You can't do this!"

Ollie continued to complain, whine, and cry all the way out to the vehicles. Nick instructed Conner and Rafe to take Ollie to Central Booking and Lockup. As they pulled off, Nick climbed behind the wheel of his own SUV and before the key was even in the ignition, he turned on Steven. "Where were you? Sleeping out there?"

"Of course not! I had no idea you might have needed me. You told me to cover the back and I covered the back."

Marti knew what was coming and tried to head it off. "Was your radio working, Steven? I don't think you arrived at the office in time for Jenna to change out your batteries."

"It worked fine," Steven retorted, slapping down Marti's attempt to help him out. "What if Ollie had gotten away from you guys and headed out the back? You'd have yelled at me for not being where you posted me."

"I need you to think, Steven. Like Marti does. She looks at a situation and if she sees a better way of dealing it out, she makes the change. She went in there and got the cooperation of everyone in the house and it went down smooth."

"And I looked at the situation and decided that I'd stay where I was just in case something went wrong. There were four of you up there in that bedroom on Ollie. You didn't need me in the way."

Sitting in the backseat, Marti wanted to knock their heads together. "What if we needed him in the back? What if we needed him in the hall? What if we didn't need him at all? Give it a rest, Nick. Steven didn't do anything wrong."

"He may not have done anything wrong, but he wants to know why I don't leave him in charge, here's the perfect example of why. He doesn't take initiative. He doesn't think on his feet. He just takes orders." Nick pulled up to a red light. "I need to know that when I'm not there, someone is handling things in a proactive way."

Steven yanked open the door of the SUV and got out. "No, you just want to know that someone is handling things your way." He slammed the door and started walking down the street.

"Steven!" Nick yelled out.

Marti put her hand on his arm. "Let him go. You've done enough damage for the day."

"I've done? How is this my fault?"

"Be proactive and think about it, brother-mine."

Saturday, 2:15 pm
Baltimore, Md

Peter Chamberland unwrapped his burger and lifted the bun.

"Ketchup, pickles, mustard and onions. Just the way you asked." Lisa bit into her chicken sandwich.

"Just checking," Peter replied. He knew that he should probably stay as far away from burgers as he could get and still be in the United States, but he was addicted. It didn't matter where they came from, although Johnny's Burgers and Buns was his favorite. How he could eat burgers five days out of seven and never gain an ounce was a bone of contention with Lisa. She ate her broiled chicken and tuna salads and power drinks and fretted over every ounce. He didn't think she weighed more than a feather soaking wet, but you couldn't tell her that.

"I hate you." Lisa glared at his burger with a longing in her eyes that wouldn't take a genius to interpret.

"It wouldn't kill you to eat a burger once in a while. All that heart-healthy food is fine, but the way you stress over every ounce and gram has to be worse for you than a burger."

She shifted a shoulder, half-turning away from him, as if that would dismiss him and his opinion.

"You know, Lisa, if you just ate half a burger a week, I'll bet you'd be a much happier person."

"I'm perfectly happy," she retorted.

"You're an uptight, nagging, lonely woman with a mean streak a mile high."

"Mile wide."

"What?"

She turned around, a half-smirk curving on her lips. "It's supposed to be a mile wide, not a mile high. And I'm not lonely. I have a wonderful cat."

Chamberland smirked. "Oh. She has a cat. Strike the lonely part."

"Absolutely. How can I have a husband expecting me to be home at a certain time to make dinner when I have you demanding that I work eighteen out of every twenty-four hours?"

"You wouldn't have it any other way. Look at all the losers I save you from having to go out with." He stuffed a few fries in his mouth.

"They say you have to kiss a lot of frogs before you find your prince. Do you have warts?"

Peter raised one eyebrow as he unwrapped his straw and stuck it down in his iced tea. "What makes you think I'm a frog and not a prince?"

"I know you too well."

The door to the office swung open and Chip burst into the room, grinning broadly. "We got it. The Baltimore Lady."

Lisa set her sandwich down. "And what is the Baltimore Lady?"

Chip pulled out a chair, spun it around and straddled it. "She's supposed to be a fishing vessel registered out of the Baltimore Harbor. And guess what?"

"She's a boat."

"Funny girl." Chip looked over at Peter. "That's how they're getting the guns into Baltimore. And here's the best part. She's coming in from Charleston in about three hours. And guess what happened in Charleston over the last week?"

Peter grabbed his burger as he stood up. "Three gun stores were hit. Call everyone in. Let's see what kind of fish this fishing vessel is bringing in today."

Chapter 10

Saturday, 3:45 pm
Prodigal Offices, Baltimore, Md

Steven grabbed a cab and was a bit surprised that he beat Nick and the team back to the offices. He went inside, tossed his radio on Jenna's desk, walked straight down the hall and out the back door. Within minutes, he was driving away. His cell phone rang. He checked it, saw that it was Nick, and tossed the phone down on the console. Nick was the last person he wanted to talk to right now.

He did his job. But it was never good enough for Nick. He loved his brother—when they were anywhere but work. Nick was dependable, responsible, and loved his family beyond measure, but he could also be hard-headed, controlling, and aggravating to the max. And no where did those negative qualities rear their ugly heads more than when Nick was at Prodigal.

His cell phone rang again. This time it was Marti. "What?"

"Why did you leave like that?"

"Because I have a lot going on in my life right now and I'm not in the mood for Nick's overbearing second-guessing. I know his adrenalin rush after a job demands that he look at every detail and criticize, but I can't handle that today. Frankly, I'm tired of being the brunt of his whippings."

He heard Marti sigh. "You know how he is. He doesn't mean anything by it."

"He means everything by it. It's why Dad left him in charge. And it's why he's so incredibly good at his job. But while Prodigal may be Nick's life outside of Jessica and Krystal, it's not mine."

"It's not mine, either, but I know not to take Nick so seriously. Like you said, it's why he's so good at what he does."

"Well, I've been taking it for years and it's been fine, but not today."

"What's going on?"

"I'll tell you if you tell me."

There was a moment of silence. "What are you talking about?"

"You know what I'm talking about, Marti. The secret phone calls. The papers you hide when someone comes close. The file you have locked in your desk."

"Have you been snooping in my things?"

He easily ignored the outrage in her voice. Marti wouldn't think twice about snooping in her brother's business, homes, and lives, but heaven forbid anyone invade any aspect of her life. "No. I'm just observant. And I know you. I know you have something going on that you don't want anyone to know about. Are you getting ready to leave again?"

"No more so than last month or last week. But I didn't call to talk about my life. I want to know what's going on with you that has you so on edge." Her voice lost the sharp edge and softened. "Talk to me, Steven."

"Nothing I want to talk about right now. Look, I have to go. I'll talk to you later." Steven hung up the phone and tossed it back to the console. It took him forty-five minutes to get to Holy Cross Hospital. And another ten to get to the room. When he walked in, he was surprised not to see anyone else there.

His old friend Kevin had bruises all over his face and his nose was swollen. His right arm was bandaged and in a sling. He was dressed in his street clothes and perched on the edge of the bed. He tried to offer up a smile to Steven but it came across more of a grimace. "You came."

Steven walked over to the bed. "Of course I came. Where is Sara?"

Kevin looked away. "Can you take me home or not? They tell me my car is totaled."

"Of course I can, but I don't understand what happened."

Kevin eased off the bed, flinching as he stood up. "Not much to understand. I was in an accident. Flipped my car off the Beltway. Ended up here."

A nurse appeared in the doorway with a wheelchair. "Here you go, Mr. Fitz."

"I can walk."

"That's against hospital policy." Her smile remained firmly in place, but her eyes flashed a signal that she wasn't in the mood for games. This wasn't a suggestion. It was an order. "Have a seat."

Steven waited until he had Kevin in the car before he tried again. "Where is Sara?"

"I have no idea. The hospital tried to call her, but she didn't answer."

Kevin was withdrawn and refusing to look Steven in the eyes. Sara, devoted wife and best friend, was nowhere to be found. Everything was wrong with this picture.

Steven started the car and backed out of the parking space. Then he stopped and looked over at Kevin. "You want to tell me what's going on?"

Kevin shook his head. "Not right now."

They rode in silence until Steven went to take the ramp at the Connecticut Avenue exit on the Beltway. "We're not going to the condo. Take the exit for Rockville Pike. You're dropping me off at the Marriott in Bethesda."

"You and Sara are separated?" It all started to make sense. Kevin's depressed air. Sara's absence.

"She left me."

"What did you do?" As if Steven even had to ask. He'd known Kevin for years. He loved Kevin. Best friends and all that, but he wasn't blind to Kevin's faults.

Kevin's eyes were blazing when he whipped his head around and looked at Steven. "Why does have to be me? How do you know Sara didn't do something? Maybe I was angry at her for something and she asked me to leave. Give us time to cool off."

The temper in Kevin's face didn't intimidate Steven at all. They'd been friends far too long for that. "Because if the two of you were having a spat and were just cooling off, nothing short of a nuclear bomb would have kept that woman from your side. She worships the ground you walk on. Besides, this is me you're talking to. Sara would never be so angry at you that she'd let you leave unless you did something like cheat on her again."

Kevin turned and looked out the passenger window and the hint of color amid the bruises on Kevin's face told

Steven he'd hit the target dead on center. "You didn't. *Kevin*."

"It was nothing. A minor fling with some waitress. No big deal. Sara will get over it. I just need to give her some time to realize that I mean more to her than her silly pride."

"Is that what you think this is about? Her silly pride?" Steven blew out a heavy breath, trying to push all the frustration out of his body. There was no point getting angry. "I don't think Sara is going to get over betrayal."

"I confessed to her. That should tell her something."

"Yeah. It told her that you cheated on her. Again."

Steven turned and drove up the entrance to the hotel. As he turned toward the patron's parking lot, Kevin shook his head. "Just drop me off up front. I just need to get some sleep."

Steven complied, knowing that Kevin just wanted to get away from the conversation. "Look," he said as he pulled up front and put the car in park. "I know you're hurting and we've been friends a long, long time. If you need me, you call me. I'm here for you, pal, okay?"

"Yeah. Okay." Kevin eased out of the car and then leaned down over the open car door. "I really do appreciate the ride. I'm just not in the mood to talk right now."

"I understand. Call me when you are."

Kevin nodded and then shut the door. Steven watched Kevin limp up to the revolving brass door and then disappear inside.

As he pulled back on the Washington Beltway, heading toward the Baltimore-Washington Parkway, he tried calling Sara. He got her answering machine and left a message.

He had just taken the ramp to get on the BW Parkway when she called him back. "Is Kevin with you?"

"No. How are you doing?"

"I've been better, all things considered. I gather you've talked to him. If you're calling to ask me to forgive him and take him back, the answer is no."

"That's not why I called. I just picked him up at the hospital and drove him to his hotel. He was in an accident last night. Flipped his car on the Beltway."

The silence hung for so long, Steven started to think his cell had dropped the call. Or that she had hung up. "How bad was he hurt?"

"A few cracked ribs, sprained ankle, bumps, bruises and I think he'll have black eyes for a few days." A police car up ahead had a car pulled over. Steven automatically checked his speed to make sure he didn't draw the officer's attention.

"He was drinking heavily."

"I thought as much. He's hurting pretty bad and I'm not talking about the accident."

"He's not hurting nearly as bad as he'd like everyone to think. I'm tired of it, Steven. I'm just tired."

"He does love you, Sara."

"Sure, but he loves himself more. And that is the problem. If he wants another woman to make himself feel better, it doesn't matter how much it's going to hurt me. Nothing matters except what he wants at that given moment."

"I can't argue with that. What are you going to do?"

"Live my life."

"I mean, are you okay? Do you need anything?"

There was a soft sigh and he could almost see her pulling into herself. "I'm okay, Steven. Honest. I think I've been preparing myself for this for a long time."

"I'll take your word on that, but if you need anything, let me know. I mean anything. Money, a shoulder, advice, opinion, the lawn mowed. Whatever. You call me."

She laughed then, but it vibrated with a ribbon of pain. "Thanks, Steven. You're a good man."

By six-thirty, Steven was back in Baltimore, heading around the I-695 loop toward home when his stomach growled, reminding him that he hadn't eaten since breakfast. He stopped at Subway and picked up a sub to take home with him. When he pulled into the driveway, he could hear Killer howling inside. His neighbors must be thrilled.

Marti had suggested a dog cage to keep Killer out of trouble while Steven was at work. Second day in the cage wasn't going any better than the first.

Once inside, he saw it was actually worse. Killer had shredded the dog bed he was supposed to be sleeping on, scattering fabric and foam as far as eight feet from the cage. His water bowl was empty and there were multiple tooth marks in the stainless steel. Even his favorite toy had felt the brunt of Killer's discontent. It was now in about five pieces on the bottom of the cage.

As soon as Killer saw Steven, the howling intensified.

"I honestly don't know what I'm going to do with you." He fed the dog, put him out in the back yard, checked through the mail, changed clothes, and then settled down in front of his computer with his meal to check on the portfolio.

Two hours later, the phone rang. Jarred from his work, he started, glancing up at the clock as he picked up the phone. "Your dime."

"Shepherd?" It was Chamberland. "Are you hiding Miss Morrow?"

"Hiding her? What are you talking about?"

"She's gone."

Steven closed his eyes as the possibilities assaulted him. "Explain gone."

"Missing, unable to be found, not home, not at work, not here, not anywhere. Are you telling me she's not with you?"

"I have no idea where she is. Last time I talked to her, she was at home."

"When was that?"

"Last night."

Chamberland was silent for a moment and Steven used the opportunity to hit him as hard as he could. "I thought you had people watching out for her."

"There was a glitch."

"A glitch." Steven turned off his computer and shoved his chair back from his desk. "Explain glitch."

"If you hear from her, let me know." And Chamberland was gone.

Saturday, 9:30 pm
Marriott Hotel, Bethesda, Md.

Kevin had never been so miserable, so lonely, or in so much pain. The medications were barely taking the edge off now. He'd tried to call Sara four times, but she never picked up the phone. He'd left three messages and on the fourth call, just slammed the phone down. Didn't she understand this was not the time to leave him? Didn't she care that he was hurt?

He kept his thumb on the remote, flipping from channel to channel. Nothing amused him. Nothing distracted him.

There had been a time when he couldn't have imagined cheating on Sara. Racing home from work to be with her, sharing every detail of his day with her, watching her laugh, smile, make dinner. It was all good. He wasn't sure when she didn't laugh as quickly or smile as much, or when he stop rushing home. But somewhere along the line, he started to notice other women and then he started to notice that they were looking at him the way Sara once had—as if he was the most intriguing man in the world.

At first, he just flirted with them. Spent a little money on them. Flattered them as much as they flattered him. And from flirting, it wasn't a far jump to more. The first time, he felt so guilty, so ashamed, he'd driven around for two hours before going home, hoping that Sara would be asleep before he came crawling in. The second time was a little easier. And soon, it didn't bother his conscience much at all. In fact, he'd convinced himself that Sara didn't care what he did and was content with the way things were between them.

But he'd been wrong. She had cared very much and now he was sitting in a hotel room with sore ribs, a splitting headache, and no idea how to get Sara to be reasonable and let him come home. There was a time when you dealt with little problems in a relationship and there were times when you set it all aside to take care of each other. He needed her to take care of him right now.

Grabbing the phone, he dialed home again. Four rings and he heard himself asking himself to leave a message. "Sara, it's me. Look, I know you're upset and you have every right to be, but I'm in a bad way here and I need you. Call me."

He hung up the phone. If she didn't call soon, he was just going to go home whether she liked it or not. It was, after all, his house, too.

Saturday, 10:35 pm
Timonium, Md.

Steven heard Killer scratching at the back door, wanting to come back in. But his thoughts were racing around Andrea Morrow. If those men had found her, she could be dead. She didn't have the money to give them and they wouldn't take kindly to that.

He called her home and cell phone number. No answer on either line. He left a message for her to call him as soon as possible, but he didn't have much hope that she would. If Chamberland was concerned, there was a good reason for it.

It didn't take more than five minutes to make up his mind. He couldn't trust Chamberland to do this right. And there was no way he could sleep knowing that she was in trouble and needed help.

He called Nick first, only to have Jessica tell him that Nick had taken Krystal and some of her friends to the movies. No point calling his cell phone. It would be off. Then he made a call to Conner, only to get an answering machine.

He was just setting the phone down when it rang. He picked it up, assuming it was Conner. "That was fast."

"Mr. Shepherd?"

The woman was whispering so low, he put one finger in his open ear. "Hello?"

"It's me. Andrea. I'm in trouble."

"Can you speak up?"

"No. They'll hear me."

"Who will hear you?"

"They have me in the back of a van. They'll be back soon."

"Where are you?"

"Parked at the 75 Park and Ride. Please."

"I'm on my way."

"They're coming back. They're going to kill me."

"Andrea. I'm coming. Okay? Andrea? Andrea!"

But the line had gone dead.

He tried to call Conner, Rafe, and Nick one more time as he sped down the highway. He left messages everywhere.

In all the years since he'd quit college and joined his brother at Prodigal, he'd never led on a capture. He was always the look-out, the backup to the backup. Nick, Conner, and Rafe were the type to go charging in, ready for action, and more than capable, and ready, to handle anything they had to face at a moment's notice. Not Steven.

He knew that doing this without backup wasn't the smartest move, but it was all Andrea had at the moment. And he couldn't let her down. Not just because it would cost him ten grand he could ill-afford to lose, but because the thought that Chamberland was using another innocent, just the way he had Nick's daughter, was intolerable.

As he passed by the Prodigal Offices, he debated whether to use his Mustang or a company SUV and decided on the Mustang. If he hit trouble, he knew that little machine would outrun most anything chasing it and leave them in the dust. If it went off-road, well, he could regret not taking the SUV then.

He pushed the speed as best he could, slowing down for red lights, but running them when he could. As he hit the ramp onto 695, he began to sweat and wiped it off with the back of his hand. Would he be in time?

Saturday, 10:45 pm
ATF Headquarters, Baltimore, Md

Peter Chamberland was furious. He wasn't sure exactly who he was the most angry with. Chip for misunderstanding when Peter gave the order to assemble *everyone* to go after the Baltimore Lady, or himself for not clarifying that he meant everyone *except* those keeping Andrea under surveillance. Either way, the woman was gone and whatever chance they had of catching the man or men behind the gun sale was blown.

Chip was keeping his distance, manning the phones and keeping track of their efforts to find the woman. Lisa was out on the streets with one of the teams.

He leaned back and yelled over to Chip. "Do we have that PEN order yet?" As soon as they discovered Andrea was missing, Peter had called his boss to push through a PEN order which would give them permission from the courts to track Andrea's cell phone in hopes that she had it on and even better, was using it.

Chip shook his head at Peter as he continued to talk on the phone with someone.

All in all, it had been a really bad day. They had descended on the harbor in force, only to find the Baltimore Lady sitting in the water, peacefully docked and not a crew member in site. After an hour of waiting to see if anyone was going to show up, Peter had sent one of his men to talk to the marina supervisor, only to find out that the Baltimore Lady hadn't been out of the harbor in over a month. Owned by an old man who vacationed in Florida until April and returned for the crab season, the boat was rarely used and then only by the old man's nephew for short fishing trips in the bay.

The whole thing had been a wild goose chase and it accomplished exactly what someone wanted. The ATF, thinking they had a shipment of guns coming in, had gone running, leaving Andrea unprotected.

What bothered Peter, and was consuming his thoughts, was how they did it. Who had enough clout to put out that kind of information? Misinformation, exactly. It was pulled off with such perfection that it was maddening.

The answer was there, just out of reach—much like a word dancing on the tip of your tongue that just seems to elude you. He knew he'd figure it out, given time. The question that seems to taunt him was simple. Would he figure it out before the next shipment of guns made it out onto the streets?

Saturday, 10:55 pm
Baltimore, Md

Steven wove through traffic praying the whole way that he didn't blow past a cop who would stop him for speeding. He was afraid if he saw those flashing lights, he'd give them reason to charge him for a high speed chase. Of course, he'd probably appreciate their help when he got to the Park and Ride, but that's providing they didn't just lock him up before he found Andrea.

As he spotted the Security Boulevard exit up ahead, he moved into the right lane. Just beyond the exit, he saw the ramp for I-70. The ramp split and he stayed left, curving around and heading east into the Park and Ride. As the road straightened out, he increased his speed. It had been close to twenty minutes. What were the chances that they were still there or that she was still alive?

He didn't want to calculate.

As the Park and Ride came into view, he looked over to the left, trying to spot a van. There were three. One white Econoline with ladders secured to the top. The second was a red minivan and he knew he could discount that one. Too many windows.

And then, at the far end of the first lot, he saw a dark panel van parked across two spots.

Steven slowed down, taking the sharp curve into the first lot. So far, not a sign of anyone around the van. When he was just a few car lengths away from the van, he saw a big black dog circle around to the driver's door. The dog jumped up and barked at the window, then started scratching furiously.

Stopping the Mustang, Steven jumped out and ran toward the van. "Chaos?"

The dog dropped to all fours and looked over at Steven, whining loudly.

The doors to the van were locked. Steven tried to look in, but couldn't see anything. But if Chaos was trying to get in, then Andrea was there somewhere.

He ran back over to the Mustang and retrieved a tire iron from the trunk. Keeping his head turned sideways, he swung the tire iron at the driver's window, shattering it. Dropping the tire iron, he reached in the window and popped the locks. Then he slid the side door open. "Andrea?"

Chaos nearly knocked him over, jumping into the van. Immediately, he started pawing at a sack against the far wall. Steven crawled in, pushing the dog out of his way. "Good boy, now let me help her."

He pulled the blankets away and found Andrea, duct taped and bound. She gazed up at him, eyes wide with a mix of tears, fear, and relief. He carefully pulled the tape off her mouth. "I'm sorry if this hurts."

"It's a trap! Get out of here!"

"I assumed as much. Now, come on."

"He's out there. You have to go. Please, hurry."

He sat her up and pulling his knife out of his pocket, sawed at the ropes around her wrists. As soon as he pulled the rope away, she rubbed her wrists, watching him work on the ropes around her ankles. "You have to go!"

Steven backed out of the van, looking around. He didn't see anyone lurking nearby, but he did see a car enter the parking lot. Grabbing Andrea's arm, he helped her out of the van. "Let's go. Now."

The car stopped and a man got out. "Is everything okay here, Ma'am?"

Steven saw the twinkle of a badge on the man's shirt. "It's okay. My name is Steven Shepherd. I'm a fugitive recovery agent."

"I don't care who you are, buddy. Step away from the woman."

Steven slowly raised his hands and sidestepped away from Andrea. "This isn't what you think it is."

"I want you to take out your weapon and toss it on the ground."

It was ridiculous. Why in the world was this officer acting like this? Slowly, Steven pulled his gun from his holster and gently tossed it away. Then he glanced over at Andrea. She was backing away from him, shaking her head. "I'm sorry."

He was still trying to figure it out when seconds later, the officer raised his weapon and pulled the trigger.

Chapter 11

Saturday, 11:15 pm
I-70 Park and Ride, Baltimore, Md

Steven dropped and rolled, hoping to hold on to his gun as he slammed into gravel and concrete. Pain racked up his body and the knee that had just healed screamed at him as it twisted under him. He knew he'd been shot in the side, but had no idea how deeply or how badly.

"So, she was smart enough to have a partner." The shooter took a step in Steven's direction. "Where's the money?"

"Who are you?"

"If I shoot you again, I will make it count. Now where is the money?"

"The ATF have it. They're just trying to flush you out." Groaning, Steven half-rolled over, tucking one hand beneath him as he fished for the small revolver tucked in the small of his back. "Andrea? Get in the car! Now!"

Sure enough, the shooter was distracted by Steven's shout and turned his head to look over at Andrea. Steven came up on one knee—his good one—aimed and fired. The shooter spun and hit the ground. But as Steven scrambled to his feet, two men jumped out of one of the white vans. He should have known they wouldn't have just one man holding Andrea.

The two men started shooting as they jumped behind the concrete barrier. Limping as he ran and skipped his way to the car, Steven kept firing without even looking to see if he was even coming close to hitting anything.

By the time he was behind the wheel, the Mustang was running, Andrea was in the passenger seat and Chaos was in the back. "Get down and stay down," he yelled as another shot rang out and the back window of the Mustang shattered. Andrea screamed, covering her head with her hands and ducking down, her head between her knees.

Steven shifted into first gear and slammed his foot on the gas pedal. The car responded as if hit by a train—tires screeching, engine screaming. It roared up the strip of parking lot but then Steven hit another problem. The parking lot looped around and exited right next to the entrance. There was only one way out and that meant driving right by the two remaining shooters.

For the first time, Steven wished the old car had power windows as he cranked the window down. When he'd inherited the classic from his dad, he thought he'd died and gone to heaven. How he loved that car! He never changed anything in it, including the fact that all it had was an AM radio.

Gripping the steering wheel with his right hand and the gun with his left, Steven readied himself. He'd never shot a gun with his left hand, but he figured he really didn't have to hit anything if he could at least come close enough to force the other guy to keep his head down.

"Can you shift for me?"

"What?" Andrea peered up at him.

"Shift when I tell you to shift!"

"I know how to drive a stick shift. Just go."

"Hold on," he said, gritting his teeth. He slammed his foot down on the accelerator and the old car gave him everything she had and then some. The engine began to whine. He pushed in the clutch and smooth as silk, Andrea shifted into 2nd gear for him. The shooters stood up and aimed at the car. Steven began shooting and lucked out. Two of his shots hit the concrete close enough to send concrete chips flying up at the shooter. They dived down and out of view. Steven shot twice more, just to make his point and hit the curve, dropping his gun in his lap, grabbing the wheel with his left and the shifter with his right. The tires skidded as the rear end caught and propelled the car out of the turn as smooth as silk. He shifted again.

Say what you would about a sports car, there was little that could compete with the old '65 Mustang. It was just pure power on wheels. But Steven could only take a momentary delight in the feel of the car beneath him. The shooter was running toward the van and another car was racing in. Steven was willing to bet it was the rest of the men that had taken Andrea.

"Well, that was fun."

"I'm glad you think so." Andrea swiped at the tears trickling down her face.

Steven glanced in the rear view mirror. It wouldn't take long for the men to jump in that van and start pursuing them. "They knew you called me?"

"They heard me on the phone with you and set this up to take you out or however you say it."

He whipped the wheel, taking the ramp back onto the Beltway, heading north.

"Where are we going?"

If they wanted him out of the picture, they knew where he lived, so his home wasn't going to be safe. "In my pocket. Get out my cell phone please." Now was when he really missed the Bluetooth technology in the SUV. "Look in the address book for Nick. Call his cell."

Hopefully he was out of the movie theater.

"Right to voice mail."

Steven smacked the steering wheel. "Try Conner."

"Cell?"

"Yeah." Why not? He wasn't having much luck finding anyone tonight.

"Voice mail."

"Where is everyone tonight? Look up Rafe."

Rafe answered the phone on the second ring and Andrea handed the phone to Steven. "Rafe? Look, I'm in a bit of trouble." He explained the circumstances and then asked. "If they're looking for me, my house isn't safe, is it?"

"Not a chance. Head for the office. They'll be looking for that Mustang and it's not exactly a car that will blend on the roads. Switch over to one of the SUV's. Get your gear bag. And then get out of there as fast as you can. Hopefully they'll go to your house first."

"And then what?"

"By then, I'll have assembled Nick and Conner and we'll get this fixed. Just drive and stay on the road and keep your cell phone on."

"Will do."

"And Steven?"

"Yeah?"

"Keep your head down."

Sunday, 12:05 am
White Marsh, Maryland

"What do you mean, he's on the run? On the run from whom?" Nick had been on his way to bed when he realized he'd forgotten to turn his cell phone back on after leaving the theater with Krystal and her three friends. Blame it on the headache four screeching, laughing, demanding teenager girls can cause. As soon as he turned it on, it rang. It was Rafe.

Nick eased the bedroom door closed and turned on the hall light. He didn't want to wake up Jessica who had gone to bed early. They hadn't told anyone yet, but Jessica was pregnant again and the fatigue was sending her to bed early and keeping her in bed late. He tried to give her as much rest as he could.

He listened to Rafe explain as he headed downstairs. "I can't believe this. Why would they want to hurt Steven? All he did was bail the woman out. It's not like he's been playing bodyguard over her."

"I don't know, Nick. This does not pass the smell test at all."

"See if you can get in touch with Conner. I think he and Ria were going to her parents for an anniversary party. They should be home by now. I'm going to get dressed and I'll meet you guys at the office."

When Nick stepped into his bedroom, Jessica raised her head. "Is everything okay?"

"Steven is in a bit of trouble. I'll fix it. Go back to sleep."

She yawned and burrowed down under the covers. "Love you."

He leaned over and kissed her on the forehead. "Love you more. Now sleep."

Within ten minutes, Nick had changed into jeans and a sweatshirt and was on his way to the office. He thought briefly about calling Marti, but there wasn't much she could do, so why disturb her sleep, too?

When he pulled up to the Prodigal building, he expected to be the first one there, so it surprised him to see all the lights on. He drove around to the back and saw Steven's Mustang parked askew, Rafe's Hybrid tucked close to the back door, and Conner's pickup truck pulling in behind him.

Nick walked around Steven's car with a flashlight and counted four bullet holes in addition to the back window being blown out. Someone had been very determined.

"I don't like the feel of this." Conner knelt down, running his finger over a bullet hole near the rear bumper. "This guy was seriously trying to stop Steven. If this had penetrated the gas tank, he'd be toast."

"Thank you for that visual," Nick replied as he leaned in the driver's window and looked around. Blood on the seat.

Inside, they found Rafe going through the gear bags. "About time you guys got here."

"Steven's hurt," Nick said to no one in particular.

"I saw that," Rafe relied.

"Did you make coffee or buy that on the way here?" Conner eyed the coffee.

"Both."

Conner turned and left the room. Nick yelled out at him, "I'll take a Dew."

"Duh," Rafe muttered.

"What do we know?"

"Nothing more than I've told you."

Conner appeared in the doorway. "Police are here."

Nick glanced at Rafe and then back to Conner. "Let them in."

Rafe dropped his feet to the floor. "Why are they here?"

"We're about to find out, I'm sure." Nick edged his hip on the corner of his desk and folded his arms across his chest.

Two officers followed Conner into the office. They must have been relatively new to the department because Nick didn't know either of them and he knew most of the officers from his days on the force. He glanced at the names badges. Harford and Weingard.

Weingard stepped forward, his hand on the grip of his gun. It was a posture that Nick was more than familiar with. "We're looking for Steven Shepherd."

"I'm Nick Shepherd. His brother. He's not here right now. What's this about?"

"Are you expecting him? Or can we find him at home?" Harford glanced around the room.

Nick didn't like the way Harford was dodging his question. Well, if this guy wanted to mark his territory, he was about to find out who was the bigger dog in the yard. Nick leaned back and picked up the phone and hit one of the speed dial buttons. "Hi, Judy. Nick Shepherd here. I'm sorry for calling so late, but is Mitchell there?"

"Sure, Nick. Hold on."

Nick noticed he was starting to get Harford's attention. "Who are you calling, Mr. Shepherd?"

"Mitchell Scott. An old friend from my days on the force." He didn't bother stating the obvious—Police Chief, your boss.

Harford dropped his eyes. Point won. *Woof.*

"Nick? What's going on? Do you know what time it is?"

"Were you asleep?"

"You know better than that, but if I don't give you a hard time, who will? So what's up?"

Nick made a point of staring at Harford. "I have two of your officers here in my office looking for Steven. What's going on?"

"I have no idea. Hold on a sec."

Nick smiled. "Sure. I'll hold."

Harford stepped forward. "There was no need to call the Chief. I would have told you that we need to talk to your brother about the murder of a police officer tonight."

"Are you trying to tell me that you think my brother murdered a police officer?" Nick didn't know whether to deck the guy or laugh in his face. But then Mitchell came back on the line and the change in his voice hit Nick hard.

"Nick. We have a problem. A police officer was shot and killed tonight and Steven's gun was found at the scene. The officer's gun is missing. And a car was seen racing from the scene and it was a '65 Mustang. Where is he, Nick?"

"I honestly don't know, but just because his gun was there doesn't mean he shot anyone. Steven wouldn't do that. You know him."

"I do. But we need to talk to him, Nick. Bring him to me."

"Mitchell."

"I know, Nick. I know. But innocent or not, you have to bring him in. The longer he's out there in the wind, the guiltier he looks. Find him, Nick. *Now.*"

Sunday, 2:05 am
Baltimore, Md near Camden Yards

"It's done. He's dead. It went off perfect. After he left, I got Ralph to bring the cop down to the parking lot, shot him, and left the bounty hunter's gun there with him."

Parked at the entrance to Camden Yards, he let his car idle as he sat, arm propped on the open window, observing the driver of the other car. He didn't like Tony. Didn't like having anything to do with him, but sometimes, like now, he came in handy. A sociopath with a love of killing, he'd hire out to anyone for the chance to kill for money.

He hated having the officer killed, but the man had nosed around a little too much and overheard something he wasn't meant to hear. Unfortunately, it cost a good man his life.

Tony grinned at him. "Did you hear me? I said I killed him. Put a good scare into the bounty hunter, too. Another couple of inches and he'd be dead as your cop."

"I heard you. What did you do with Joey's body?"

"Hid real good. No worries. No one will ever find it."

Sitting behind the wheel of his F-250, Tony looked like a little kid playing in his daddy's truck. Short, a little bald, a little too happy with the idea of death. "Now, you gonna pay me or what?"

He picked up the envelope from the console between the seats and passed it through the window to Tony who grabbed it, looked it in, grinned again and tipped his head as he sped off.

He sat there a minute, coming to terms with it. No turning back now. It was done. And now he had to make the next move. Shifting the car into drive, he slowly pulled out of the lot and turning on his flashing lights, sped down the street toward the station.

Sunday 2:35 am
Catoctin Mountains, Maryland

Steven pulled off Route 15 and headed up the mountain. After driving on the highway for the last thirty miles, he had to make a conscious effort to slow down for the twisting, winding mountain road. Some of the turns were so sharp, he practically had to slow to a crawl to keep from going off the road. More than once, a deer jumped out in front of him, leading others across the narrow road.

Andrea had been asleep for the past hour, but as he made a sharp turn, she stirred, then yawned. "Where are we?"

"Near Thurmont."

"Is that in Maryland?"

"You've never heard of Thurmont? Camp David? Presidential retreat?"

"I've heard of Camp David." She sat up a little straighter, rubbing her eyes with hands.

"Well, Thurmont is the closest town to Camp David. Many a President has come down from the retreat to dine at one of the restaurants in town. Usually McDonalds."

"You're making that up?"

"Actually, I'm not. In fact, there was a little brouhaha a few years back because Clinton didn't come down to eat at McDonalds and they took it a little personal since every other President has dropped by at least once." He glanced in his rearview mirror again, satisfied that they weren't being followed. For the past hour and a half, he'd been winding around down one road and up another with no real destination in mind. But now he was tired of driving and he needed some time to think.

"So, we're going to Camp David?"

"Not in this lifetime. No way we'd get anywhere close to it. But there is a camp ground up here. My dad used to bring the family up here at least once every summer."

"And we're going camping?"

"Sort of. I'm tired and I need to just park and rest for a little while. I need to figure out what to do next." And he had a temple-pounding headache that was either rooted in fatigue, lack of food, or a deadly sense of mixed anger and dread.

"I'm really sorry I got you into trouble."

"Trouble?" he was dimly aware of his voice rising in with a hint of temper and fully aware of the fact that she was as much a victim as he was. "I killed a police officer tonight. Obviously, he was a dirty cop, but still."

"Oh, that guy wasn't a cop. I don't know where he got the uniform and badge from but he was one of the guys that kidnapped me. He changed into the uniform after I called you."

"Well, my brother called while you were asleep. It seems I am now wanted for killing a police officer."

Andrea shook her head. "They can't do that! He was obviously working for the bad guys. He kidnaps me and shoots you, but you defend me and yourself and you're the one in trouble?"

"The whole thing feels like a setup, but why would those guys want me out of the way? I was no threat to them at all. None. So this makes no sense. Right now, I have the police out there just waiting for the opportunity to call me a fugitive on the run and Nick is waiting for me to call him back and I don't know what to do."

"But you didn't do it."

"Just like you didn't try to sell a shipment of guns." He glanced over at her for a second and saw her turn away to look out the window. The last thing he wanted was to poke at her, but nothing in his life had gone right from the moment he'd met her. "You'll have to forgive me if I'm a little hostile right now, but the first time I meet you, you help a fugitive escape by attacking me. Now you help someone murder a police officer and frame me for the murder. Nice work for an innocent school teacher."

Backing into a campsite so that he was partially hidden by trees and brush but could keep an eye on the road coming into the campground, he parked. The sudden silence was broken only by the ticking of the engine and the soft sniffles as Andrea wiped away her tears.

"I didn't sell those guns. I don't know anything about guns. I've never even fired one. This is all a big mistake."

"Oh, this is a mistake, all right. And I'm the one that made it. Chamberland must be laughing hard enough to shake Baltimore."

He stared out the windshield, watching two deer slip out of the woods and look over at the truck as if wondering how dangerous it was. They must have decided it wasn't too friendly because they turned with their tails up in alarm mode and darted off into the brush. If only someone had flagged a warning at him before he got involved with this woman.

"Steven?"

"What?"

"Your cell phone is ringing."

Steven reached down into the console and picked it up. "Talk to me and you better have good news."

"I wish I did." Nick told him. "It's going to take time to get the ballistics report but they're not waiting. They want you to come in and answer questions."

"If I do, I'll have to bring Andrea in with me and once she's back in the system, they'll probably find a way to kill her while she's sleeping or something."

"You still think she's innocent?"

He reached up and rubbed his forehead. The conflict between what he could see and what he believed was torturing him. Was she as innocent as he believed she was? Or was she as guilty as it appeared?

"I don't know what to think, Nick. Nothing about any of this is making any sense at all. Why lure me down there? Why kill that officer? Why leave Andrea in the van? Why use Andrea to broker the guns in the first place? Why ask me to bail her out? Why lie about the money?"

"All good questions and so far, we don't have any good answers. What do you want to do?"

"Take two aspirin and sleep for about ten hours, but since that's not going to happen any time soon, I don't know."

"Why are you up in the mountains?"

Steven sat up straighter and then slumped down. "You're tracking me."

"Well, it's not like it's hard since all of our vehicles have tracking on them, Steven. And we're probably not the only ones. They may not be able to find your vehicle yet, but they will be. And there's your cell phone. And Andrea's."

"What kind of world is it when we can't disappear anymore?"

"Welcome to the new world of Big Brother. Steven, you need to come in."

Steven glanced over at Andrea, staring at him with wide, glassy eyes, as if her whole future rested in his hands and she was holding her breath to find out how it would turn out. "I just can't help feeling that if I do, it would be a huge mistake. Nick, something is going on. Why kill that police officer? And why was he there? That keeps rolling around in my head and all I can figure is that he was set-up same as I was. So why? Why did they want him dead?"

Sunday, 3:25 am
Prodigal Offices, Baltimore, Md

Marti parked the Vette in front of the building and climbed out. She didn't expect the whole place to be lit up and everyone here. They must have gotten a lead on a fugitive. Well, didn't that just step all over her privacy? She wasn't going to be able to send that fax now.

The street was quiet. Lights out in the surrounding buildings. People tucked securely in their beds. The street lamps dotted the empty avenue like runway lights down a deserted runway.

She almost turned around and headed back home. *Well, as long as I'm up, might as well put it to good use.*

She found Nick on the phone, Conner pacing in front of the window and Rafe sprawled out on Nick's sofa. "Off to bring someone in?"

Nick held up a finger in her direction. Rafe moved his feet to the coffee table so she could sit down. "The police think Steven killed an officer. He's in hiding while Nick is trying to get to the bottom of it."

"Steven? Kill? Never happen. Why in the world would they think such a thing?" Her brother was about as capable of murder as this building was of flying.

Conner rolled his shoulders and then stretched. "Supposedly, they have a witness and they found Steven's gun at the scene."

"A witness?" Marti shrugged out of her jacket. "Give me five minutes with this so-called witness. No way did he see Steven shoot a cop. Not happening."

"We may know that, but unfortunately, there are a lot of police officers ready to believe the worst."

Nick hung up the phone. "What brings you in at this hour?"

Dodging the question, Marti quickly bombarded him with questions. "What's this about Steven? They don't really think he'd kill a cop, do they? They all know Steven. He has trouble killing a mouse because it has big eyes. What are you going to do? How can we help him?"

Nick gave her a quick run down of the events and then ran a hand down his face. "We all know Steven didn't do this and that he's not capable of doing anything remotely like this. Right now, I'm burning up the phone lines with every source I have on the force trying to calm things down and hopefully convince them that Steven is innocent. Cooler heads need to prevail right now."

"Where is Steven?"

"Up in the mountains." He pushed back from his desk and stretched out his legs. "Can anyone get me a Dew?"

Rafe slowly ambled to his feet. "I'll get it."

"I'll die of thirst before he gets back." Nick looked back over at Marti. "As long as you're here, we might as well put you to work. The officer's name was Ryan Stewart. Been with the force three years. Married. One child. That's all I know. I want you to dig into his life. Find out why someone wanted him dead."

Marti nodded. "I can do that. But first I want to know what the plan is. Besides calling your friends and asking them not to lynch Steven."

She could see the fatigue on his face, pulling down on his eyes and mouth. In the way his shoulders were slumped. There was no doubt that Nick would move heaven and earth to protect his family and that included Steven and her, but she also knew sometimes there was nothing you could do to save the ones you loved.

"Honestly? I don't know. My first suggestion was that Steven go on in and talk to the police. Show that he has nothing to hide. But he's with Andrea Morrow and he's afraid that part of this is to set her up for a jailhouse murder."

"They could have murdered her when they had her. Call him. Tell him to get back here. Hide Andrea first, if that'll make him feel better, but he has to come in."

"At first, I thought the same thing, but something's very wrong here, Sis. And I'm a little wary of tossing Steven into a situation we can't control."

Marti rolled her eyes as she came to her feet. "You can't control everything, Nick. I thought you learned that lesson with the Carvers."

"I know I can't control everything, but when things don't feel right to me, I pay attention to my instincts. It's kept me alive a long time and I'm not giving up on that now. The more I think about this, the less I like it. I told Steven to stay in the wind as long as possible. In the meantime, we try to figure out who did shoot that officer and why."

Chapter 12

Sunday, 4:15 am
Catoctin Mountains, Central Maryland

"Why did you become a bounty hunter?"

Steven opened his eyes. He'd reclined his seat and was deep in thought, trying to figure out why the police officer was killed. Why he was being framed. Why the police honestly thought he'd pulled the trigger. The puzzle was laid out in a hundred pieces and while Steven enjoyed puzzles, this one was pressing in on him like a ticking clock.

"Why do you ask?"

Andrea shrugged. "I've walked the dog, pulled all the lose threads in my sweater and pretty much ruined it. A conversation would be nice."

Steven closed his eyes again. "Because I inherited one-third of the business when my father died a few years back."

"So, it wasn't like you grew up with dreams of chasing fugitives."

"No. Far from it. My degrees are in finance."

"Finance? As in banking?"

Turning his head, he opened his eyes and looked over at her. "I have a Masters in International Banking and another in Business Economics and a Bachelor's in

International Commerce. Can you believe that?" He knew there was probably a touch of longing in his voice but he couldn't help it. He loved everything about numbers—the way they could tell a story, their consistency, their reliability. Two plus two was always four.

Her eyes widened a bit and he could see the fatigue lurking there. She needed rest. So did he. But until he heard back from Nick, he didn't want to move.

The temperature had dropped a few more degrees and he could see the goose bumps on her arms. He cranked the engine and turned on the heat. All around the vehicle, the pitch black night seemed to wrap them a cloak of silence. Up here, on top of the mountain, they seemed years away from the trouble they were in.

"Wow. So why are you a bounty hunter?"

"I told you. I own a third of the business."

She shook her head as she leaned forward toward the heat vents. "That's the dumbest thing I ever heard. So what if you own it? You should be doing what you love to do. You don't think I'm a teacher because of the money, do you?" She smiled and it made him return it.

"It doesn't matter. Nick needs me at the agency. End of story." He was about to cut the engine when he saw headlights flicker through the trees. Someone was coming into the park and he doubted that it was a camper looking for a place to set up a tent. He hit the power buttons and lowered the front two windows before turning the SUV off.

"I want you to crawl out the window. Do not open the car door. When you get out, get the dog out and go to the back of the SUV. Wait there for me."

"What's going on?" Andrea unbuckled her seat belt.

"We've got company and I don't know if it's friend or foe. But friends don't drop in without calling first. Go."

He reached back and hauled the gear bag between the seats. Then he crawled out the window, grabbed the bag and hurried back to Andrea. "Keep the dog quiet and stay with me."

Taking her hand, he led her into the woods about a hundred yards and then stopped. Kneeling down, he opened the bag and pulled out the night vision goggles. He slipped them on and looked back toward the SUV. Two figures were slowly walking toward his vehicle. Not good.

Gary Albert didn't like the woods. It was too dark, too quiet, and he could just imagine the eyes of bears and coyotes and wolves stalking him. He preferred the city—the lights, the noise, the people. He'd never been camping, never hiked a mountain trail, and had no desire to ever try either one. "Hurry up, will ya?" he nudged his partner.

Phil just shot him a glare as he whispered. "Hush. You want him to hear us?"

"It ain't here."

"He's here. He's out there in the woods. Now quiet." Phil leaned in the SUV window and tucked the pistol under the front seat.

Gary leaned in, keeping his voice low. "What if he finds it? He's gonna wonder what we're doing? He'll look."

"Not if we give him reason to think we're here to kill him." Phil grinned as he pulled out the pistol he had tucked in his waistband. "Come on."

"Are you nuts? You wanna go truckin' through them woods?"

"No big deal. Nothing out there but that bounty hunter and the girl. Now, come on. We stomp around a bit, then let him think we gave up and we're outta here. The minute the cops check his car, they find the gun and he goes down for murder."

"What if he finds it first?"

"He ain't gonna know we put it there. Now, come on."

Steven led Andrea deeper into the woods and higher up the mountain. He gave her credit, she climbed over rocks, walked through shallow creeks, and took branches in the face without a word. Finally, he found an outcropping of boulders.

"Stay here," he whispered as he pointed to the top of the rocks. "I'm going to go up and look around. Be ready to run if I tell you to."

He wished for his boots as his loafers slipped on the rocks but he finally made it to the top. Sweeping his gaze slowly from left to right, he finally picked up two figures in the woods, spread out, approaching slowly. And the fools were using flashlights.

Steven hurried, slipping and sliding, back down the rocks and grabbed his holster and gun out of the bag and strapped it on. "We've got a bit of a lead on them, but not much. They're using flashlights to find our tracks."

"What do we do?" she whispered.

"We're going to try and circle back, hit that creek and this time, head downstream a ways. Hopefully, we'll lose them."

She leaned in close and he picked up the scent of lavender and vanilla. "Why don't you just shoot them?"

"If they shoot first, it's self-defense. If I shoot first, it's murder." He swung the bag over his shoulder, grabbed her hand and headed straight south, through the woods, looking back from time to time to see if he was well beyond the flashlights.

Finally, he turned and started back downhill.

A few minutes later he stopped and knelt down. Andrea sat down on the edge of a fallen log. "What's wrong?"

"They're making way too much noise. I know they're probably city boys, but I doubt they're stupid. Do me a favor. I want you to hide over there behind those rocks and tell me what command I need to give Chaos to take one of the guys down and hold him without killing him."

It surprised him that she actually laughed. "Easy." She leaned over and whispered in his ear." Then she moved over to the rock outcropping.

"Come on, Chaos." The dog just stared up at him. *Duh*. "Chaos, heel." The German Shepherd moved to Steven's side. Okay. Now to set a little trap and see what he could catch.

Moving quicker now that he didn't have Andrea to worry about, he circled around behind the two men. They were moving about twenty-five feet apart and talking to each from time to time. Especially when one of them tripped or was hit in the face with thorny brush.

It was cold and clear; the moon shifting in and out behind the occasional cloud, casting light through the darkness. For a moment, Steven let himself remember all the times he and his father would slip out into the night in these very woods, looking for owls, raccoons, and possums. You needed to walk softly, be patient, and wait for the right opportunity.

Steven knelt down and pointed to the man farthest away. Speaking softly, he said, "Chaos, get 'em."

The dog was off like a Chinese rocket on the 4th of July. Taking a deep breath, Steven ran up behind the other man whose attention had now been directed toward his partner who had a dog hanging from his throat. He slammed into the man from behind, knocking the man to the ground. He heard him grunt a split second before he started to fight back.

Steven took a blow to the ribs by the guy's elbow. It felt as though all the air in his body had just been sucked out but he just rolled back and swept his left foot out, kicking the man in the face.

Roaring with anger, the man lunged. Steven kicked him again, this time in the kneecap. The man went down like a tree under a chainsaw. Grabbing the man's arm, he snapped a cuff tie around the wrist and then reached for the other arm. The man tried to tuck it under his body.

"I can just shoot you, if you prefer."

"You're a dead man."

"Not from where I stand." Steven pressed his knee into the small of the man's back. Immediately, the man reached back to push him off, and Steven cuffed him. He rolled the man over then glanced over at Chaos who had the other man pinned to the ground by the throat. He was thin with long hair, tattoos all around his neck, and enough of his face pierced to make a magnet jump. In spite of trying to look tough and mean, he was frozen with fear. Smart man.

The man he'd just tackled was a little shorter with short blond hair and a pockmarked face. He must have hated his teen years. "Why are you looking for me?"

"I don't know what you're talking about."

"Why did you kill that police officer?"

The man turned his head.

"Okay, be that way. It's your hide. You see . . . if you're not going to tell me what I want to know, you're of no use to me. I'm going to tie you and your partner to that tree of over there and leave you here. Since it's only early April and the camping season doesn't really open until May, I figure the bears, coyotes, and foxes will keep you company."

"You can't do that!"

"Sure I can." He stood up and cupping his mouth, yelled. "Andrea!"

The man lifted his head and looked up at Steven. "Don't do this, man. If I tell you anything, he'll kill me."

"Who will?"

The man just shook his head.

Steven walked over toward the spot where Chaos still had the tattoo man pinned. "I'm only going to say this once, so I want you to listen to me very carefully if you don't want this dog to rip your throat out. I'm going to give him a command and he's going to release you. If you try to move, he won't wait for me to tell him what to do. He'll be on you before you can get an inch. And the next time he takes your neck in his mouth, he will come away with flesh and blood, do you understand me?"

The man glared up at him. "Yeah. Just get him off me."

"When I release him, I want you to slowly and I mean *slowly* roll over on your stomach and put your hands behind you." He saw something flicker in the man's eyes and he knew this fight wasn't over yet. "Chaos, break."

Chaos pulled back, but kept his snarling, drooling mouth very close to the man's face. The man slowly started to roll and then attempted to scramble to his feet. Shaking his head, Steven just watched as Chaos lunged.

The man screamed as the dog grabbed him by the throat once again. Granted, the dog didn't draw blood, but Steven honestly thought the threat of it was enough to keep the man from trying to escape. So much for that idea.

With Chaos still holding on to the man, Steven cuffed him. There was a little bit of a struggled but every time the man moved, Chaos bore down a little bit harder and that proved to be sufficient deterrence.

When Steven stood up and stepped back, Andrea was standing there with his gear bag. "You rang?"

"Yeah, there's some more of these cuff ties in the bag. Get me some will you?" Then he turned to the dog. "Chaos, break, break."

This time, Chaos released and walked over to Andrea and sat down.

"Good dog."

"He's a great dog," Andrea replied handing him the ties.

"You can't just leave us here," one of the men pleaded.

"Just tell me why you're trying to kill me and I won't." Steven hauled the man to his feet and shoved him over to the tree he was going to tie him to.

"We weren't supposed to kill you. Just scare you into running."

That made no sense at all. All this to make him run? He was already running. Okay, he wasn't exactly running. More like avoiding being seen. Big difference. "Why me?"

"You were just convenient, that's all. Nothing personal, man."

Steven sat the man down. "Then the police officer was the target?"

"Yeah. We was to kill him and pin it on you. That's all I can tell you, man. You gotta let us go. I tell you anything else and he'll cut my throat, don't you get that?"

Steven shook him. "Who will kill you?"

The man just shook his head, his thin lips tight over his teeth.

"Then you stay here and hope for some early campers."

"Man, don't you get it? I tell you and you go after him and you can't touch him. But he'll know I talked and I'm dead."

"Why can't I touch him?" Steven crouched down to look the man in the eyes. He saw the fear and realized this guy wasn't just trying to stay quiet. He was trying to stay alive.

The man stared at Steven. Blinked. "Cause he's a cop, man. The dude that hired us was a cop."

Chapter 13

Sunday, 5:50 am
Prodigal Offices, Baltimore, Md.

Marti picked up the reports from the printer and walked into Nick's office. Rafe was on the sofa, talking to his sources on his cell phone. Conner was sitting in front of Nick's desk, talking to her brother. She walked over and tossed the report down in front of Nick.

"What I say something isn't right, I'm never wrong. The girl? Andrea Morrow? She's a fruitcake. Ten years ago, she was employed as a teacher in Montgomery County. Started calling 9-1-1 every night, claiming she was being stalked, that someone was in her house, or that someone had been in her house. The police never found any indication of stalking or break-ins. Then stuff started disappearing from the school. She shows up one day and starts hauling all the stolen merchandise back into the school, claiming she found it in her garage and had no idea how it got there."

Nick leaned back, resting his temple on the tips of his finger. "I don't want to hear this."

"Yeah, I'm not real happy either. The woman was politely asked to find another job. She moves to Richmond, gets another teaching position. Two years later, here we go again. Someone is stalking her. Hang up calls on her phone. Stolen merchandise. Break-ins. Slashed tires on her car. Then she starts running into the principals office, claiming there were snakes, scorpions, and bloody knives on her desk. Each time, it was checked out and no one ever found anything. Not a single varmint in the entire school. The principal sends her for a psych eval."

Marti reached over and pulled a document out of the stack. "She was tormented and tortured as a child by a father that delighted in abusing her and her mother. Physical and emotional. Kid would be sitting in class, look out the window and see her father watching her from across the street. Come out of the drug store with her friends and see him watching her from his car parked at the curb. Wake up in the middle of the night and find him standing over with a belt in his hand. He'd beat her and then warn her it would happen again if she didn't obey him. Mother was sent to the hospital on numerous occasions. The child on four. The doctor diagnosed her with post traumatic stress disorder. Says that she is still living the nightmare of her father stalking her, waiting to pounce on her."

Conner shook his head. "Why didn't the mother get her out of there?"

"She did. Finally. The father went too far and killed a man in a fight. The mother's co-worker. He thought she was having an affair with the man. He's arrested and sent to prison. The wife packed up her and the kid and were gone before the hearing. She changed her name and the Andrea's and started a new life in Pennsylvania.

"Bottom line, she's delusional. Does things and then blames some imaginary stalker."

Nick reached over and picked up the phone. "Do me a favor. Fax that over to Chamberland," he instructed as he dialed. "Chamberland? Nick Shepherd. My sister is about to fax you a report you need to see. And the next time you get my family embroiled in any of your messes, I'm personally going to find you and move your ears to your elbows, you got that?"

Nick slammed the phone down. Looked up at Marti. Smiled. "It was his voice mail."

Marti laughed as she picked up the report. "I'll get this faxed over to him."

Nick rubbed his temple as his sister left the office. He stared at the phone. Steven was not going to like this. His brother had a good heart but lousy instincts. If there was a woman pulling a con within a hundred miles, Steven would find her. And get involved with her.

Finally he picked up the phone and dialed. Conner rose to his feet. "I think I'm going to make a pot of coffee."

"Steven, answer the phone."

Rafe looked over at him. "Why isn't he answering?"

"I don't know, he isn't telling me."

"Funny guy. Okay, you need sleep."

Nick hung up and then dialed again. He ended up in Steven's voice mail again. "Call me. It's urgent. I mean immediately, Steven."

Rafe stood up and stretched. "I can't find anything, Nick. This cop, Ryan? Clean as a whistle. Looks to be a real good guy. Been with the force about four years, married, two young children, father was a cop in Philadelphia, coached Little League. If there's dirt, it's buried. His bank accounts don't show any unusual deposits or withdrawals, his mortgage is paid on time and it's a moderate home. Nothing he couldn't afford on his salary. Wife works for Verizon. They have maybe four grand in credit card debt, two vehicles. He drives an old Ford pickup which is paid for and she drives a little Toyota but the payments are low. I don't see that he's on the take. No word on the streets of any problems."

Nick drummed his fingers on the desk, trying to figure out who he knew on the force that might be able to tell him more about Ryan. If the man wasn't dirty, he knew that someone was.

"Check out his partner. See if he had something to hide."

Rafe nodded as he stepped over the coffee table. "Back in a minute."

Conner came in just as Rafe departed. He set a can of Mountain Dew in front of Nick. "How did he take it?"

"He didn't answer."

Conner turned the computer screen around and worked the mouse, bringing up the tracking program. "He's still parked up on the mountain. You want me to just go get him and bring him in?"

"That's nearly an hour from here. He'll answer in a few minutes and I'll get him to come on in."

"This isn't going to go over well with him. He's always championed the underdog."

"Ah, man." Nick stood up and yelled, "Marti!"

A few seconds later she stuck her head in the doorway. "What?"

"Steven's dog. He'll never forgive us if that dog isn't given food, water, and a walk."

She tipped her head, the scathing look thinning her lips. "So, you want me to drive all the way out to his house and walk his dog?"

"Do you see any other way for that to happen?"

"Yeah. Send Rafe."

"You have a key to Steven's house."

"I can give it to Rafe."

"I'm asking you to do this."

"No, you're ordering me, as you always do, but I'll take care of it."

"How was that an order?" Nick dropped back down in his chair.

"You didn't ask me to go, did you?" She gave him another look and walked away.

"I'll never figure her out in a million years. Did I order her to go?"

"No. You did that thing you do. *This has to be done.* And then you let us take it from there, knowing we'll do it."

"And that's giving an order?"

"In a manner of speaking. Yes." Conner grinned at him. "But if it's any consolation, you're getting better about that whole control thing."

Sunday, 6:15 am
Catoctin Mountains, Maryland

Steven leaned against the bumper of the Prodigal SUV. He wasn't sure what to do with the two men he'd tied to the tree. He couldn't leave them here to die. He couldn't take them with him. And he wasn't sure that if he called it in, the Park Police would find them.

"Steven?"

He looked over at Andrea. She'd been holding up pretty well, all things considered. Her hair was matted with leaves and twigs, her clothes streaked with dirt, and her coat had a nasty tear at the shoulder. Still, she wasn't whining or complaining. Two points in her favor. He rubbed his cheek.

"Maybe if a leave a couple of flashlights pointing at them, the Park Police will see them."

"Another hour and it will be daylight. They'll find them. They aren't gagged, so if they see the Park Police, I'm sure they'll get their attention. In the meantime, I think your cell phone is ringing."

Steven pushed off the bumper, walked around to the driver's door, reached in through the window and picked up his cell. Sure enough, he had missed calls. All of them from Nick. He listened to his messages and then called Nick back.

"What's going on?"

"She's delusional."

"What?"

"The woman you're with. She's done this before. Several times. I have a psych evaluation here. Steven, get in here."

"Explain this to me and not in your usual shorthand. I want the whole story."

He leaned against the SUV as Nick went through the entire job history, psych evaluation and final analysis. Each word was like a dagger. Once again, he'd been fooled. This time, it led to more trouble than he knew what to do with. He looked over at Andrea. She was kneeling on the ground, rubbing on Chaos' ears. There was no Paul framing her. There was no killer threatening her. She was in on it with them. Just as Chamberland had first thought.

"Does Chamberland know?"

"Marti just faxed the report over to him. He'll know soon enough. Steven, you need to come in. We'll go down to the station and give your statement. I'll call our lawyers and make sure they're with you every step of the way."

"It's a cop, Nick."

"The man that died? Yes. We know."

"No. The man that ordered the hit on that officer. It was a cop. So what do you think my chances are walking into that station? You think he hasn't planned all this out? Somehow, all the evidence in my favor will disappear and all they'll have is evidence to charge me with murder. I can't come in, Nick. Not until I find out who is doing this and why."

"Then ask Miss Morrow. And don't fall for the tears. She's in this up to her pretty little neck."

"Help me."

"I'm on it, little brother. So is Conn, Rafe, and Marti. We're going to get to the bottom of this. But I really think you need to come in."

"I can't, Nick. I won't go to prison for something I didn't do."

"Steven—"

"Keep digging. In the meantime, I'm leaving two men tied up to a tree right near the campsite Dad used to use when we'd go camping. They know more than they're saying but I can't stay here and waste time trying to convince them to talk."

"I'll send Conner out to pick them up."

"I won't tell them that. Maybe an hour of listening to the animals in the woods will loosen their tongues for Conner."

Suddenly, he felt very tired. It was more than just the hours without sleep or the hangover from the adrenalin. As he closed his phone, he shut his eyes and took a deep breath. The air was cool and clean but it didn't help. He wanted very much to say '*why me*,' but he knew that was a waste of mental energy. Looking back, he wasn't sure he'd have done anything differently.

"What did he say?"

Steven opened his eyes and looked over at Andrea. "He told me about your last few jobs and why you don't have them anymore."

She turned her head, staring out into the darkness. He couldn't read her expression and wasn't sure he wanted to. Obviously, he couldn't even trust himself to judge a pie at the county fair, much less people.

"I'm not crazy, Steven." She tilted her head, her eyes bright with tears and the vulnerability he saw there chipped at his resolve. He mentally shook it off. "I really was being stalked." She pulled up her knees and wrapped her arms around them. "I'd come home from work and all my living room furniture was completely rearranged. But they couldn't find anyone's fingerprints but mine. So I was nuts as far as they were concerned. I'd put the furniture back and a few days later, it would happen again."

"You had a rough childhood, Andrea. No one can blame you for having residual effects from that."

Her laugh was rough, choked, and full of despair. "Residual effects? That's what everyone thinks is happening? I just happen to have the key to a storage unit full of stolen guns and it's because of residual effects?"

"No. But the nonexistent boyfriend. The threats against you." It sounded ridiculous just coming off his tongue. He ran a frustrated hand through his hair. "It doesn't make any sense. Unless you were in on it from the start, none of this adds up. Why did you call me? Why me?"

She glanced at the faint streaks of pink to the east and he suddenly realized that she was hiding something from him. Something important.

"You have ten seconds to come clean or I'm leaving you here with them."

Tears started running down her face again but this time, he ignored them.

"I'm sorry. They threatened to kill me."

"They told you to call me?"

She nodded.

"And you have no idea why me and not some other Tom, Dick, or Harry?"

This time she shook her head.

"Did you know any other them? Ever see them before? Know their names?"

"There was one they called Tony, but he left as soon as we reached the Park and Ride. He had his car parked there. He told these two to call him as soon as it was done."

Steven pushed off the vehicle. "Get in. We have to go." He walked over to the two men tied back to back to the tree. "We're leaving now. You had your chance. Good luck, guys. I hear the bears coming out of hibernation can be pretty hungry this time of year."

They both started struggling, screaming, cursing him, and pleading for their lives as he walked away. He didn't bother to respond. If either of them had bothered to tell him anything he needed to know, he might have hung around for a few more minutes, but they didn't. Maybe Conner would have better luck with them.

As he started the engine and buckled his seat belt, Andrea asked, "What do we do now?"

"We need to get rid of this vehicle and find another one. This one is too easy to track."

"What? Steal a car?"

Easing out of the campsite, he shook his head. "I haven't committed as single crime so far. I'm not going to start now."

As soon as he got them out of the campgrounds and back out on a main road, he picked up his cell phone and called Kevin. He could tell by Kevin's gruff greeting that he'd woken the man up. "Dude, did the insurance company give you a loaner?"

"Good morning. Or is it the middle of the night?"

"It's going on seven. Time to get up and greet the day. Did they give you a loaner?"

"Yeah, they gave me a loaner. Not that I'm up to driving it yet, but it's parked down in the lot. Why?"

"I need to borrow it. I'll leave you my SUV."

"Why?"

"It's important, Kevin. Can you do this for me?"

"Of course. I'm just asking."

"I'd rather you know as little as possible right now. Do me a favor. Take the keys and the rental agreement down to the front desk. Leave it in an envelope for me. Then you can just go back to bed and sleep for a few more hours."

There a moment of silence before Kevin spoke again. "It's the silver Lexus under the light on the right. First space past the handicapped parking."

"I'll find it. Thanks, Kev. I owe you one."

"We'll just deduct it from all that I owe you."

Steven ended the call and tossed the cell phone in the console. "Okay, we have a car that no one will know to track. Now, we have to find out who this Tony is and who is pulling the strings."

"Can I ask you a question?"

"Shoot."

"I really want to know. Do you believe me? That I'm innocent of all this?"

"Honestly?"

"Honestly."

"I don't know. I wish I did."

Chapter 14

Sunday, 7:30 am
Project Exile Task Force Headquarters, Baltimore, Md

Nick leaned against a file cabinet waiting for Chamberland to finish reading the reports that Marti had faxed over. When Chamberland hadn't returned his phone call, Nick drove over only to run into Chamberland coming in for the morning, coffee in hand.

He took a moment to look around the room. He'd been on his share of task forces during his time with the Baltimore County Police Department, but they'd never had the accommodations this task force had. Desks were grouped in threes and fours, all equipped with brand new computer monitors. A conference table stretched along the far wall flanked with chairs and next to three white boards, currently filled with notes, photos, and crime scene pictures.

"I wish I could have had this when I interviewed her. Good work. Tell your sister I said thanks."

Nick watched Chamberland hand off the notes to someone. "That's it?"

"What exactly is it you were expecting me to do?"

"Oh, I don't know, maybe believe me when I tell you that my brother didn't kill that police officer."

Chamberland took his time answering, taking another sip from his coffee. "I'm not in charge of that investigation and I don't have any clout over there at all. You need to talk to Lt. Chicca in Homicide."

Nick didn't know Neil Chicca except by reputation. Fifteen years or so on the force, worked his way up from patrol through Vice and eventually to Homicide. He was said to be as tough as nails but fair, and strictly by the book. He wouldn't fix a parking ticket for his own wife much less give the benefit of the doubt to someone like Steven.

"Is your brother with Miss Morrow?"

Nick wasn't sure how to answer that, but he had to go with the truth. "Yes."

Chamberland seemed satisfied with that answer and nodded. "Well, like I said, the best thing I can advise right now is for you to talk to Chicca and tell your brother to turn himself in for questioning."

"One of the men he questioned fingered a cop. How safe do you think Steven feels right about now?"

Chamberland straightened a bit. "Your brother questioned these men? Where?"

"He caught them trying to come after him. Conner is on his way to pick them both up as we speak."

"I want them."

"Sure, Chamberland. Go see Chicca. I'm sure he'll turn them over to you once I turn them over to him."

Nick made sure his grin was as sarcastic as possible as he strode out of the room. Chamberland was only out for himself and Nick knew exactly how to play the agent's game.

Halfway down the hall, Nick heard Chamberland call out to him. He wiped the grin off his face before turning around. With a somber, straight face, he watched Chamberland eat up the hallway with long strides. "What now?"

"I will tell you this. The officer was shot with two different guns. One was a .44, registered to your brother. One shot to the chest. The other was a 9 mm. Two shots—one to the shoulder, the other to the heart. They recovered the .44 on the scene, but not the 9 mm. Here's the interesting part. Your brother's gun was wiped clean."

"Wiped clean?" Nick shoved both hands in his pockets as he rocked back on his heels. "Why would Steven stop to wipe his gun clean in the middle of a shootout and then toss the gun down, knowing that it was registered to this agency? And you don't think there's something fishy going on?"

Chamberland glanced furtively over his shoulder, then nudged Nick's arm and started walking down the hall and out the front door. Nick waited patiently for Chamberland to speak his mind. They were on the sidewalk and half-way up the street before he started talking again.

"You and me, we're a lot alike." He threw up his hand to stop Nick's denial. "I know you wouldn't agree, but we are. Both of us have law enforcement in our blood. We live it, breathe it. Your men—Rafe, Conner—they're the same. None of us could imagine doing anything else with our lives. We're addicted to the adrenalin. We love the rush. Oh, we may have some differences of opinion on how to carry it all out, but at the core, we're two of a kind. Your brother is a different breed altogether. Frankly, I don't know why he's in the business, but I'm sure he has his reasons.

The bottom line is that he's in over his head. If there is a cop behind this, and I'm inclined to agree with that assumption, this isn't going to go well for him. Get him a really good attorney and get him in here to give a statement."

"And if the cop is from this department?"

"And if he's from the County? Look, Shepherd, I don't like this any better than you do. How do I do my job when I have a cop messing with my evidence?"

When Nick raised an eyebrow, Chamberland nodded. "Yeah, I've had my suspicions. Things have been coming up that only an insider could have pulled off. But what insider? It could be any officer on the city force or the county, or it might even be someone on the task force."

"Why did you release Miss Morrow and then let the public think she had gotten away with the money?"

Chamberland stopped and stared out across the city. Nick glanced down the street. It was empty of pedestrians and only two cars were moving. Church bells were ringing, reminding some that mass was about to start. The sky was gray and overcast, adding making it feel chillier than it really was. "It wasn't my decision. It came from above me. I refused to do it, so they put the pressure on one of my men."

No wonder Chamberland wanted to talk out here where no one could overhear them. While crooked cops were no where near as prevalent as movies and books liked to portray it, they did exist. Human nature being what it was, power attracted the good and the bad. Unlike politicians, police departments tended to root out the bad as quickly and as efficiently as possible, and with as little fanfare as possible.

"What has Steven stepped in the middle of, Chamberland?"

The agent took a deep breath as he rolled his shoulders. "Let's just hope he survives it."

Sunday, 7:45 am
Marriott Hotel Parking Lot, Bethesda, Md

After picking up the keys to Kevin's rental at the front desk, Steven parked the Prodigal SUV a few spots away from the Lexus, transferred everything out of the SUV, and then drove around to the front door so that Andrea could run in and leave the keys for Kevin. Within ten minutes, they were back out on Rockville Pike, heading toward Virginia.

"I could use some coffee," Andrea told him. "And Chaos needs food and water. Which reminds me. I'm hungry. Can't we stop somewhere?"

"Sure." But where? What he wanted more than food was sleep. And if he didn't get some soon, he was going to fall asleep at the wheel and they wouldn't do any of them any good.

Nick promised to call him as soon as Conner picked up the two men at the campsite and interrogated them. So far, he hadn't heard anything, but it was probably going to be another hour or more. Until then, his mind kept running in loops that were slowly short-circuiting his brain. Never in his life, including college finals, had he ever been so stressed out and he wasn't sure he knew how to deal with it.

He was ready to snap and trying very hard to hold it together. "If you don't mind, I'm going to find us a hotel. You can order up room service if you like, but I need to sleep."

"That's fine. I'm sorry. I should have realized. I've taken a few catnaps through the night, but you haven't slept a wink. You must be dead on your feet."

"Oh, I'm well beyond that point now."

Steven found an Embassy Suites on Leesburg Pike about ten minutes later and checked in. While he was taking care of that, Andrea walked Chaos and then met Steven in the lobby. He held up the key card. "I told them you need food and they promised to send it up right away."

"One room?" Andrea asked, obviously not too keen on the idea.

"I can't protect you if you're off in a different room, but relax. There are two bedrooms."

Steven was barely in the room when his cell phone rang. He flipped it open. "Talk to me, Nick. What's going on?"

"The two men you left in the park?"

"Yeah?"

"They're dead."

Chapter 15

Sunday, 9:10 am
Police Headquarters, Baltimore, Md

Lt. Neil Chicca could name off the three worst days of his life with ease—the day Buck Jensen gave him a wedgie in the eighth grade in front of the entire assembly, the day his best friend, Robbie, died in a car crash coming home from college on spring break, and the day his father died.

He was pretty sure this was going to be chalked up as number four.

Splashing water on his face, he braced his hands on the sink and stared into the mirror. His eyes were bloodshot and underscored with dark circles, and the lines on his face looked deeper than yesterday. It was doubtful they really were, but he felt as if he could feel each groove digging deeper around his mouth.

When he'd gotten the call about Ryan, he couldn't believe it. They had been friends since the academy and while their careers had taken different paths within the force—he going on to homicide while Ryan went to vice—they remained close friends. And to hear he'd been shot down in the street like a bad habit.

He'd gone to Ryan's wife, tried to comfort her, but what do you say to a woman who would never see her husband again? His words seemed inadequate even though she thanked him. As soon as her sister arrived at the house, he'd made his excuses and hurried over to the station.

Now he was being haunted by the what-ifs. Ryan had called him yesterday afternoon, asking to meet with him. Supposedly, he had uncovered something that scared him and he wanted to share it with Neil. Ask for advice on how to handle it. Ryan put him off—he had promised to attend his daughter's ballet recital.

And now Ryan was dead, taking whatever he feared with him. He couldn't bring Ryan back, but he would do everything in his power to see to it that the killer paid dearly.

Drying his face with stiff brown paper towels, he headed back to his office. Another cup of bitter, black coffee, another antacid, another look at the witness's statement. A witness they couldn't find.

He'd barely dropped into his chair when one of his fellow officers strode quickly up to his desk. "Your witness? He's dead. We just got the word. Park police found him and another man shot and killed up in the Catoctin National Park."

Neil picked up a pencil and wove it through his fingers. "Any idea why he was there?"

"According to Matt Conner of Prodigal Recovery, they were there to kill Steven Shepherd. Allegedly, Mr. Shepherd managed to get the jump on the two men, tied them to a tree and left them for Mr. Conner."

Neil couldn't keep the skepticism out of his voice if he tried. "And he left them alive, right? Where have I heard that story before? Find Steven Shepherd and find him now."

As the officer hurried off, Neil picked up the phone and called Ryan's partner. "Darrell. Our witness is dead."

"What? What happened?"

Neil leaned back, tossing his pencil to the desk. "He went after Shepherd. Shepherd said he left the man alive for one of his men to pick up and when the man arrived, our wit was dead."

"He points the finger at Shepherd. Shepherd walks away and our witness is dead. Do we have people out looking for this guy?"

"Yes." Neil picked the pencil up again. "Look, Darrell, I need to ask you a question."

"Ask away."

"Ryan called me and said he needed to talk to me about something important. Do you have any idea what it was?"

There was a slight pause before Darrell responded, "I seriously have no idea, Neil. He didn't say anything to me."

"Okay. Just checking. I'll keep you posted."

The phone was barely hung up before it started ringing again. Neil picked it back up. "Chicca."

"We just got a call from Montgomery County. They found Shepherd's SUV. It just left the Marriott and is headed into DC."

"Notify DC with a BOLO. Tell them to pull him over and hold him."

"You got it."

Opening his desk drawer, he pulled out his gun and strapped on his holster. Then he grabbed his car keys off his desk and headed out the door. He could be in Montgomery County in half an hour and at the DC line a few minutes later. Hopefully DC would cooperate in turning over Shepherd to him.

Sunday, 9:20 am
Dupont Circle, Washington, DC

Keith pulled the SUV over to the curb and parked. If he'd had to stay in that hotel room another minute, he'd have jumped from the roof. Pocketing the keys, he slowly limped his way up the street to his favorite coffee shop, stopping at the newspaper stand first to pick up the Washington Post. Spreading the paper out on the table, he sipped his coffee and read the paper while waiting for his breakfast bagel.

He glanced at the article about a police officer shot and killed in Baltimore and then moved on to something a little more interesting—a senator caught in a hotel with his eighteen-year-old intern by his wife. She proceeded to shoot the senator in the kneecaps with a .22 pistol he'd bought her to protect herself at the house when he wasn't home. Leaving her husband bleeding and howling on the floor, the wife then cut all the intern's hair off, telling her she was getting off easy for messing around with a married man and sent her home. The intern couldn't be reached for a comment.

Neil lifted the paper as the waitress slid his bagel across the table. His cell phone rang. Closing the paper and folding it next to his plate, he answered the call. "This is Keith."

"This is Steven's brother, Nick. Do you happen to have Steven's SUV?"

"Yeah, why?"

"And are you parked at Dupont Circle?"

"Having breakfast. What's this about?"

"So you aren't in the vehicle?"

"No. It's parked down the street. Nick?"

"Don't go back to it, Keith. The police are heading there now to take possession of it. I called Steven, but his cell phone is Frederick County, so I had a feeling he dumped it somewhere."

"Dumped it?" Keith stood up and walked over to the picture window at the front of the restaurant and looked down the street toward the SUV. Sure enough, a police car was sitting next to it, blocking it in. "What's going on?"

"Steven's in a bit of trouble. Nothing we can't handle. I just don't think Steven would want you hauled in and questioned, so don't go back to the SUV. Eat your breakfast and walk away. Grab a cab or something. You don't know who owns it and you never saw it before."

"Okay. What kind of trouble is he in?"

"I can't talk long. If someone hears me and realizes I'm shadowing everything they do, they'll toss me out of here. We'll explain later. Just walk away."

"Okay. As soon as I finish my breakfast."

"Take care, Keith."

Keith hung up the call and returned to his table. Steven in trouble? And here he thought he'd never see the day. He picked up his bagel, wrapped it in a napkin and stuck it in his pocket. After tossing money down on the table to pay the bill, he walked over to the waitress. "Out of curiosity, is there a back way out of here?"

Sunday, 9:25 am
Embassy Suites Hotel, Leesburg, VA

Andrea finished her breakfast, took Chaos out for another walk and then stretched out across the bed with the dog curled up next to her. Normally, she didn't allow him up on the bed with her, but nothing was normal now.

She had called Liz and when it went straight to voicemail, left a message.

Curling her fingers into the dog's fur, she allowed the tears to slip through. Why was Paul doing this to her? What had she ever done to him? Now people were getting killed, she and Steven were hiding from everyone while his brother tried to get to the truth, and it was all her fault.

Swiping at the tears, she punched in Paul's number. It rang twice and then he picked up. "Well, well. Isn't this a nice surprise. Where are you, Andi?"

"What is going on, Paul? Why are people getting killed?"

"You know what I always liked about you? You're more concerned with other people than you are with yourself. Wouldn't you rather know why I chose you? Don't you want to know why I used to re-arrange your furniture? Or move things around in your closet?"

She scooted back to sit up. Chaos lifted his head. "That was you?"

"I had to amuse myself somehow."

"I lost jobs because of you."

"Oh, boo-hoo."

"Why, Paul? Why would you do that to me?"

"Because I hate you. I've always hated you. And now, I have the chance to destroy you and I'm loving every minute of it."

"But that was before you even met me." None of this made any sense. Why would someone hate her without knowing her and go to such lengths to ruin her life?

"I knew who you were. So when I was told to keep an eye on you, it was all the chance I needed to give a little payback."

Her head shot up. "Someone told you to stalk me? Who would do that?"

"You can't guess?" He laughed, early choking with it. "This is so rich. No, I want to enjoy this a little while longer. Why don't you think on it. I'll tell you when you give me back the money."

"I told you, I don't have the money! The police just did that to lure you out. They have the money. And the guns."

"I'm starting to believe you. So why did you call me?"

"To stop this before anyone else gets hurt. Steven didn't kill that that police officer. Or the two men at the campsite."

"Didn't have anything to do with it. Not my problem."

"Wait a minute, if you weren't involved, who is?"

"There are some very important people that make a lot of money off those guns and they have a lot to lose if it comes out they're involved. They're just tying up loose ends."

"And you're not a loose end?"

He laughed again. "No. I have a strong connection. No one is going to bother me. They're not too happy that I used you to pick up the money, but they won't do anything about it."

"They're going to kill me?"

"Probably. You can identify me."

"But I don't know who you really are! How can I hurt you?"

"Now there's a million dollar question."

"It's about who hired you to watch me, isn't it?"

"Give the girl a lollipop."

Sunday, 10:00 am
Project Exile Task Force Headquarters, Baltimore, Md

Nick leaned against the building with his shoulder as he listened to Conner update him on the scene at the campsite. The Park Police had taken over with the Baltimore Officers shadowing their every move, ready to take over as soon as they could. A gun had been found at the scene. Until ballistics and the coroner proved it one way or another, it was merely an assumption that it was the murder weapon.

Feeling a hand clamp down on his shoulder, Nick interrupted Conner. "Let me call you back, Conn." Closing his phone, he turned around to face Chamberland. "What?"

"You can't keep Steven in the wind like this, Shepherd. I know you think you're protecting him, but you're really not doing him any favors. He needs to come in and give his side of this. As long as they believe Steven killed that officer, they aren't going to be looking for the real killer.

Nick couldn't argue with Chamberland's logic, but he was skeptical that Steven would be given the benefit of the doubt. Once they had him in custody, they'd ram him through the system, charging him as fast as they could.

"They may not be looking for the real killer, but we are."

Chamberland looked around. "Who is? Conner? Because you're here watching and listening to everything that goes on and using it to keep Steven one step ahead of us."

"Caught on to that, did you?" Nick wasn't even going to apologize. "Rafe is on the streets following up some leads." As a former city police officer, Rafe knew the streets inside out. If anyone could dig deep enough to find out anything, it was Rafe.

"You be careful, Shepherd. I'd hate to see you on the other side of those bars."

"I may be walking a fine line, but I'm clearly not breaking any laws. Steven has not been charged with a single thing. He's a person of interest. Not a suspect. I am not helping a fugitive elude the police. Until Steven is formally charged with a crime, he's free to be wherever he wishes to be."

"And that fine line you're walking could smudge. They just searched your brother's SUV. They found a 9mm tucked under the front seat. It looks like it may be the weapon used to murder Officer Ryan."

"They had no cause to search his SUV."

"They say it looked abandoned."

Nick snorted. "See, this is why I am not insisting Steven come in yet. They are determined to nail him to the wall for this and he's innocent. That SUV hadn't been parked there for more than half an hour. No way could they claim it was abandoned."

Chamberland shrugged. "I'm just giving you the latest."

Good news—Chamberland was being helpful. Bad news— you couldn't always trust the man not to have an ulterior motive that could blow up in your face. Nick combed his hand through his hair. "Too many pieces to this puzzle for it make sense. First Andrea and the guns. Then Steven and this officer. Then the two men try to kill Steven and end up dead. Now they're determined Steven's going to take the fall for it."

"Get him an attorney. Now. And I doubt I need to tell you this, but I'm going to anyway. I'm pretty sure a cop was involved, but I don't think he's at the top of this pyramid. Someone is orchestrating all of this. I played right into their hands when I released Andrea, but I couldn't do anything else. I have no doubt that they're going to kill her if they find her. Why they picked Steven to be the fall guy on Ryan . . . I don't know. I haven't quite figured that one out yet."

"I haven't either."

Nick's cell phone rang and he looked at the screen. "It's Jessica. I need to take this."

"I have to get back inside anyway. Check in with me later."

Nick nodded as he flipped the phone open and strolled down the street. "Hi, Hon."

"Where are you? Church starts in forty-five minutes."

Grimacing, Nick glanced at his watch. "I'm sorry. I really am, but I don't think I'm going to be able to make it."

"Nick, we talked about this. Business does not interfere with Church or Krystal's school events. You promised."

"This isn't business, Jess. It's Steven. They're trying to pin the murder of a cop on him."

"No way."

"Very way. You and Krys go on without me. I can't leave right now."

"No, you can't. We'll say a prayer for him. Will you be home for dinner?"

"I don't know yet. I'll call you a bit later and we'll see how things are going."

"Okay. Love you."

"Right back at ya in multiples." Nick ended the call and then dialed Rafe. As soon as he answered, Nick said, "Tell me you have something. Anything."

"Well, I found out that Marco is really upset about the last shipment. And word is someone is playing both sides of the field. He arrests them on a minor charge and then warns them when something worse is coming down."

"So it is a police officer."

"Yep. But so far, I haven't been able to find out if it's city or county. But I have a rumor I'd like to chase."

"What's that?"

"The man running this whole thing? He's running it from prison."

Nick could feel the groan down deep in his chest. What was the world coming to? In the old days, cops just took a little money from bars and hookers to look the other way. "See if you can verify that."

"I'm working on it. But finding the officer is still priority, right?"

"Absolutely."

"Steven still in the wind?"

"Catching a few winks, but in the wind."

"Nick, something about all this doesn't smell right. I just can't put my finger on it."

"I hear that loud and clear." Nick took a deep breath. "While you're sniffing around, see if you hear anything about something scheduled to happen in the next day or two."

"Like?"

"I don't know. I may be crazy, but this is all a little convoluted for me. I wouldn't be surprised if it was happening because something bigger is about to happen."

"You're right. You're crazy. Isn't this enough?"

"Yes. It is. Keep me posted."

Sunday, 11:12 am
Prodigal Offices, Baltimore, Md

Marti's fingers flew across the keyboard as she went from one search result to another. She was slowly taking Andrea Morrow's life apart from seam to hem. Everything started with her. She had to be the key. But how? So far, nothing in Andrea's life indicated associations with any criminal element. She rarely dated. There was no Facebook, Twitter, Website, or internet dating service.

Calls to fellow teachers at the school had been a dead end. She'd only reached six of them, but not one of the six had anything negative to say about the woman. She was quiet, kept to herself, never said anything bad about anyone else, her students loved her, the parents liked her.

No one was that big of a saint.

There had to be a skeleton somewhere and Marti was determined to find it.

The biggest question mark so far was the mother. No trace of her anywhere. Andrea's employment records stated that her mother, Leona Morrow, resided in Phoenix. But the number actually belonged to a hair salon and they never heard of a Leona Morrow. The address was not a residence; it was a tire store. They never heard of her either.

The woman was a ghost.

Or Andrea was lying about her mother's name and residence.

Conner set a cup of hot tea down next to her keyboard. "Anything?"

She shook her head as she picked up the cup. "Not a thing, Conn. And that's suspicious all in itself. I tried Social Security. Four Leona Morrows in the county, but not one with the same birth date. I talked to the one in Binghamton, New York. She's a retired sales associate from Sears. Her husband answered the phone. I don't think she's our lady. The one in Indiana died a year ago. It's too early to check on the one in Nebraska or the one in Oregon."

Conn grabbed Jenna's chair and dragged it over next to her. He sat down, elbows on his knees, hands clasped as he studied the screen. "Okay, let's go another route. Go back to her birth certificate. What was her name? She had to have aunts, uncles, grandparents. Something. Maybe that will lead us to the mother. She's probably living close to her parents if they're living."

Marti shook her head. "I tried that. Court records on the change of name were sealed. I can't access them."

Conn frowned. "Let me see the employment records again. All of them. I can't believe that she wouldn't have an emergency contact. There has to be something there somewhere."

Sipping her tea, Marti lifted an eyebrow. "Like I didn't think of that? It's a different number on each application and none of them led anywhere."

"You sure learned how to do this kind of work fast. Sure you haven't done this before?"

Shrugging, she looked at the computer screen again. "I've ordered her phone records, but it will be at least another hour."

"Phone records? We don't have that capability."

She smiled at him, reaching over to pat his cheek. "I do."

A few minutes later, Conn went back in Nick's office to talk to Rafe and she was left alone with her work. Glancing at the office door, she switched screens and went back to reading the email from Jackson Hillman. His last lead hadn't panned out but he was sure he was getting closer. *Yeah. Right.* She was starting to think the man was just drumming up leads to keep her writing checks. She hit reply and wrote him back: *You have 24 hours and the money runs out. Make it count.*

Time to find another P.I.

In the meantime, back to helping Steven.

Had Steven fallen into the situation or had Chamberland pushed him? If Steven hadn't been there, would Andrea have been offered bail? Or were they just holding her until someone from Prodigal showed up? If Chamberland was behind it, he knew that Steven was usually the one that was responsible for turning in the fugitives. How hard would it have been to just hold Andrea until Steven showed up?

She didn't trust Chamberland one bit. Nick might be willing to cut the man some slack, but she knew men like him all too well. You counted your fingers after shaking their hand.

But why would Chamberland set Steven up? That was the big question mark in her mind.

She checked her email again and sure enough there was one from her friend. She opened up the attachment and studied the phone records. She started by checking off the numbers she had in Andrea's file, and then moved to the rest of the numbers. She was able to track most of the numbers with reverse lookup—the dry cleaners, veterinarian, pizza delivery, Chinese restaurant, car mechanic, and a dentist. But there were three numbers she couldn't get information on.

Dialing the first one, she tapped her pencil, watching little dots of pencil marks appear on the file folder cover. It rang and rang and no one ever answered. She finally moved on to the second number.

"Hello?"

Marti sat up straighter. "Hello? My name is Marti. I'm calling about Andrea Morrow."

"Andrea? Is she okay?"

"She's fine. Not hurt or anything. May I ask who I'm talking to?"

There was a long pause and she started mentally kicking herself. She should have played this a little differently.

"Who are you?" The suspicion in the woman's voice was palpable. She decided the only way to play it now was straight-up honest and hope for the best.

"My name is Marti Shepherd. We own the bail bond company that is holding Andrea's bail."

"What do you want?"

"Whoever set Andrea up and got her arrested is now messing with my brother, framing him for murder. I was just hoping you might be able to tell me if Andrea ever mentioned anyone stalking her or threatening her."

"Why don't you just ask Andrea?"

"It's complicated. She and Steven are in hiding right now and I'm trying—"

"In hiding? With a man? My daughter does not run off in hiding with some man she barely knows! Are you telling me she is in danger?"

Marti stepped down on her impatience. "Yes, ma'am. They are in danger and I'm really trying to figure out who is doing this as fast as I can. Please. Is there anything you can tell us that would help us find out who is trying to frame your daughter and my brother?"

"Oh, my. There's not much I can tell you, really. Andrea doesn't date much. There's this young man, Paul, that she's been seeing lately, and I understand he's the one involved in all this."

"Anyone else?"

"Last year she was seeing this young man. Oh, what was his name? Rusty? No. Randy. He was a police officer. Got a little too controlling. Pushy. Then she found out he was married. She broke it off and he harassed her for quite a while before he gave up."

Marti wrote down the name. "Do you happen to have a last name?"

"No."

"Do you know if he was a city officer or county?"

"I have no idea, honey. Andrea never said. Mostly she talked about her kids."

Marti started to reach for her tea, but the woman's words stilled her hand. "Andrea has children?"

"Her students. She thinks of them as her kids. Loves each and every one of them, so she's always telling me stories about what they're doing and who is improving and which one she's worried about. That sort of thing."

She sipped from her tea as her mind raced through possible questions. "So, other than this Paul and possibly Randy, you can't think of anyone that would hurt Andrea."

"Not a soul, hon. Andrea is a good girl. Kind, considerate, minds her own business. Not the type to attract trouble."

Conner came out of Nick's office and walked over to stand behind her. He must have read her notes because he picked up a pen under where she had written the name Randy, controlling, married, and police officer, he wrote: car type? Residence?

Marti nodded. "By any chance, did Andrea ever mention what type of car Randy drove? Or where he might have lived?"

"Oh, I have no idea where he lived. I don't think she knew either. He was very secretive about all that. It's what led her to be suspicious about his being single or not. But I think she said he drove some fancy sports car. What was it? Oh, my memory isn't what it was. I remember she was surprised that a police officer could afford something like that. Had heated leather seats. Convertible. Silver. You know, I think she said it was a Mercedes."

Marti wrote down all the information and underlined the make of the car. Conner tore the sheet of her pad and smiled as he hurried back into Nick's office. Knowing Conn, he'd have the owner of the car in a matter of minutes.

"Thank you so much. You've been a big help."

"You'll keep me informed, won't you? Let me know how Andrea is?"

"I will, yes."

Marti hung up and grabbing her tea, joined Conner in Nick's office. "Have it yet?"

He laughed. "No. So this guy was involved with Andrea? When?"

"Last year. Didn't want to let her go. Stalked her for a while. But if we're looking for a crooked cop with a connection to Andrea, he fits the bill."

"He sure does. But it's not going to be all that easy. Randy could stand for something as obvious as Randall, or it could be a nickname."

Marti sank down in a chair. "Call Andrea and see if she knows if it was real name or not."

He glanced up at the clock. "You think they're awake yet?"

Chapter 16

Sunday, 12:12 am
Embassy Suites, Leesburg, VA.

He ran through the woods, pulling Andrea behind him, trying to find the trail. The sun beat down on them, growing hotter and hotter as they climbed higher. Where was the trail? It was supposed to be here. He and his father had used it many times. Now there was only a tangle of brush, vines, thorns, and rocks.

"Where are we going?" Andrea asked, breathing hard, sweat soaking her hair.

"I don't know anymore. I thought I knew, but nothing is the way it was supposed to be. I can't find the way. It was supposed to be so clear."

"Maybe we're going the wrong way."

Steven shook his head. "It can't be the wrong way. This was the way my father went. It has to be right."

"I don't think so, Steven. I think it's the wrong way!"

"No! It has to be here!"

Steven jerked awake. He went perfectly still, trying to figure out where he was and why he wasn't in the woods. Little by little, images danced through his mind—tying up the two men, trading vehicles with Keith, finding a hotel.

He eased up and off the bed. Rolling his shoulders, he stumbled into the bathroom. When he stared into the mirror, he almost laughed. His hair was sticking straight up in the air and there were bits of leaves and brambles caught in it. No wonder the front desk clerk looked at him a bit oddly when they checked in.

He washed his face, running water through his hair as he tried to put some order into it. Longing for his toothbrush, he opened the door to the living room area and glanced around. Andrea's bedroom door was closed. She was probably still sleeping. He started a pot of coffee in the kitchenette and then walked over to the window and pushed back the curtain.

He still felt groggy and disoriented. Stretching out the stiff muscles, he looked out as traffic below moved slowly down the highway. This was the wrong area to be in if they had to move fast. The entire DC area was a huge traffic jam twenty out of every twenty-four hours. Time to move.

He poured a cup of coffee, wincing at the bitter taste and added another sugar to it. The clicking sound of someone disengaging the locks had him stepping back and looking around for a weapon. Why did he leave his gun on the nightstand? Idiot. He finally decided hot coffee was about as deadly as he was going to get and prepared to launch.

It was the jingling sound of Chaos's dog tags that warned him to set the mug down. Andrea came into view and startled, stopped in her tracks. "Oh. I didn't know you were awake."

"That is debatable. Where did you go?"

She held up a bag. "Took Chaos out for a walk and then stopped and picked up toothbrushes, toothpaste, and some deodorant. I hope that's okay?"

"Keep this up and I may have to marry you." He took the bag from her and dumped the contents out on the counter. "I think we need to get cleaned up and get out of here. Did you sleep at all?"

"A little," she replied with a shrug. "Marti called me. Somehow she tracked down my mother. I'm not happy about that, but it's too late for me to do anything about it. You guys had no right to bring her into this. Now she's all stressed, worrying about me."

"I'm sorry." Steven picked up a toothbrush and travel size toothpaste. "I didn't know she was going to do that."

"Well, she did. I told her all she had to do was ask me, but I don't suppose she trusts me. Anyway, she's running down information on a police officer I dated briefly last year. I doubt that will lead to anything, but if she wants to waste her time, better she spend it chasing some creep like Randy than bothering my mother."

He was about to just go brush his teeth when he saw the high color in her cheeks and clenched fists. "You're really upset about this."

"Yes. I am."

"I told you, I'm sorry, but I didn't know anything about it."

"I'm not blaming you. And I had words with your sister. I'm just not over it yet."

"Wow." Steven reached out and tucked a strand of hair behind her ear. "You never cease to amaze me."

She stepped back away from his hand. "Why?"

"Because most people in your situation would have been screaming at me even though I had nothing to do with it."

"I don't think that lashing out at you is going to help my mother right now." She turned on her heel. "I'll be ready to go in five minutes."

Ah, Marti. I know why you did it, but I can't help wishing you hadn't.

When he stepped back into his room, he saw his cell phone flashing that he had voicemail. He put it on speaker and dialed in for his messages, listening to them while he brushed his teeth.

"Steven. Conner. Call me when you get this."

"Steven. This is Nick. Get out of Virginia. They found a gun in your SUV and it looks like it's the murder weapon they've been searching for. They won't stop now and if they find you, they're not going to play fair. Keep your head down and move."

He rinsed his mouth and grabbed a towel. It looked like everything had been imploding while he'd been sleeping. He half expected to wake up and find out it was all over and he could go home. Nope. It was way worse.

"It's Kevin. I had to abandon your SUV, dude. I'm guessing Nick has already called you about it. So far, no one has come looking for me, but I'm going to check out of the Marriott and move to another hotel. Hopefully that will help you get a head start. I don't know what they think you did, but I don't believe it. You need me, call me."

Ah, Kevin. Your life is spinning out of control and you're worried about me. Shaking his head, he capped the toothpaste.

"Steven?" It was Marti this time. "We need to get you an alternative vehicle. If I know you have Kevin's rental, it won't be long before the cops know. I called Vic and told him we needed a decoy car."

Vic owned a used car lot in Baltimore and provided Prodigal with nondescript sedans and hockey-mom minivans when they needed to do surveillance.

"Jenna picked it up and is going to meet you down at the shopping center at 29 on 40. Look for a blue and gray Jeep Cherokee. And keep your head down, bro. Love you."

He didn't like the idea of heading back toward the office, but hopefully, they'd be able to get in and get out without being caught. Picking up the phone, he dialed Kevin's number. "Hey. I need to get rid of your car and Marti has one set up for me. You want me to pick you up and you can drop me off?"

"Sure. I'm just checking in at the Crowne Plaza. It's just up Rockville Pike a couple miles from the Marriott."

"We'll be there in about half an hour. Meet us out front. You'll be driving."

"Okay."

"I really appreciate this, Kev."

"Hey, it's more exciting than anything going on in my life, right now. I'm enjoying the distraction from my troubles."

Yep. That's was Kevin. Forget studying for those classes he was failing in college. There was a party somewhere he had to go to. Forget his marriage was falling apart. He wanted to play cops and robbers with Steven.

"Andrea! Let's go."

He stepped into the living room area and found her leaning against the door. "I was ready five minutes ago. What took you so long? Primping?"

She still had a bit of attitude hovering around the edges but it was obvious she didn't want it to show.

"I don't look this good without a little work."

She snorted as she opened the door.

Sunday, 1:05 pm
Geri's Subs, Baltimore, Md

Rafe worked slowly on his sub as he kept a close watch on everyone coming and going. The sub shop was known for its great food, but it was also known to attract certain key criminal minds in the area. You could always tell when they were coming in; they sent in one or two big, burly bodyguard types in first to secure a table in the back, away from the glass windows.

But, this was Sunday, most of the businesses in the area were closed, and the place was nearly empty. Slumped down in a booth, he had taken pains to blend into the woodwork of the neighborhood, and with the bandana, starter jacket, and sneakers, he looked like just another sullen Hispanic punk on the streets.

He saw Bennie saunter in and waved him over. Bennie was in his early thirties and a career criminal. With limited ambitions, Bennie managed to live on the fringe between small time crimes and felonies. There was little that happened in this neighborhood that he wasn't aware of on some level. People talked to Bennie because they trusted Bennie. He kept his head down and his mouth shut.

But Bennie owed Rafe. And it was time to collect.

Bennie warily slid in across from him. "Long time, Rafael. What brings chu down here? Chu lookin' for trouble, bro?"

"Answers, Bernardo."

Bennie scooted the salt and pepper shakers over in front of him and started moving them around. "Yeah?" There was enough negativity in that one word to force Rafe to lean forward and say softly, "You owe me, cuz. Time to pay up."

Ten years earlier, Bennie had been in the wrong place at the wrong time and was arrested along with four other young punks who were guilty of assaulting a couple of tourists. Bennie had used his one phone call to find his cousin, Rafe, who happened to be a police officer. Rafe had gone out a long limb, convincing the D.A. that Bennie had been with him at the time of the assault and could not possibly be guilty. The D.A. cut Bennie loose. Rafe had no idea where Bennie had actually been, but he knew that assaulting tourists was not Bennie's style.

"Man, that was a long time ago."

And the years hadn't been all that kind to a man that had never been all that good looking to begin with. A little too skinny with big ears that stuck out from the side of his face like side doors on a van, he had taken to wearing his hair long to cover them, but it was thin and lank and fell over the ears like waterfalls over rocks. Crooked teeth, tiny nose, and lush mouth, he had struggled to keep up with his Constanza cousins and had always fallen short. Rafe felt bad about that, but it didn't excuse the man for just giving up and taking the easy way out, quitting school and running drugs. "Should I add a little interest to that?"

Bennie rolled his head, slumping his shoulders. "I wasn't with those guys that night."

"I believe that. Otherwise I wouldn't have given you an alibi, but I put my reputation and my job at risk for you." Rafe sprinkled a little more vinegar over his fries and then offered Bennie one.

Bennie declined. "Chu gonna tell about this?"

Rafe shook his head as bit into a fry. "Haven't seen or talked to you since Christmas at Abuela's.

Bennie looked around before pushing the salt and pepper shakers aside. "What chu need?"

"You hear about that police officer shot and killed last night down at the Park and Ride?"

Bennie tipped his head in silent acknowledgment.

"Word I have is that a man named Tony was behind it. What have you heard?"

"Tony is just hired help, chu know? But he's bad news, cuz. Bad news. Likes to kill. But he got no head for bizness. Chu hire him, he duz the job. That's all."

"You see him as good for this?"

Bennie stared at Rafe, his dark eyes nearly dead of emotion. What had he seen through the years that had done this to him? "So they say."

"Any idea who hired him?"

Bennie coughed up a bitter laugh. "The man, Rafael. You look to the man. Word is, that cop stuck his nose in someone's bizness and got it cut off. All I know."

"Where can I find this Tony?"

"He and Marco are tight now. Usually hanging down around the pool hall with Marco's guys."

"What about these weapons Marco was buying? Any idea where they're coming from?"

"What I hear, a guy in prison has connections with a cop at city. They doin' bizness on this. The Man tells him where the shipments are, the guy sets up the heist and they move the guns here and sell them. Nice and clean."

It didn't make any sense, but Rafe didn't have time to ask anything more specific as he spotted one of Bennie's old friends coming through the door. "Yeah, Gina, she's got five kids now and Maria is finishing up college."

Bennie looked totally confused until he spotted his friend. A wink at Rafe and he eased right in to the conversation. "Never saw Maria going to college, man. Figured her to be like her sister and marry someone from the neighborhood and start dropping kids."

Rafe shrugged. "I think Leo broke her heart in high school, running off to marry that girl."

Bernie shrugged again. "He's lucky we didn't break his face for that." Then Bernie slid out of the booth. "Later, Cuz."

Rafe watched Bernie drape an arm over the man's shoulders as they disappeared into the back of the store. More than likely a drug sale.

Tossing money down on the table, he left the sub shop and headed for his car. Three doors down from the shop, he was yanked into an alley and slammed against the brick wall. The impact against his head had him stunned and seeing stars and fireworks. "You're asking too many questions. It could get you killed."

"I'm just catching up with old friends from the hood." He studied the two men that had him pinned. One of them was black and practically dancing on the balls of his feet, obviously hyped out on something. The other was Hispanic and had a .38 pressed against Rafe's cheek. He couldn't recall ever seeing either one of them before, but the one with the gun was definitely going to be a problem.

"You from the hood, eh? Why don't I know you?"

"Was. Grew up just three blocks from here. I still have cousins here. Like Bennie. Just had lunch with him."

"Yeah? Well, you've been wandering all morning asking questions about things that ain't none of your business, you get my drift? You've upset some people."

Rafe let his smile grow ever so slowly until it was a toothy grin as he eased one hand behind his back. "Yeah? Cool. To think that *some people* would be the least bit concerned with someone like me."

"Yo man, you got a smart mouth on you, esse."

"That's cause I'm smarter than you, *esse*." Rafe swung his left arm up, clipping the man's arm at the wrist and knocking the gun away while reaching up with his left hand to place his .44 right between the man's eyes. "You see, I know who I'm dealing with before I'm stupid enough to pull a gun on him. Especially when's he's smarter, faster, and carries a bigger gun. You got that... *esse?*"

Sunday, 3:45 pm
Prodigal offices, Baltimore, Md

The conference room table was littered with coffee cups, water bottles, soda cans, notepads, pencils, cell phones, and laptops. After half an hour of everyone sharing what information they had, it was time for figuring out what to do. And it was bringing on one massive headache for Nick.

"Okay, Conner. I want you to go after this cop, Randy. Marti's digging into his finances right now, but I want you to talk to people who know him, including his partner. See if you can find anything that would convince me he's the dirty cop."

"Will do," Conner replied.

"Rafe, I'm a little concerned about you going after this Tony. You've already had one run-in with his buddies. They're going to see you coming a mile away and they won't be taken by surprise a second time."

"I'm not worried about them. I can hold my own."

"I know you can. But I'm thinking that Chamberland's men might take lead on that." Nick still wasn't sure that having Chamberland helping them out was a smart move, but the man kept insisting he wanted to do whatever he could to clear Steven's name. At this point, Nick was willing to take what he could get and pray for the best.

Chamberland glanced over at Rafe. "We can do that."

"Oh, sure. You guys go running in there with your black jackets with the letters ATF blazed on them and they won't notice a thing."

Nick tapped his finger on the table. "Rafe, I understand what you're saying and in some respects, I agree with you, but time is running out for Steven. Chamberland can go in with guns blazing if he wants to, as long as he finds out from Tony who hired him and why."

Rafe threw his hands up. "Fine. I'm cool. Where do you want me?"

"I need you take my place at the station. Everyone was starting to get suspicious about my hovering."

Chamberland's cell phone rang. He excused himself to answer it. Nick took the opportunity to talk to Rafe. "I know you'd be better down there than he will, but I need you at the police station. Things are starting to heat up and the clock is seriously ticking. I don't know how much longer we can protect Steven."

Chamberland stepped back into the room. "They just matched the gun in Steven's SUV to the gun that shot the police officer. They're going charge him with murder."

Chapter 17

Sunday, 4:10 pm
Gettysburg Battlefield, Gettysburg, PA

Sitting on a concrete bench overlooking the battlefield, Steven stretched out his long legs and lifted his face to the sun. If it wasn't for the circumstances, he might actually enjoy spending time at the battlefield with a pretty lady.

"What are we going to do?" Andrea asked.

"I'm still trying to work that out. I can't run forever and now that they're issuing a warrant for my arrest, it's just a matter of time."

"Then do what your brother said to do. Turn yourself in."

"And then what happens to you, Andrea? Who will watch out for you? Chaos is a great dog, but as you so aptly stated, he can't stop a bullet." At the sound of his name, the dog lifted his head and looked at Steven, then lay back down. "Can you go stay with your mom?"

"I won't do that. I could lead trouble straight to her door."

"Take the car and go on vacation for a week or two. Go see New England. Or Chicago."

"I'm not supposed to leave the state, remember? They could revoke my bail."

He glanced over at her. "I am your bail bondsman, remember? I'm not going to revoke your bail. I'm practically ordering you to leave the area."

She didn't respond, choosing to stare out across the battlefield. It didn't look much like a battlefield from this bench. Just an open field with some farm houses on the other side. "Hard to believe such a bloody battle was fought here, isn't it?"

"I've never been here before. It's not quite what I expected, but there's something about it that just makes you want to whisper in respect."

"I know what you mean. When I was a kid, my dad was friends with the guy who had a horse farm. We used to go up there all the time in the summer and ride the horses. Nick and Marti took to it like they born in the saddle. Once, Mr. Weber loaded up all the horses in a stock trailer and we all came here—my dad, Nick, Marti, myself, Mr. Weber, and his two daughters. We had lunch in our saddle bags and we rode across that field right there and then circled up on Little Round Top and back around. It took a couple of hours to ride the entire battlefield and we stopped up on Little Round Top for lunch. It was the most amazing experience. Sometimes, I could almost swear I could smell the gunpowder and hear the cries of the wounded."

"Wow. I can't even begin to imagine."

"Riding up there in the woods toward Round Top, you'll just be riding along and then all of a sudden, you look over and there's a cannon, still sitting exactly where it was left at the end of the battle." He ran a hand through is hair. "A couple years later, one of my cousins started working on the family genealogy and found out that we had three great-great grandfathers here. They weren't related to each other at the time, of course. And they wouldn't have known each other—one was from Virginia and two were from North Carolina, but they were all here for this battle. I wondered if in the evenings, they sat in their different campsites, listening to the same cries of the wounded, smelled the same smoke from the cooking fires. Maybe one of them pulled out a harmonica and played something sad. And my ancestors would have sat out here somewhere, all listening to that same mournful song, wondering if they would live to see their families again."

"Oh, Steven," she said softly. "I can almost see it, smell it. How horrifying it must have been for them."

"Some of them came here because they believed with every fiber of their being that their cause was the right one. Others were here because they had no choice. Some lived. Some died. None were ever quite the same again." He stood up. "Now I'm just getting myself depressed."

He wasn't sure if he was here because he believed his cause was the right one or because someone, circumstances had taken his choice away, but he couldn't help feeling this entire situation was going to change his life forever. He just wasn't sure if it meant going to jail for murder.

"I'm going to ask you again, go away from here. Get in the car, head North or West and don't stop until you're at least five hours away. Don't come back until you hear from one of us."

"And leave you to face this alone? I was there at the Park and Ride, Steven. I know what happened. Don't you need me to tell them you're innocent?"

Shoving his hands in his pockets, he stood watching a young couple reading the inscription on one of the monuments. "They won't believe you. As far as they are concerned, you may have even planned it with me. You can't help me now."

"Then you're going to turn yourself in?"

He didn't answer as he strolled over to one of the monuments. The truth was he didn't know what to do. The honorable thing was to turn himself in, have his attorney present, and see how it played out. But honestly, he was terrified. What if he ended up in jail? What if he was charged with murder? What if his life as he knew it was over? Could he handle that? Could he accept it?

He wasn't sure he could. There was so much he still wanted to do with his life. In some respects, he hadn't even started yet. And wasn't that just a shock? All this time, he'd been working, living, paying bills, walking the dog, taking his car in for annual maintenance, and now he realizes he was just biding his time, waiting for something. But what? In July, he'd be turning thirty-four. And what had he honestly done with his life? Sure, he'd helped a few people here and there, but was it enough? Did it really count as having accomplished everything he wanted? Not even close.

"Steven?"

"I have to." He turned and looked down at Andrea. He hated that she kept looking at him as just waiting for him to prove that he was no different than any other man she'd ever know. There was no way he wouldn't let her down somehow, sometime.

"Just be careful, okay? This morning, Paul said that—"

"You talked to Paul this morning?" His mind shifted gears so fast, he could almost smell the burning rubber. "How?"

"I called him. On my cell phone. I wanted him to leave you alone, but he said that he wasn't the one behind this." She stared down at the sidewalk. "He said that very powerful people were involved and they were just tying up loose ends."

"Why didn't you tell me this before?"

"I don't know. You were sleeping and then we had to leave so quickly, and then your friend had to drive us to the car dealership."

He started pacing the sidewalk, trying to figure out exactly why that piece of information felt like a ray of hope. She talked to Paul. She could reach him. Maybe they could get their hands on him and this madness could stop.

"So, if you call him, he takes your calls?"

"Sometimes. He did this morning."

"Does he still believe that you have the money?"

Her shoulders lifted in a small shrug. "I've been trying to convince him I don't and he says he almost believes me."

He whipped out his cell phone. "Let's see if we can convince him you do."

"Why would we do that?"

"Cheese for the trap."

Sunday, 4:45 pm
Prodigal Offices, Baltimore, Md.

Nick watched his wife and daughter come through the front door of the offices. Jessica was carrying a platter covered in foil and Krystal was lost in her music, earbuds firmly in place as her head bopped in time to whatever she was listening to.

Jessica reached up to kiss his cheek. "We decided if you couldn't come home for dinner, we'd bring dinner to you."

"Thanks, hon. I'm sorry about all this." He peeled back the foil and the savory scent of pot roast, onions, potatoes and carrots tickled his nose and his stomach growled.

"This is Steven, not some fugitive."

Nick had lost his wife over his habit of putting work first and when they reconciled, they'd had long talks about what it would take to make their marriage—and their family—work. He'd promised not to ever work on a Sunday or on family night. It was a promise he'd kept until today.

Jessica followed him into his office where Krystal was already sprawled on the sofa, her feet up on the coffee table. She grinned up at him. He leaned down and kissed her forehead before settling down behind his desk with his dinner. Jessica took the chair across from him and pulled silverware wrapped in a linen napkin from her purse. "What's the latest?"

"They feel they have enough to arrest him now." He unwrapped the silverware and removed the foil from the platter. "This is going to taste so good."

"I can't believe anyone could believe Steven capable of any of this. It's surreal."

As he loaded the fork for the first bite, Krystal pulled the earbuds from her ears. "Daddy? Is Uncle Steven going to go to jail?"

"Not if I have anything to say about it."

She stared at him a second, smiled, and then stuck her earbuds back in. If only he had her confidence. Ever since he saved her from the Carver brothers, she seemed to believe he could and would do anything. But getting Steven out of this trouble was going to take more than a few prayers and a well-orchestrated rescue mission.

"Where's Conner and Rafe?"

"Rafe is down at the police station, keeping me posted on what's happening there and Conner is trying to find out what he can about the man that shot that police officer."

"Did you know him? The police officer?"

"Ryan?" Nick shook his head. "He hasn't been with the force that long." He pointed to the pot roast with his fork. "This is excellent."

"I'm glad you're enjoying it." She glanced over at Krystal and then turned back to him and now he saw the worry in her eyes. "Can you clear Steven of all this? Find the real killer?"

Everything in him wanted to beat his chest and assure the women in the family that he was more than capable of saving his family and winning against the bad guys, but he knew that would be more ego than logic. They had a killer who didn't want to be found and he wasn't going to just throw his hands up and walk into Prodigal because Nick wanted him to confess.

"I think we have a good chance, Jess, but I can't lie to you and tell you it's in the bag. We're treading on thin ice around the police station. I believe we have a rogue cop. They don't want to hear it. Better a rogue bounty hunter than one of their own gone bad."

"I know you and the guys will do everything that can be done. The rest we'll have to leave to God."

He pushed a bit of potato around on the dish. "There are times when I can believe God for anything and trust Him with everything. And then there are times like this when I'm not sure I know how to trust Him to come through for us. I want to rush in and handle it all myself to make sure it's done right. And I know I'm wrong. I've been down that road before."

"And God is not going to appreciate you trying to run His business for Him. We may not like it, but we're going to have to believe He has Steven's best interests at heart and will do what's best for him."

"I'm trying, Jess. But every time I think we have a handle on this, they come up with more evidence against him. Someone is very determined to make sure Steven goes down for this."

She leaned forward, her eyes blazing. "And we're just as determined that he won't."

Nick set his fork down and pushed the plate aside. "I'm scared, Jess. I haven't been this afraid since—" He glanced over at Krystal who was now stretched out across the sofa, her feet tapping out a rhythm only she could hear.

There were still nights were he dreamed that she was dead on the floor of that warehouse. Where he could still see the blood and the lifelessness in her body.

"You saved Krys. You'll save Steven. God has something up His sleeve. He always does. We just have to be ready to roll when He reveals it to us."

"Well, I hope He does it soon. Time is running out for Steven."

"Well, if it's any consolation, I know a bail bondsman that will post his bail if it comes to that."

Nick found himself smiling at her humor. "Yeah. Me, too."

Nick's cell phone chirped and glanced over at it. "It's Steven." Quickly, he flipped it open. "Talk to me."

"I just found out that Andrea has been in touch with this Paul guy. The one that set her up with the guns. He's the key to this, Nick. If we can get him, the rest of the house of cards will tumble in."

Nick leaned back in his chair. "I'm not so sure. He may not be willing to tell us anything about his accomplices."

"Nick, it's all we've got right now. They're about to put me in cuffs and charge me with murder."

"I wasn't saying it wasn't worth a try. Where are you now?"

"Pennsylvania."

Nick glanced at his watch, trying to calculate how much time it would take to bring everyone together. "Do you honestly think she can convince him to meet?"

"I think if we dangle the money in front of him, he'll jump at the chance."

"What money?"

"The money that Andrea took from the gun buyers."

"But Chamberland has that money."

"But Paul doesn't know that for sure. Andrea calls him and tells him that she has the money and will give it to him if he promises to back off and leave her alone. Something like that. I think he'll go for it. Then we take him into custody and help him understand that talking to us is the only chance he has."

Nick rolled it around in his mind for a minute, trying to quickly access the pros and cons. "Okay, let me call Conn and Rafe back in. We're going to need them. It'll take them about half an hour to get in here. Then we'll need to plan this out. I'll call you back in about two hours or so and we'll take it from there."

"Andrea and I will go get some dinner while you do what you do best."

Nick slowly hung up the phone. Do what he does best. *God help me.*

Sunday, 6:00 pm
Hagerstown Correctional Facility, Hagerstown, Md.

Norman Rotterback walked out of the prison gates and took a deep breath. He was free. Finally. Slowly, a grin spread across his craggy face. A few strings pulled in the right direction, a few dollars well spent, and he was released early. Sure, he was supposed to report to his probation officer once a week and stay away from criminals, drugs, and firearms, but if anyone actually believed he was going to turn into a choir boy at this stage of his life, they were the ones that needed to be locked up.

A green F-250 pickup pulled up to the curb and stopped. Norman walked over and climbed in. "You're late."

Paul shifted to drive. "By what, two minutes?"

"Late is late." He buckled his seat belt. "Where do we stand?"

"Everything is still set. The cops are running around in circles."

Norman chuckled. "What do we have on the girl?"

"She's all upset because you framed her boyfriend for murder."

"Cryin' a river here. Where is she?"

"Don't know. She's on the run with him."

Norman wasn't sure he liked that, but it didn't matter at the moment. He looked out at the Washington County countryside—farms and hills and cattle and corn. Boring. Reclining his seat a nudge, he closed his eyes. "What about Tony? Any word?"

"I was told he decided to visit his aunt in New Jersey until it cools off."

"Good."

Paul turned on the radio to some rock station that instantly hit Norman's nerves like a tazer. "Turn that noise off."

The music stopped. Paul muttered something under his breath but Norman didn't care enough to ask him to repeat himself. The boy had done fairly well, all things considered. There was that one little glitch with the girl that had worked out in the long run. It was a perfect setup to get rid of Ryan. Too bad he had to go snooping where he didn't belong. Some people were just like that. And it usually cost them.

He must have dozed off because when he heard Paul's cell phone ring and opened his eyes, he saw the sign for Ellicott City. They were almost home. He sat up straighter and rubbed his face with his hands.

"Hold on a minute." Paul muted his phone. "It's Andi. She's saying that she has the money and will turn it over to me if I promise to tell her who killed Ryan so that her friend can clear his name."

Norman's mind scrambled for a foothold. He knew for a fact that the ATF had the money, so what was the girl's game? "Tell her you'll do it."

"What?"

How the kid could be so smart sometimes and still so stupid was beyond him. "I want her close. This will get her out of their hands and into ours."

Something flashed in Paul's eyes but Norman just ignored it. It didn't matter what Paul liked or didn't like. He was calling the shots.

He listened to Paul give her the message and get the details. When the boy hung up, Norman looked over at him. "What's the deal?"

"Ten tonight at the IHOP."

"Public place. Smart girl. It won't do her any good, but what she don't know only helps us." Norman rubbed his hands together.

Sunday, 7:20 pm
Enroute to Baltimore from Gettysburg

Andrea had been trying to convince herself that Steven was just like every other man her mother had warned her about. But so far, regardless of how bad things had gotten, he hadn't once yelled at her, blamed her, or insulted her.

Trying to focus on analyzing Steven was better than contemplating what could happen over the next few hours. She wasn't sure she wanted to see Paul, but she needed to feel proactive for a change. And she wanted Steven proved innocent and free to go on with his life.

"Scared?" Steven asked her.

She wanted to lie, but couldn't find it within herself to even bother. "Yes."

"You don't have to do this, you know. We can find another way."

"Yes, I do have to do this. If it wasn't for me, you wouldn't be in this trouble. I brought this down on you and I need to help make it go away."

"It's not your fault. Someone else planned this."

"I'm sorry this happened to you."

"Don't worry about it."

She looked over at him, admiring the calm that seemed to emanate from the center of his being. If only she felt that calm. Then she noticed that he kept glancing in the rearview and side mirrors. "What's wrong?"

"I think we've picked up a tail."

"What do you mean?"

He didn't have to answer. The siren burst was enough to make her jump in her seat and then the lights started flashing. She looked back over at Steven. Other than the knitting of his brows, he still looked calm.

"What are you going to do?"

"Pull over."

"Are you crazy? They'll arrest you!"

"Probably. Take my cell. Call Nick and let him know I've been arrested."

"But can't you just outrun them?" She glanced back at the unmarked police car following them even closer now.

"You can't outrun the police, Andrea. And it only makes it worse when you try. Call Nick. They shouldn't arrest you. No reason to. You go straight over to Prodigal. Nick will take over from there."

"But what about the meeting with Paul?"

"Nick will handle it. Just let him know, okay? I need him to get in touch with an attorney and I need him there to bail me out if I make bail."

"Steven? What happens now?"

He had pulled the Jeep over to the side of the road and put it in park. The officer in the car hadn't attempted to approach them yet. Probably waiting for backup. Steven reached over, grabbed her hand and squeezed it. Then he put both hands high up on the wheel. "It'll be fine. I promise. But I need to know I can count on you to get to Nick."

She nodded and flipped open the phone. "Why can't you call him?"

"Because if I make one move, it will be all the excuse these people need to shoot me. As long as I keep both hands on the wheel, I pose no threat."

It took her three tries to get her shaking hands to scroll through Steven's address book and find Nick's cell phone. She was about to hit dial when there was a tap on the driver's window. Steven rolled the window down.

"Yes, sir?"

The police officer stayed just behind Steven's shoulder, one hand on the butt of his gun. "Driver's license and registration, please."

"Sure." Steven lifted up to pull his wallet out. "What was I doing wrong?"

"One of your brake lights is out."

Steven handed over the documents. Andrea sat frozen in her seat. *What to do, what to do, what to do.*

"Could you get out of the car, Mr. Shepherd?"

"Dial," Steven said as he unbuckled his seat belt.

Andrea hit dial and as it started to ring, she watched Steven climb out of the car and walk back to the front of the police car. There he placed both hands on the hood of the car and spread his legs.

"Talk to me."

"Nick?"

"Yes? Who is this?"

"The police have Steven. They just pulled us over. They have him back there at their car. What do I do?"

"Which police jurisdiction?"

"I don't know."

"Andrea, calm down. What does it say on the side of the police car?"

"It's unmarked."

"Okay, what are they doing?"

Tears started to run down her face. "They're putting him in handcuffs."

"Okay, more than likely, they're not going to bother with you. There is no warrant for your arrest. I need you to calm down so that you can drive straight here to the office. Do you know where you are?"

"On the highway." She watched as another police car pulled up and Steven was placed in the back of the unmarked car.

"*Which* highway, Andrea?"

"Oh, uhm, Route 15. No, wait. We just got off 15 a few minutes ago. We're on 70."

One of the police officers started walking toward the Jeep. "They're coming for me."

"Andrea. Calm down. They have no reason to arrest you."

"They didn't have any reason to arrest me before, but they did. And Steven didn't kill that man, but they've arrested him."

The police officer leaned down in the driver's window. "Ma'am? We're taking Mr. Shepherd to the County Police Headquarters up ahead where he will be picked up and transferred to Baltimore Intake. Can you drive yourself?"

"Yes."

The officer nodded and walked away. Andrea felt as if she'd just melted into a mass on the seat. "Did you hear him?"

"I heard. Now get behind the wheel and come straight here to the office."

Chapter 18

Sunday, 7:45 pm
Prodigal Offices, Baltimore, Md.

Marti stood at the front door, arms folded, staring out at the street. She was worried about Steven. Nothing was coming together the way it should. Rafe hadn't been able to penetrate the wall of silence in his old neighborhood. She hadn't found a thing in Andrea's background that gave them any clues at all. The officer she'd been dating was a dead-end. He'd moved to Atlanta six months ago, transferring to the department there.

Jenna came into view, marching toward the door with a furious look on her face. Marti stepped back away from the door as Jenna yanked it open, eyes blazing. "Steven is arrested for murder and no one around her bothers to call me? Have you all lost your mind?"

"Probably. How did you hear about it?"

"It's all over the news. Where's Nick?"

"In his office with Conner and Rafe."

She unbuttoned her coat. "And what is he doing to help our boy?"

"Everything he can."

Tossing her purse and coat down on her desk, she headed for Nick's office. *This should be interesting.* Marti trailed right behind her. In truth, she was sure that everyone missed not having Jenna there over the past twenty-some hours, but no had thought to bother her. Well, they'd be paying for it now.

Nick was just hanging up the phone when Jenna slapped her hands down on his desk. "I thought we mattered to one another. I thought we were family. That when one hurt, we all hurt. So why did I have to hear about this on the news?"

"I'm sorry, Jenna. Honestly we didn't think it was going to go on like this. It should have been a two hour blip on our radar and over."

Marti couldn't help smiling. *Way to go, Nick. Always was a fast thinker.*

"Steven is charged with three counts of murder and you think it's going to be a little blip on your radar?"

"Three?" Nick lost his soft smile. "What three?"

"A police officer and two men up in some national park somewhere."

Conner slammed his fist down on the arm of the sofa. "They knew Steven didn't kill those men! They were alive when he left them!"

"Someone better explain everything to me—in detail—and right now." Jenna kicked Rafe's feet and he jumped up out of the chair to let her have it, retreating to join Conner on the sofa.

"One second." He turned to Marti. "Lance is going to meet Steven at Intake. As soon as he finds out when the bail hearing is, he'll call you. Have everything ready. I don't care how much it is, bail him out."

"Of course. Any chance we can get him out tonight?"

Nick shook his head. "Doubtful. On a Sunday night?"

"It was worth a try. You know we could try and call Judge Rogan. He owes us a favor."

"I doubt he'll be able to convince a magistrate to go down just for one bail. It's only going to be one night and Lance says he can get Steven into a cell by himself and he'll stay there with him."

"He better." Marti didn't doubt for a second that someone might try to silence Steven before he had a chance to prove his innocence. Her biggest concern was for his safety in the midst of a large police presence. And wasn't that ironic?

Marti's cell phone buzzed in her pocket and she excused herself to take the call. Closing Nick's office door, she perched on the corner of her desk. "What's up, Jack?"

"I think I found him."

She felt something lurch in her chest and tried to step on it. How many times had she heard this only to be disappointed? "Where?"

"Winston-Salem, North Carolina."

"How sure are you?"

"Positive. How soon can you get here?"

Marti's mouth went dry. "You've been sure before."

"I'm going to send you an email with some pictures I took. Then call me back with your flight information. I'll pick you up at the airport."

She wanted to kick something in frustration. Of all times for Jack to find him. Steven needed her right now. She couldn't just leave. Sitting down at her desk, she brought up her email. "Jack, I have something here that needs my attention. As soon as I've handled it, I'll jump on the first flight out."

"Marti, you've been breathing down my back for what? Three years? And now that I've hit the jackpot, you can't get here?"

She opened Jack's email and downloaded the pictures from the zip file. Then she opened them and there he was. Finally. She'd found him. "I'm sorry, Jack. You have no idea how much I want to run to the airport right this minute, but I can't. Hopefully I can be out of here in the next day or two. Just keep an eye on him. Don't let him slip away."

"You see the pictures?"

"I'm looking at them right now. It's him."

"So get down here."

"As soon as I possibly can." She closed her cell phone as she continued to stare at the pictures. Finally. The search was finally over. All the years. All the miles. "Got you."

"Got who?" Jenna asked as she picked up her coat and shook it out.

Marti quickly closed the file. "No one. Did Nick bring you up to date?"

Jenna's lips pursed as she hung up her coat. "Yes, but it will be a long time before I let him think I've forgiven him for not contacting me immediately." She walked over to stand in front of Marti's desk. She pointed to the computer. "This no one that you *got*—does it involve Steven?"

"No."

Jenna stood there, eyeing her carefully as if waiting for more of an answer. "But you don't want to talk about it."

Marti took a deep breath. "Correct."

Jenna nodded and moved away. "Fine. I don't pry into people's secrets. If you need anything, let me know."

She'd found him. And it was eating at her like a fire licking up starter fluid. Standing up, she followed Jenna into the conference room where the office manager set about making a pot of coffee. "Jenna, you're good at keeping things to yourself, aren't you?"

"I like to think so."

"I may have to go away again. I just want you to dissuade Nick or Steven from trying to come after me."

Jenna leaned against the counter, tilting her head. "So you won't be coming back?"

Marti blew out a heavy breath and dropped down in the nearest chair. "I don't know. I hope I will, but I don't want to make any promises."

Jenna pulled out the chair next to Marti and sat down, reaching out to take one of Marti's hands. "Honey, you do what you have to do, but you keep in mind that you have family here. Those boys love you to within an inch of your life and while Nick may bluster a bit, they would both lay down their lives for you and neither of them would judge you for anything. You go and you do whatever it is you need to do to find that peace you're trying to find. But then you come home."

Tears welled, but Marti refused to give let them go. "You sure you haven't been snooping around my stuff?"

Jenna laughed. "You know better. But I know a woman with a mission and I know you're searching for something in your life that you haven't found yet. I don't know what it is, but it doesn't matter to me. What matters is that you understand that whether you ever find it or not, there are people here that love you. And that includes me and Conner and Rafe. It would break our hearts to lose you again. We need you here. And I think you need us. So do what you have to do, but then come home."

Marti wanted so desperately to just spill it all—the pain, the frustration, the hurt. She shook off that need. "I've done things I'm not proud of, Jenna. Things that still haunt me each and every day. I don't know if I could stand seeing that mirrored in my brother's eyes and it would. Neither of them have a clue and I don't want them to have to think about it."

"Honey, the not knowing makes them think much worse, believe me."

"They've said something?"

Jenna shook her head. "While you were gone, I'd hear them, talking, considering, worrying. Wondering if you were dead or alive, wondering if you had joined a cult or been sold off into the sex trade. You think that doesn't hurt them? To wonder like that?"

Marti listened to the coffee maker sputter and spew as the aroma of fresh brewed coffee filled the room. "Just let them know that I'm safe and sound and maybe someday, I'll be able to come back."

"Don't do this to them, Marti."

"What about me? What about what's important to me?"

"I'm not trying to keep you from going, Marti. I can see it burning in you like revenge. I'm just trying to convince you to come right back when you're done."

Marti choked out a bitter laugh. "Burning like revenge. That about sums it up."

"Who hurt you like this, Marti?"

Marti stood up, shaking her head. "We never had this conversation." Then she left the room, coffee forgotten.

Sunday, 8:15 pm
Task Force Headquarters, Baltimore, Md.

Chamberland nodded to Lisa and stood up, stretching. "I'm going to go get some dinner."

"I think I'll join you," Lisa snagged her jacket from the back of her chair. "How about something substantial for a change? I'm tired of subs and pizza."

"What do you have in mind?"

"How about that Italian place down by the harbor?" She strolled through the door and into the hallway.

"I don't know if I'm up for something that heavy."

They stood together in the elevator, saying nothing. Side-by-side, they strolled out of the building and climbed into Peter's car. As he pulled away from the curb, Lisa turned to him. "What did you find out?"

"I'll explain in a few minutes."

Half an hour later, they pulled into the parking lot of a steak house in Ellicott City where Chip was waiting a table for them. He'd ordered them drinks and was buttering a slice of hot bread when they sat down.

"All this cloak and dagger. Don't you love it?"

Chamberland set his cell phone down on the table next to his keys. "Not when I'm looking at a cop for my suspect and I'm working in a building full of cops. I'm walking around feeling like a have a target on my back."

Lisa picked up the menu and perused it. "They wouldn't dare strike at us."

Chip waved a slice of bread through the air. "I beg to differ. They killed a cop that knew too much. We would mean even less to them."

"But we're Feds," she protested.

Chamberland snorted as he lifted his glass of water. "All the more reason to get rid of us." He turned to Chip. "What did you find out?"

"Ryan's partner is in this up to his weak chin. He's living way above his means but he has it all in his wife's name to defer suspicion. I asked for phone records but haven't received them yet. But I think this goes up further than Darrell."

"What makes you believe that?"

Chip leaned back as the waiter appeared. They all ordered and as soon as the waiter stepped away, Chip folded his hands over his plate and leaned in again. "I found a homeless man down by Camden Yards. I was down there following up on the lead Lisa got. About this guy Tony hanging out at a pool hall down there. Anyway, this homeless man tells me that he saw Tony, in his truck, pull up about two in the morning, just after Ryan was killed. He pulled up next to an unmarked police car and they talked for a few minutes. Then the cop handed over an envelope and Tony left."

"If it was two in the morning and an unmarked car, how did he know it was a cop?"

"Because right after Tony left, the car pulled out, turned on its flashing lights, and took off up the street."

Chamberland traced the condensation on his water glass with his thumb. "And no way to know who was in that car."

"Ah contraire. Our homeless man has a near photographic memory." Chip pulled out his notebook, flipped it open and set it down in front of Chamberland. "He saw the plate number. I ran it. Discreetly. Belongs to Detective Randy Shiff."

Chamberland felt as if he'd just been slammed in the chest by a semi. "Great." Shiff and his partner were on the task force. He had access to everything they were doing and every move they were making. And he'd know minute by minute exactly how the investigation was going.

This was so not good. He looked at Lisa. "I want you to discreetly check with the motor pool. Make sure Shiff was driving his own car that night. We have to have him cold on this. I'm going to go see Benedict. If anyone can pull some strings quick, he can. Maybe he can get us some phone records."

"Of what? Schiff calling Ryan? One officer calling a friend of his on the force? That's not going to help us. We're going to practically have to catch the man in the act of selling one of the stolen guns. Or find the guns in his basement." She combed both hands through her hair. "This is wrong on so many levels. Steven Shepherd doesn't stand a chance against this."

Sunday, 9:30 pm
Baltimore Central Booking and Intake Center, Baltimore

Steven shifted in the hard metal chair, trying to find a comfortable position. He knew this is what cops did—left you waiting in an interview room until you were so uncomfortable and so miserable, you'd be willing to talk just to get out. His attorney, Lance Fielding, leaned against the wall. "You okay?"

Steven looked up at him. "I guess. At least I know understand why fugitives are so determined not to come back here."

Lance smiled as he folded his arms across his chest. "It helps that you have a few friends around here. That one officer seemed almost embarrassed to process you in."

"Rachel? She's a good cop. I hated to put her through this."

He reached up and rubbed his eyes. How in heaven's name did he get in this situation? He'd never seen anything spin out of control so fast.

The door opened. Lance pushed off the wall, putting on his lawyer face—stern, annoyed. Two officers came in, but only one pulled out the chair across from Steven and sat down.

"Steven, I'm Lt. Neil Chicca and this is Detective Shiff. I'm going to record this conversation, okay?"

"Fine with me." He leaned back, folding his arms across his chest. He knew they'd take it as a defensive move, but the truth was, he was just tired and wanted to rest his arms.

"I'd like to get your story, Steven. Why don't you start at the beginning?"

"Sure. ATF Agent Peter Chamberland asked me to post bail for a woman named Andrea Morrow." He watched the annoyance building on Chicca's face. "Oh, you don't want go back that close to the beginning?"

"The smart attitude isn't going to help you, Steven."

Steven jerked forward. "And neither is this let's-be-buddies act. Andrea called me on my cell and told me that she was being abducted and that they were going to kill her. I ran to the rescue. When I arrived, she was tied up in the back of a van. I got her out of the van and a police officer pulled up. I identified myself and he ordered me to toss my gun. I complied, trying to explain to him what was happening. Before I could get a word out, he shot me. I returned fire. Two men jumped out of a nearby van and started shooting. Andrea and I took off."

Lance walked over and sat down next to him. Steven slowly went through the story, right up until he heard that the two men in the campground were dead. Then Chicca started poking at his story, trying to get him to say something that contradicted the original story.

"No, I did not fire my weapon. It was on the ground. I couldn't get to it so I went for the .32 I keep as a backup."

".32?" Chicca leaned forward in his chair. "Ryan wasn't shot with a .32." He opened the file in front of him and began reading quickly. Steven glanced at the file and then jerked in his chair.

"Wait. That's Officer Ryan?"

Chicca slid the photo over toward Steven. "Yes."

"That's not the man I shot. This guy was blond, tall, thin, had a scar on his chin. Your photo of Ryan shows a man with brown hair, mustache, and glasses. We are talking about two different men."

Shiff snorted. "Oh, so now we have a dead cop who isn't a dead cop? You'll say just about anything to get out of this, won't you?"

"I'm telling you straight. If this is a photo of Officer Ryan, then I didn't shoot him."

"Then why did you run?" Shiff asked.

"Because there were two other men shooting at us."

"What did they look like?"

"I did not get a good look at them. It was dark. I was under fire."

"But not dark enough for you to see Officer Ryan clearly."

"He was standing ten feet in front of me. The other guys were half way across the parking lot. Do the math."

Shiff slapped the table. "You shot and killed a law enforcement officer in cold blood!"

Lance leaned forward. "Are you charging Steven with murder?"

Lt. Chicca tapped his pen on his notebook and turned off the recorder. "I have evidence against him."

"But not enough for a conviction. Let him go. You can see he's totally exhausted. He's agreed to tell you whatever he can. He's agreed to a polygraph. There's nothing more he can give you right now."

"And my head will be chopped off if I let him walk out of here."

"Do you have enough to charge him?" Lance asked.

"Honestly? Yes."

"Then charge him and let him get some sleep." He glanced at his watch. "I have news conference to hold."

Chicca's head snapped up and his body stiffened. "News conference?"

"Absolutely. My client is an upstanding member of the law enforcement community. His father and his brother were both police officers. Their company has been serving the courts now for over thirty years. Add that to the fact that he's offered to take a polygraph, that the evidence against him is so obviously planted a child could figure it out, that he was in the process of saving a kindergarten school teacher when he was shot and nearly killed himself, his car was shot up, and his family has been a constant presence throughout this fiasco, trying to help bring the true killer to justice."

Steven slapped the table. "That's it!" He grabbed Lance's arm. "Call Nick. Tell him to call some of the county police he knows from his days on the force. Have him call the Chief. My car! I put Officer Ryan's gun down between the seat and console so that I could shift gears. The whole back window was shot out. Have them look for the bullet. They can determine by the angle and force of the round how far away the shooter was when he shot out my window. And the ballistics. I guarantee it will be the same as the round that killed Officer Ryan. That will prove that I was being shot at the same as Officer Ryan. Between the ballistics evidence, Andrea's testimony, and a polygraph, they'd have to believe me."

Lance nodded. "I'm on it. I'll be right back."
Chicca stood up. "We can send our people"
Shiff stood up. "I'll get on it."
"I don't think so, Lieutenant. No offence, but I wouldn't trust anyone in your department to handle walking my dog at this point."

Chicca obviously wasn't too happy with the insult but he sat back down and watched as Shiff quickly left the room.

"You believe me, don't you?" Steven asked. "It's in your eyes."

Chicca wearily rubbed a hand down his cheek as he looked down at his notebook. "Honestly? I don't know."

Steven leaned forward, his arms on the table, hands on top of each other. "Then let me go and let my brother and our team help you. We're getting close."

Chicca slowly rose. "I wish I could, Steven. But I have orders from the Captain to charge you and hold you. He's even told the D.A. to argue for no bail."

"And that doesn't make you a little suspicious?"
"It's not the first time a cop killer has been held tighter than someone else."

"Oh, please. You know as well as I do that this has nothing to do with me being some cop killer. It's a frame job and they're protecting their backsides." Steven stood. "Where are you going?"

"There's evidence to collect."
"Don't you dare let anyone in your department know, Lieutenant! They'll destroy it! You can't!"
"I have an obligation to my department."
"Lieutenant!"

Chicca just left the room and locked the door behind him.

Sunday, 10:30 pm
International House of Pancakes, Baltimore

Andrea pulled the Jeep into the parking lot and then chose a space under a parking lot light. Chaos whined as she pulled the keys from the ignition.

"I don't know why I'm doing this either, boy." She'd been second-guessing herself into exhaustion. Steven had been trying to help her and look what happened to him. She'd been trying to help Paul and look what happened to her. There had to be some way of getting Paul to help her and Steven.

Slowly, she opened the door and stepped out. What if he wouldn't help? He blamed her for everything because she had given his name to the police. But hadn't he sent her there in the first place? Didn't he understand that regardless of what kind of mix-up had occurred, he had to help. If there was a mix-up. The longer this went on, the more she doubted.

"Hello, Andi. You're late."

Startled, Andrea jumped and then spun around. "Don't do that."

"Do what?" Paul asked. And that's when she saw it in his eyes. He'd done it deliberately and was enjoying the fact that he'd scared her.

"Paul, you have to help me. And Steven."

"I don't know exactly what you want."

"You set all this up, Paul. I don't know why, but you did. And now an innocent man is sitting in jail and you're the only one that can do anything about it."

"Wrong, honey. I didn't shoot that cop. And I didn't have anything to do with his murder. There's nothing I can do for your boyfriend."

"He's not my boyfriend."

"Then don't worry about it. It's not your problem." He took her arm. "Come on. There's someone I want you to meet."

Chaos leapt out of the Jeep, barking furiously. Paul dropped her arm. "If you want that dog to see another day, I suggest you tell him to back off." He swept back the corner of his jacket and she saw the gun there. For the first time in all the time she'd known Paul, she was truly terrified of him. Who was this man? Why hadn't she seen the truth long ago?

"Chaos, down."

The dog responded but whined in protest. She didn't blame him. She felt like whining herself.

Paul grabbed her arm again, but she noticed that he kept on eye on Chaos. "Let's go."

"Why?" she tried to pull back, but he held firm, nearly dragging her across the parking lot.

"Someone that has been waiting a long time to see you."

"I don't want to go with you, Paul. Let me go."

"Sorry, Andi, but what you want or don't want no longer matters at all."

Paul stopped in front of his truck. The truck passenger side door opened and a man stepped out.

And Andrea felt the ground beneath her shift. Her mouth went dry. Her heart started jumping. This could not be happening.

"Hello, girl. Don't you have a hug for your daddy?"

She opened her mouth, but nothing came out. How could he be here? How did he find her? If he'd found her, had he found her mother? Fear crawled up her body and wrapped around her in a familiar embrace. The devil was back in her life.

"Stupid as you ever were," Norman spat. "Put her in the truck, Paul. We gotta go."

Andrea put up a little bit of resistance, but she was still staring at Norman as if she'd seen a ghost. In some ways, she felt as if she was seeing a ghost.

Paul practically had to pick her up and shove her into the truck. Norman climbed in after her.

Running around the truck, Paul climbed in behind the wheel. The he hit the steering wheel."

"What's wrong," Norman asked.

"That dog of hers. He just jumped in the bed of the truck."

"So what? It's just a dog. Let's go."

As soon as Paul pulled out into traffic, Norman asked Andrea, "Now, where is your mother?"

There was an instant mix of relief and despair. He didn't know where her mom was. And she couldn't tell him. He'd make her miserable until he got what he wanted from her. She spent too many years under his roof not to dread what was coming. She braced herself for it.

Norman smacked her upside the head. Pain exploded in her head and she couldn't help the fact that she started crying, slumping her shoulders, and folding herself in, but she still didn't answer him.

"Where is your mother, girl? Don't make me hit you again. She's my wife. I have a right to know where she is."

Andrea's only response was to sob even harder. *Oh, Mom. I'm trying.*

"I'm not in the mood to be very patient, girl. I got a big thing going down and when it's over, I'll have a lot of money. Then you, your momma and me, we're going to Mexico. I got a piece of land down there. Nice spread. Gonna make a nice life."

Paul stopped at a red light. "But, I thought you wanted me, too."

"Sure, boy. Sure." Norman seemed almost dismissive of Paul, keeping his attention on her. "So, you're gonna tell me where your momma is. And the sooner you do, the sooner it gets easier on you. You know I never could stand that stubborn streak of yours. You're gonna obey me, girl. You know that, don't you?"

Andrea felt her head nodding, almost as if it were responding by habit alone. But inside, she was screaming. *I'll never tell you where she is. Not even if you kill me.*

Chapter 19

Sunday, 10:45 pm
Prodigal Offices, Baltimore

Nick stood under the parking lot light, legs braced slightly apart, arms folded, watching the forensics team go over Steven's Mustang. They had a tow truck standing by to take it to the forensics lab garage.

Lance had called twice. The first time to give Nick Steve's message about the Mustang. The second call to warn him that Chicca's team may try to intervene. Nick pulled in every favor he had to get the county team working on the car before Chicca's team could assemble on site.

Now, he was just impatient. He wanted them to secure the car and get it out of here before Chicca's team showed up. Time was not on his side. If they took much longer, it was going to turn into a jurisdiction turf war. And he couldn't afford for Chicca to win on any level.

Finally, he saw one of the officers wave to the truck driver, but Nick wasn't breathing easier just yet. They still had to get it loaded, secured and down the road. Once it was gone, Chicca would have to jump through a whole lot of hoops to prove he had a right to the car.

Conner came out of the offices and walked over to Nick. "How's it going?"

"Slow. Any word from Lance?"

"They've settled Steven in a cell for a while. Lance is staying with him."

Nick nodded. "I have to admit, Conn. I'm worried."

"You want this car gone?"

"Like five minutes ago."

"Done." Conner walked over to the tow truck driver. He heard Conn say something along the lines of "What's this for?" The truck driver started moving at twice the speed as Conner started messing around with the controls on the side of the truck.

Nick brought his hand up and covered his mouth, hiding the smile. This tow truck driver would now be trying to get off this lot for no other reason than to get away from Conner.

Nick turned as he heard footsteps crunching on the gravel trim around the parking lot. It was one of his old friends from his days on the force, Sergeant Colin Mullinex. "Hey, Colin."

"Nick. We're taking it in now, but I wanted to let you know that we found the weapon, just as Steven said. And while it's just an initial finding, it sure looks like the round through the back window came from at least fifty yards away."

"Thanks, Colin. I appreciate this."

"I'm not really doing anything, Nick. This is going to be by the book all the way. It has to be if it's going to help Steven."

"I know. That's why I called you. I don't want any favors other than making sure that someone honest handles the evidence. That's all. Let the evidence speak for itself."

Colin held out his hand and Nick shook it. "It'll probably be sometime tomorrow afternoon before I have anything solid for you."

"That's fine." He would have preferred far sooner, but he could only push so far and like Colin said, it couldn't smack of favoritism or it wouldn't help Steven at all.

Marti stepped just outside the back door. "Nick!" she yelled.

"I have to go."

"Take care, Nick."

Nick gave Colin's shoulder a pat and then strode over to Marti. "What's going on?"

"I finally made some progress and you are not going to believe what I found."

He followed her back inside the building. "What?"

"Okay, so I kept digging into Andrea's past."

"Why Andrea? I thought we were looking for a crooked cop?"

"Rafe is. But I still think the key is Andrea."

Nick didn't agree, but as long as Rafe was looking for any police officers that might be involved, he wasn't going to argue. "Okay, what did you find?"

She dropped down behind her desk. "Weaving through that woman's life was like being two feet high playing in a six foot high maze." She turned her computer screen around. "Okay, first off, I want you to know that since she didn't return the Jeep the way she was supposed to some three hours ago, I called Vic and told him to go ahead and report it stolen."

"Marti," Nick started to object. What was the point?
"Wait. Just hear me out."
"Go ahead."

Marti's eyes sparkled with a life he hadn't seen in them in a long time. This is where she could really shine, digging through the labyrinths of a puzzle and getting to the truth.

"Okay, so I kept digging and I finally found something interesting. On her first rental application, right after college, she listed the name of a young woman—Kathy Illes—as a reference. I found Kathy. But she didn't recognize Andrea's name as Andrea Morrow. When she knew Andrea in high school, it was Andrea Caspren. So, I started tracking Caspren and I found an old phone listing for a Leona Caspren. So, then I looked for a Leona Morrow in the same town. Bingo. A tiny little news article about a woman that witnessed a car accident."

Nick was growing impatient and while he hated to stop Marti while she was on a roll, he had to. "Marti. I'm thrilled. Really. Could we get to the point here?"

"Leona Caspren was married and gave birth to a daughter. Andrea. Her married name was Rotterbach. She was married to a Norman Rotterbach. Who is in prison as we speak."

"Prison?"

"Yep. Nasty man, this Rotterbach. All that abuse Andrea suffered as a child? It was no joke. This guy as a rap sheet you wouldn't believe."

Nick leaned over her shoulder, reading her notes on Rotterbach. "Okay, how does this help us with Steven?"

"Okay, I've spent the last two hours going over Rotterbach's life with a fine toothed comb. Rotterbach had a mistress. And this mistress bore him a child. Born just six months after Andrea was born."

Nick winced. "Ouch."

"Oh, it gets better. The mistress? Helen Unger."

"Okay." This wasn't going anywhere.

"She had a son. I pulled records on him and I don't mean school records. This guy has been in and out of the system his whole life. His rap sheet reads like a who's who of how to be a career criminal. But get this, his list of aliases. Paul Ungerford, Paul Rotterdam, Paul Paulson, and Paul Rousch."

"Okay, why does that name ring a bell?"

"Think Andrea and think Paul Roush."

Nick's head snapped back. "You're kidding me? Paul is Andrea's brother?"

"Half-brother. Now tell me again that she isn't in this up to her pretty little neck?"

Nick pulled Jenna's chair over and dropped down in to it. "Okay, so Paul is her brother. You think he's keeping dad's business running while dad's in prison?"

"That's my guess. With Andrea's help."

"It doesn't play for me. Why set your sister up?"

"Set her up? I don't think he set her up. She went to deliver the guns and pick up the money. Then she blames it all on some mysterious boyfriend, who isn't a boyfriend at all."

Nick held up his hand as questions bombarded him. "Yeah, but if you're arrested and you're trying to protect yourself and your brother, do you give them your brother's name? Wouldn't you give them a phony name?"

Marti pursed her lips. "Good point. That doesn't play, does it?"

"Not for me. But what if she didn't know Paul was her brother? What if Paul is just using her? The scorned child. Andrea was the legitimate child by a marriage. Paul would have been odd man out his whole life. Right?"

Marti shrugged. "Plays for me."

"Okay, so there has to be some resentment there."

"And what, he's looking to make points with the old man? I don't know, Nick. That doesn't play."

"No, it doesn't, does it?" He tapped his fingers on the desk. "We need to find Andrea."

Sunday, 11:15 pm
Ken Benedict's Office, ATF Headquarters
Orleans St, Baltimore, Md.

Peter Chamberland stood at the window, hands clasped behind his back, staring out across the city. Behind him, his boss, Ken Benedict was reading over the file Chamberland had given him.

"You realize what you're asking?" Benedict's voice moved through the quiet office, intruding on Chamberland's thoughts.

He turned around, leaning back against the credenza. "I do. The man is in this up to his hairy neck, Sir."

Ken Benedict was an icon with the agency. He was unorthodox, but his methods, while not always popular, brought in results. While he had the demeanor of a friendly old grandfather, he was incredibly sharp and tough, but fair. He gave Chamberland far more leeway than most in the agency would, and in turn, Chamberland gave Benedict what he wanted. Results.

Slipping off his glasses, Benedict placed them gently on top of the file, as if still deep in thought. "This is going to be very tricky, Paul."

"I'm aware of that, Sir. But I wouldn't ask if I wasn't positive."

"I know that, Peter." Benedict pushed up out of the chair and walked over to the bar tucked in the corner of his office. He poured himself a scotch and then lifted the bottle in Chamberland's direction in a silent offer. Chamberland shook his head.

Setting the bottle back on the shelf, Benedict walked over to stand near Peter at the window, sipping on his drink. "I don't like it when something like this happens. Abuse of power. Greed. When one falls, we all fall. It makes every branch of law enforcement look bad."

"It's worse than that, Sir. They're putting weapons out there that are killing our own, not to mention what it's doing to the citizens of this city." Chamberland clenched his fists. "We're supposed to be stopping crime and murder, not feeding it."

"I'm going to sign off on this, but Peter," he took a deep swallow and then stared down at his glass as if somewhere in the golden amber brew were the answers to the problems of the universe. "Be careful."

"I will, Sir."

Chamberland turned and strode to the door. As he reached for the doorknob, he heard Benedict. "Peter?"

He turned and looked back at his boss. "Sir?"

"Take this man down hard."

Sunday, 11:45 pm
Paul's home, Baltimore, Md

Andrea sat on the bed, her hands clasped between her thighs, her breathing shallow. Blood trickled from her nose and lip. She could feel her lip swelling and the throbbing pain in her mouth was relentless. She heard the lock on the door click into place and the tension drained.

But it wouldn't last long. She knew that. He'd come back again and again. He'd keep at her until she gave him what he wanted. He'd torment her until she'd feel as if she were going mad with it. This man whose blood ran in her veins. This evil she knew as Daddy.

Slowly, she curled up on the bed, resting her head on a near flat pillow. Not bothering with the blanket, she stared at the door. It might be ten minutes, it might be two hours, but just when she thought she could relax, he would return. She might see him coming. She might wake up and find him staring down at her with hatred in his eyes. But he would return.

He always came back.

Once, she had adored and loved her father. Her daddy. But then one day she realized that he was a bad man. How had her mother survived all those years?

A rush of desperate memories swamped her mind, yanking her back to a time she only wanted to forget. She no longer felt like a grown woman in charge of her own life, but once again, a helpless child forced to suffer the torment of her childhood once again. *You hear me, girl? You'll be sorry.* How many times had she heard those words and bore the brunt of what they represented? How many times had they come just moments before a fist? Or a slap? Or a belt?

Foolish of her to think that she'd overcome the scars. Or that she was no longer susceptible to the same crippling symptoms.

Wrapping her arms around herself, she tried to remind herself that she wasn't eight years old any more. Rocking, she kept talking to herself. *I am strong. I am strong. No one is going to beat me. No one is going to punish me for breathing. For living. He can't hurt me. I'm okay. I might feel the slap. I might bleed. But I live. And I won't tell him where you are, Mom. I promise.*

It was all about the waiting now. Letting the fear build until she was almost hysterical with it. Her stomach was clenching, her head was pounding, and she could almost smell the sweat beading her face. Jumping at every shadow. Every noise. Every footstep in the hall was *him* coming for her.

> *Monday, 12:20 am*
> *Prodigal Offices, Baltimore, Md.*

Nick was rocked back in his chair, feet crossed on top of his desk, hands clasped at his waist, eyes closed, and barely awake when a tapping began to annoy him like a mosquito buzzing around his face. It took another minute for him to realize that someone was at the front door of the building.

Slowly he eased out of his chair and walked softly in his bare feet out into the reception area. He was surprised to see Chamberland and a woman standing at there. Unlocking the door, he waved them in. "Didn't expect you."

"Did we wake you?"

"Not exactly. Another five minutes and you would have."

"You alone?"

Nick shook his head as he locked the door again. "Everyone's spread out all over my office, catching a cat nap."

Chamberland pointed to the small grouping of chairs for clients against the wall. "Can we talk here? Or do you want to go on back to the conference room?"

"Here's fine. Rafe is asleep on the conference table. What's up?"

"I don't think you've officially met, but Nick Shepherd this is Lisa Somers, one of my agents."

She was a tall, statuesque beauty with intelligent eyes, long dark hair, and a no-nonsense manner that would make any man look twice and think again before taking her lightly. Nick reached out and shook her hand. "Pleasure."

"Same," she replied in a husky voice that was soft but firm.

"Have you met my brother yet?" Nick asked, smiling.

"No, I haven't had the pleasure."

"He'd be crazy about you. If he drops at your feet and swears to love you forever, he'll half mean it."

She tipped her back and laughed, the sound of it as rich and strong as her voice. "I'll keep that in mind."

As soon as they were all seated, Chamberland clasped his hands between his knees and leaned forward. "We think we've found the head of the snake."

Nick closed his eyes. *Thank you, Lord. Forgive me for doubting You.* Then he opened his eyes. "Who is it?"

"Better yet, how much longer does he have to live?"

Everyone turned to find Marti leaning against the doorframe just outside Nick's office. "I thought you were sleeping," Nick responded.

"I was." She looked at Chamberland first. "My favorite ATF Agent. You're up late."

Chamberland smiled. "And your bite hasn't eased up a bit."

"Not likely to. Who's your friend?"

Nick made the introductions. "Marti, this is Agent Lisa Somers."

"Hi."

Lisa nodded with half a smile.

Marti looked back at Chamberland. "So you know who he is, now what are you going to do to him?"

"We're going to set him up and take him down."

"And how sure are you that you have all his accomplices?"

"We're not. That's why we need to work with you."

Marti pushed off the wall, grabbed a chair and plopped down in it. "Oh, wow. The Ice Man needs our help. Will miracles never cease."

"Marti," Nick said with a touch of warning in his voice.

"Leave her alone," Chamberland said. "If she was ever actually nice to me, I don't know that I'd like her as much."

Nick just shot her a warning with his eyes and turned back to Chamberland. "What do you need from us?"

"We need a connection between him and Andrea Morrow. That's the thread we haven't been able to tie together yet."

Marti looked over at Nick and he nodded. She walked over to her desk and returned with a notepad and handed it to Chamberland. "His name is Norman Rotterbach. His son is Paul Rotterbach. AKA Paul Roush."

"Bingo," Chamberland declared as he read her notes. "Marti, my estimation of you just went up another couple of notches."

"Which was still higher than my opinion of you. Now here's what we still haven't quite figured out yet. If Andrea's father and half-brother are bringing guns into the city, and this cop is helping them get them into the city undetected and distributed, and we know that the gangs are buying them, where does Andrea fit into this? Is she in on it? Or were they just using her?"

Lisa's cell phone rang and she excused herself to cross the room and take the call.

Chamberland tilted his head as he looked over at Marti. "I've been trying to figure that one out from the moment I met her. Once minute, I'm convinced she's a good actress and as guilty as sin. The next minute, I'm not so sure."

"That was Chip." Lisa strode across the room, tucking her cell phone on her belt. "We need to get down to the hospital. Someone shot at another cop. He's alive, but just barely."

"Who?" Chamberland asked, lifting his head.

"An officer by the name of Tim Darrell. He was Officer Ryan's partner."

Chamberland jumped to his feet, handing Marti her notebook. "We'll be back."

"Keep us posted," Nick told him as he unlocked the door and let them out.

Marti set the notebook back on her desk. "First Ryan and now his partner. Someone is getting nervous."

"Hopefully we're the ones making him nervous."

Chapter 20

Monday, 12:45 am
Union Memorial Hospital, E. University Parkway, Baltimore

    The emergency room was packed and the noise level hadn't decreased since Chamberland had arrived. Babies were crying. Women were moaning. Men were complaining. Nurses were trying to settle everyone down. The television in the corner was trying to get everyone's attention.
    It was all skating on a thin blade along Chamberland's last nerve. He paced in front of the doors leading back into the emergency care area, waiting for the nurse to return. He had to see Darrell and talk to him now. Police officers were starting to wander in and out and there

was no way he was going to let any of them near Darrell until he had a chance to talk to him.

The double doors swung open and the nurse, an overweight woman with gray hair and tired eyes, waved him in. He rushed through with half a glance at Lisa who stood nearby. Lisa barely made it through the doors before they closed behind her. The nurse didn't notice. She was already marching through the maze of curtained areas.

Finally she stopped and pointed at one curtain, drawn tight. "Just a few minutes." She then noticed Lisa and pursed her lips.

"She's a Federal Agent and required to assist me in this."

The nurse looked skeptical, but just walked off without a word.

Chamberland ducked through an opening in the curtain. Officer Darrell was hooked up to a bevy of machines that were keeping track of his vital signs. As pale as the sheets covering his body, Darrell had his eyes closed and was breathing heavily in spite of the oxygen feed into his nose.

"Darrell?"

Slowly, the man opened his eyes.

"I'm Agent Chamberland. I'm working with the Project Exile Task Force. Can you tell me who shot you?"

Darrell let his eyes slowly close.

"Darrell, this isn't going to stop. He's killing everyone connected with this operation. Are you going to let him get away with it?"

Darrell opened his eyes again. "You can't . . . stop . . . him."

"You're wrong. I can. And I will. But it would be faster and easier with your help."

"What . . . do you . . . want?"

"Why did he have Ryan killed? I don't think he was in on this."

"Overheard . . . conver . . . sation. Was . . . going . . . to I.A."

"Okay. And then he has the two men at the campground killed. And we found Tony's body about half an hour ago. Now you. Who else is in this? Anyone else on the force?"

Darrell's head barely moved side to side. "Rotter . . .bach."

"We know about Rotterbach."

"Cop killers . . . coming . . . Lady."

"What lady?"

Chamberland leaned over, trying to hear Darrell whose voice had dropped to a near whisper. "Boat. Fifty millimeter. Stop. It."

Suddenly, the machines started screaming and Chamberland stepped back as the curtain was yanked open and hospital staff flooded in, pushing him aside and then out.

He looked over at Lisa. "Make sense to you?"

"A fifty millimeter boat? No sir."

A uniformed man marched toward them, his stride long and determined, his face etched in grief. "How is he?"

"I don't think he made it, Sir."

Summerfield dropped his head. "This has got to stop."

"I agree, Sir."

"Did he tell you anything? Anything at all that would help us find out who did this?"

Chamberland shook his head. "He really wasn't making any sense at all and then he was gone. But Steven Shepherd is in custody, so we know he didn't do it."

Summerfield shoved his hands deep in his pants pockets. "No, but he had that girl with him when he killed Ryan. She might have done this."

Chamberland looked over at Lisa and then back to Summerfield. "It's a distinct possibility. She's disappeared and no one can find her."

"We'll find her, Agent Chamberland. You can count on that."

Summerfield strode off, heading back toward the emergency waiting room, most likely to inform the troops that they'd lost another good man. Chamberland glanced over at Lisa. "Thoughts?"

"We better find her first."

Chapter 21

Monday, 1:10 am
Paul's residence, Baltimore, Md

Andrea jerked up when she heard the door unlock and the door swing open. But it wasn't her father. It was Paul.

She brushed her hair back with her hands. "What do you want?"

"Where's your purse?"

"Why?"

"Because Dad wants it."

Andrea started to reach for it behind her on the bed and then stopped. "Why did you call him Dad?"

Paul's lip curled and it reminded her of a wolf baring its teeth before lunging on its prey. "Haven't you figured it out yet? I'm your brother. Half-brother, actually. But still."

"That's impossible."

"Not really. Your mother was such a lousy wife, he fell in love with my mother. And here I am. If she'd agreed to give him the divorce he wanted, he'd have married my mom, but oh no, the princess had to have her daddy."

Andrea knew that her brain wasn't exactly firing on all cylinders at the moment, but none of that made any sense to her at all. "My mom divorced him a long time ago."

"Liar."

"No. It's true. That's why he can't find her. She divorced him, changed her name, and moved far away from him. She doesn't ever want to see him again."

"Only because she took all his money. That's all he wants back from her."

"Money?" Andrea couldn't help laughing. "There was no money. He rarely ever worked and when he did, he drank it all. Mom is the one that worked herself silly making sure we had a roof over our heads and food on the table."

Paul clenched his fists and stepped forward. Andrea drew back, afraid he was going to punch her. "That's a lie! He told me that when he was arrested she took everything and ran off. He tried to divorce her and she refused."

"If she ran off, Paul, he could have divorced her for desertion. Does he have you that buffaloed?"

"You shut up! You're the reason he couldn't be with me all the time!"

"Oh, please. I would have gladly let you have him all the time. I hate the man."

"You are so ungrateful. After everything he did for you."

"He didn't do anything for me!" She took a deep breath. If she continued yelling, it would only draw her father's attention and she didn't want to see him. "Believe what you want. I don't care."

She reached for her purse. Oh no. Her cell phone. Her dad was going to use it to get in touch with her mother. But there was no address in her contacts. Just the cell number and he couldn't trace that. Relieved, she handed her purse over to Paul. "Take it. It won't give him what he wants."

Paul left the room with her purse, locking the door behind him. As soon as she heard the lock snick into place, she went to stretch out on her back and felt something in her back pocket. Steven's cell phone!

Watching the door, she pulled it out and went to the contact page. She found Nick's number and hit call. He answered on the second ring. "I didn't think you could call me from jail, bro."

"This is Andrea."

"Where are you?"

"I don't know. My dad." She hitched a breath. "It's too much to explain right now, but please help me. He's going to kill me, I just know he is."

"Who? Your dad? Or your brother? What's the game, Andrea?"

"It's not a game, Nick. I swear to you. I didn't know Paul and I were related. I just found out! And I don't know how my dad found me, but he wants me to tell him where my mom is and I won't do it. I just won't."

"And you don't know where you are?"

"No. It's just a house on a street. But I don't know the address."

"Well, it doesn't really matter. I can track you with Steven's cell phone. Just keep it on. Put it on mute so they don't know you have it in case it rings."

"Okay. So, you're coming for me?"

"Yes, Andrea. We're coming."

"Thank you." She felt the tears welling up again. "Thank you."

But Nick was gone. She muted the phone and put it back in her pocket. Hope. Finally, a ray of hope.

Monday, 1:30 am
Prodigal Offices, Baltimore, Md.

Nick twisted the top of his bottle of Mountain Dew. "I don't know why this is a problem for you."

Marti reached for the sugar and started spooning it into her coffee. "Because the woman is trouble. How do you know this isn't a trap just like the one Steven walked into?"

"I don't, but she can lead us to Paul and her dad."

"Send Chamberland in after them."

"I called Chamberland. He hasn't called me back yet. Time is ticking by."

Marti pulled out a chair at the conference table and sat down. Rafe was sitting next to her, yawning. Conner was still asleep in Nick's office. He wouldn't bother waking him up until he knew for sure they were going after Andrea.

"Nothing is going to happen to her in an hour. Or even two. If Rotterbach was actually going to kill her he'd have done it already." Marti took a sip of coffee then set the cup down, wrapping her hands around it. "This is her father we're talking about. They've had plenty of opportunities to kill her if that was their intention. If this man is everything I think him to be, he doesn't want to kill Andrea or her mother. He wants to torment them. He wants them at his beck and call, day after day, making sure that they are so miserable they don't care whether they live or die."

Rafe raised his hand. "If anyone wants my vote, I say let Chamberland handle it. It's not like we have any authority to take Paul or Rotterbach into custody. The best we could do is walk out of there with Andrea and the minute we do, those two will be in the wind."

Nick didn't like it, but they were right. He buried his head in his hands. He was too tired, too stressed, to close to the problem emotionally. Steven was sitting in jail, waiting for him to do something, anything, to get him out and Nick was stuck here at the office doing nothing.

"Nick, it's coming together. Between what we have and what Chamberland has drudged up, we're starting to get the picture. Let's not rush in and mess everything up when we're so close."

Nick lifted his head and looked across the table at his sister. "I hear you. I just hate sitting here doing nothing."

"We all do," Rafe replied with another yawn. "But any minute now, Chamberland is going to call and tell us where to hit and we'll have plenty to do."

"You really think he's going to keep his word and bring us in on this?" Marti snorted in a very unlady-like manner.

"It might be a minor part in his play, but yeah, I think he will. He can't trust all those cops around him. He's going to need people he knows will have his back. And that's us." Rafe stood up and crossed over to the coffee pot. When he saw it was empty, he gave Marti a dirty look and started another pot.

Nick's phone rang and he grabbed it. "Yeah?"

"You were right. We were so busy running around looking at the right hand that we missed what the left hand was doing."

"What does that mean?"

"Come open the front door and I'll explain."

Nick closed his phone. "Chamberland's here."

Marti stood up. "I'll let him in."

As she went to stand up, Conner entered the conference room. "Look who I found skulking around out front."

Chamberland entered, followed by Chip and Lisa. He tossed a file and a roll of papers down on the conference table. "Miss me?"

"Like fleas."

Chamberland laughed and looked over at Rafe. "I'd love some of that."

"It's brewing."

Pulling out a chair, the ATF agents sat down. "Okay, I want to show you—"

Nick held up a hand. "Before you begin, Andrea called me. She has Steven's cell phone. Says she's being held by Rotterbach and her brother. She's begging us to get her out of there before they kill her."

"Did she tell you where she is?"

"No, but I have a lock on Steven's cell. I know where she is."

"The police think she may have been the one to shoot Officer Darrell tonight." Chamberland raised his eyebrows. "You know, since Steven couldn't have done it."

"Well, I know she couldn't have done it unless Darrell was shot at this address."

"They'll just say that she left the cell phone at the house when she went to kill Darrell."

Nick took a swig from his drink, frustration humming through him. "This is nuts."

"It doesn't matter," Chamberland stressed. "I want to run a scenario by you all and see if works for you."

"Go ahead," Rafe replied setting a cup of coffee down in front of Chamberland. "We don't have to be to work until eight."

There was scattered chuckles and smiles around the room, breaking some of the tension that had been building for hours. Nick took the opportunity to bring everyone back to the main issue. "You said that while we were all watching one hand, we were missing what the other hand was doing. Explain."

Chamberland took a sip of coffee and then set the cup down. "I think the bust at the storage unit was a set-up."

"With Andrea, you mean?"

"For us, as well. Ever since that bust, we've been running around chasing ghosts, essentially. We got a tip about a fishing vessel named the Baltimore Lady. We go running out there only to find the vessel sitting at dock. The Harbor Master tells us it belongs to some old man in who winters in Florida and is rarely out of dock until the old man," Chamberland looked at his notes, "one Charles Unger returns in May. His nephew occasionally takes it out on day trips for a little fishing and that's it. We figured it was a dead end and set it all aside."

"But Unger is Paul's last name," Marti interjected.

Chamberland held up a finger. "Hold on. Let me lay this all out, piece by piece. We didn't have that information at the time, so we just assumed it was a false lead. Which is exactly what they wanted. While we were ignoring the Baltimore Lady, they were getting it ready for another shipment. In the meantime, we're chasing Andrea, trying to find out who she was connected with and then they use Steven to get rid of Officer Ryan. I understand that he overheard a conversation he wasn't supposed to hear. Steven was the perfect fall guy."

"They didn't count on us," Conn said, leaving back, folding his massive arms across his chest.

"No, they didn't. So, all of your focus turned to defending or protecting Steven. In the meantime, we were still looking at Marcus, the buyer of the guns, and trying to connect him to Andrea. Then people started dying all around the case. The two men at the park and ride? Dead in the campground. Steven becomes the fall guy again. Why would these guys go all the way out to Thurmont? To plant the murder weapon in Steven's car. Their boss, Tony, was found shot in the back of the head and dumped in an alley on the south side."

Lisa leaned forward. "And that's when we started getting really suspicious. Why is everyone connected with that bust being killed off?"

"To eliminate witnesses," Rafe offered.

"Correct. Anyone that can point us to the two main players in this game. A specific cop and Norman Rotterbach, who was suddenly released early from prison and classified as a C.I. for the state."

"C.I?" Marti picked up her coffee mug and headed for the coffee pot.

"Confidential Informant," Chip replied.

"Now," Chamberland continued. "we come to Officer Darrell. Ryan's partner. And more than likely, the way that Ryan overheard a conversation. Darrell was one of the crooked cops."

"One of? You mean there's more than one?" Nick toyed with the cap on his Mountain Dew.

"Oh, yes. We have one more cop involved and Darrell must have either threatened him or was getting a little too nervous because he was shot. I managed to talk to him just before he died. He wasn't able to say much, but there are three specific words that rang alarm bells for me. The first was fifty millimeter. The second was boat. The third was Lady."

"A fifty millimeter boat?" Conner shook his head. "Makes no sense."

"I don't think he was telling us that the boat was fifty millimeter, " Chamberland replied.

The ramifications hit Nick hard and fast. "You're talking .50 millimeter weapons."

"I think so, yes."

Nick covered his eyes with one hand.

"What's the big deal with .50 mm weapons?" Marti asked.

Nick dropped his hand. "They are extremely lethal. They can penetrate a Kevlar vest like a hot knife through butter. And go right through a car with just as much ease."

"Uh-oh. Stuff like that out there on the streets?" Marti looked as horrified as Nick felt.

"I think this is what was going on with the left hand. We get a bust, pick up some stolen weapons, think we've done something positive, and all the while, they've got this shipment coming in undercover."

"On this boat. The Baltimore Lady." Nick stood up and started pacing. He couldn't help it. The thought of weapons like that out on the streets in the hands of kids and gangs was devastating.

"I think so, yes."

"When do you think they're coming in?"

"All indications are tomorrow." Chamberland glanced up at the clock. "Later today, actually."

"What do you want to do?" Nick asked.

"Stop them."

"What about this cop? The one you say is still out there? Won't he try to stop us?" Marti reached for the sugar.

"If he knew, he would. So, I and my team are going to be in and out of task force headquarters today like nothing has changed. As if we're still just looking for someone buying illegal guns on the street. But we'll have the boat under constant watch. And now that we know where Rotterbach is, we want to put surveillance on him and Paul, as well."

"What about Andrea," Nick asked.

Chamberland shook his head. "If we try to pull her out now, we could blow this whole thing."

Nick felt the rush of something bitter in is throat. "Here we go again."

"This is not the same at all, Nick. This is no innocent kid and I can't see why Rotterbach would want to kill her."

"I don't think Norman Rotterbach wants her dead," Marti said dryly. "I think Paul does."

Monday, 3:30 am
Paul's Residence, Baltimore

Andrea looked out the window to the front yard below where Chaos was lying near the sidewalk, staring at the house. Waiting for her. She'd tried opening the window, but it was painted shut. And after two hours of waiting for Nick to show, she'd given up hope of rescue. Why would he help her, after all? If it wasn't for her, his brother would be asleep in his own bed tonight, not in cell facing murder charges.

Moving to the second window, she tried again, putting all her strength into shoving it upward, but it never budged.

The lock at the door clicked. Andrea hurried back over to the bed and was barely seated before Paul walked in. "Dad wants to you downstairs."

Slowly, she got up off the bed and followed him down to the living room where her dad was sitting on the sofa, the contents of her purse strewn across the coffee table. He tipped back the bottle of beer and took a swallow was he watched her approach. Setting the bottle down, he picked up her cell phone.

"Sit down, girl."

She eased down to perch on the edge of a sofa chair across the coffee table from him. Swallowing hard, she tried to imagine what game he was going to play now. The man was capable of anything. He'd left her locked upstairs for hours just so she could have all that time to wonder, worry. Fear.

Norman picked up her cell phone and scrolled through the contact page. Then he hit dial. "No, it's not your daughter. It's your husband."

Andrea started to lurch off the chair. Paul looped a belt around her throat and yanked her back. She gagged, trying to catch her breath. Reaching up, she tried to pry the belt away but he only pulled it tighter.

"Andrea?" Norman looked over at her with a smirk as evil as he was. "She's here with me. I thought a little family reunion would be nice. Why don't you tell me where you are and we can get the party started?"

His face turned red and he gripped the phone a little tighter. "Well, let me put this another way, then." He nodded at Paul who slammed something up against the side of Andrea's face. She screamed as the pain shot through her.

"Now, let's try this again. Where are you?"

"No, Mom! Don't!" she screamed. Paul hit her again and this time, nausea rose up as she fought against the dizziness. Hot tears streamed down her face as her vision blurred.

Norman wrote down the address. "I'll see you in a couple of hours. And don't think about running. If you aren't there, your daughter will pay for it." He ended the call and tossed the phone down on the coffee table.

"Now, little girl. Do you see how futile it is to fight me?" Norman jerked his head at Paul who released the belt.

Crumbling to the floor, Andrea bent over, hands massaging her throat as she tried to stop the ache in her lungs by slowing her breathing.

Norman stood up and walked over, looming over her. "Next time I tell you to do something, you do it and you don't give me any backtalk, you hear me, girl?"

Andrea managed a weak nod.

"Paul? Is everything ready?"

"Yep. I had the boat fueled up on Friday. She's good to go."

"What time are you supposed to meet them?"

"Around noon."

Andrea watched Norman move away and felt a small sense of relief. He hadn't kicked her. And the further away he was, the less the chance was that he would.

"Wait. Aren't you coming with me, Dad?"

"No. The two of you can handle this part without me. I'm going to pay a little visit to my wife. I'll meet you back here later."

Two of you? Was he planning on her going with Paul? Nick, why didn't you come when I called?

"But, I thought you wanted to make sure nothing went wrong."

"Is something going to go wrong, Paul?"

Andrea recognized that tone in her dad's voice. It dared you to answer any other way except the way he wanted. And then promised you'd pay if you were wrong. She knew it was petty, but she was glad it was Paul on the other end of that tone and not her.

"No. Nothing will go wrong."

"Take the girl back to her room and lock her in. And then you better get ready to go."

Paul grabbed her arm, his fingers biting the flesh. Wincing, she crawled to her feet. The dizziness rose up again and she stumbled, but managed to stay on her feet. She used the railing to climb back upstairs and then collapsed on the bed in another rush of tears as Paul shut and locked the door.

I'm so sorry, Mom.

*Monday, 4:00 am
Prodigal Offices, Baltimore.*

The conference room looked like downtown Bagdad right after the invasion. Papers were strewn across the table, on the counter, pinned on the bulletin board, and tossed on the floor. Coffee cups, soda cans, and bottles of water—some empty, some not—scattered around the room. Styrofoam containers with the remnants of eggs, pancakes, hash browns, bacon, sausage, and toast were piled in the center of the table.

Jenna would kill them. Nick tried to ignore the mess and keep his attention on Chamberland who was standing at the blackboard, talking about the Chesapeake Bay.

"We're guestimating that he's going to leave the dock between five and six in the morning because the Harbor Master said he usually does. The destination is the problem. We don't know if he's going to dock somewhere between here and Norfolk or meet up with another boat somewhere and transfer the shipment at sea. There are plenty of places a transfer can happen." Chamberland pointed to the map. "Tangier, New Point, Cape Charles or Kiptopeke. Once he passes those, the next stop is Norfolk and I doubt he's going to get anywhere close to that port."

"So how do you plan on finding out in the next hour or so?" Conner asked.

"We don't. We've got a boat standing by that we can use to tail him from a distance. We'll also have a plane in the air. He won't get away from us."

Lisa raised her hand. "Please tell me I'm not assigned to the boat."

"Why?" Chamberland asked.

"Because I get seasick."

"You're in the plane."

"Thank you," she replied with a smile.

"We're going to have a surveillance team at the dock and another watching our police officer. I have a feeling he's going to be on the boat, but just in case he decides to sit this one out, we'll have him under our watchful eye the entire time."

"You want him on the boat, don't you?" Marti asked.

"It would make our lives so much easier," Chamberland admitted.

Nick raised his pencil. "Where do you want us?"

"I'd like you to be on the boat with some of my crew. Conner and Rafe, I'll need you on the boat next to the Baltimore Lady. We've talked to the owner and he's given us the keys. I want you to look like a cleaning crew hired to clean the boat up for the season. The owner only asks that we don't let it got shot up."

"Where do you want me?" Marti asked.

"How persuasive are you?"

She tilted her head with a frown. "Want to find out?"

Rafe chuckled, covering his mouth with his hand. Chamberland glanced at Rafe and then back to Marti. "Kidding. Do you get airsick? Because I'd like you to team up with Lisa."

She frowned. "Babysitting. I hate babysitting."

Lisa looked affronted. "Hey."

"Don't worry. I'll show you the ropes."

Lisa stared at Marti a long moment and then slowly smiled. "I think I'm going to like you."

"Don't let it get around," Marti responded. "Ruin my reputation."

Chamberland glanced at the clock. "Let's get our gear together and get to the Harbor. I want to be in place long before our guys get there."

Chapter 22

Monday, 5:15 am

Baltimore Harbor, Baltimore

Paul was furious. This was not the way it was supposed to happen. He was supposed to be sailing off this morning with his dad. After all these years, all the work, all the kowtowing, and at the last minute, he ditches Paul to go off to that woman.

Slamming the truck into park, he cut the lights. It was that girl's fault. Her and her mother. Always stepping in between him and his dad. Always interfering. Always ruining things.

Grabbing his bag, he climbed out of the truck and locked it. The salty air was crisp and cool and he couldn't help taking a deep breath and exhaling slowly. The harbor lights sprinkled the water like jewels. Boats swayed and bobbed against the dock, causing the ropes and bumpers to squeak softly. Small waves lapped and slapped against the hulls of the boats secured to the docks.

He strolled down to the Lady wondering what the old man would do if he were to take off with this shipment. It was worth a lot of money. More money than he'd ever had in his life. He could just sail off to another port, sell the guns, and disappear forever.

When he came up on the Baltimore Lady, he was surprised to see the Prime Catch lit up and a crew on board. He walked over and stood for a second, watching this hulk of a man scrubbing down the deck. He knew the man that owned the Prime and had never known Robert to have it cleaned this early in this season. When the big man stopped and looked over at him, Paul asked, "Working for Pete?"

The big guy squinted at Paul and then shook his head. "Guy hired us was named Robert."

Suspicions at rest, Paul boarded the Lady. He went down below and stowed his gear, then slipped into a heavier coat. It might be balmy in the harbor, but once he got out on the water, it would get downright cold until the sun came up and warmed things a bit.

"Ahoy, Baltimore Lady!"

Paul zipped up his coat and went up on deck. "Hey."

His father's partner jumped aboard. "Where's Norman?"

"Decided not to go." Paul climbed up to the wheel.

"This is important! How can he just decide not to go?"

Paul looked down the ladder at the man. "I don't have any say in the matter. You don't like it, call him and tell him to get his ass down here."

Standing there, Paul waited while the man did indeed call and then waited while the two men argued on the phone. Finally, the man ended the call and looked up at Paul. "Let's go."

Paul nodded and started the engines. Waiting while the man freed the ropes to the dock and then jump back on board, Paul wondered how easy it would be to dump the guy overboard after the shipment was stowed away. He was younger. Stronger. Tougher. He could do it easy enough. One well-placed shove and oops. So sorry.

Revving the engines, he slowly pulled away from the dock. He'd made this trip many times, picking up shipments of guns, ammunition, and drugs, so he knew the route. Still, he kept a sharp eye on the buoys, the lights, and other fishing vessels heading out for a day of fishing.

A small plane buzzed over the harbor and then headed off to the East and Fort McHenry. Tourists maybe, although it was a bit early for it. The sun wasn't even up yet and wouldn't be for another hour.

Turning south, Paul pushed the engines a little more, picking up speed now that he was out of the harbor. The wind picked up, snapping at the flag flying on one of the masts. The bay was choppy, but the fishing boat plowed through them.

"Paul?" His dad's partner climbed up the ladder to stand behind him, interrupting Paul's peace and quiet.

"What?"

"Doesn't it seem as though there's more traffic out here this morning than there usually is?"

Paul shrugged. "It always picks up the further we get into Spring."

"I don't know. It doesn't feel right."

"You were supposed to make sure that the task force was busy chasing their tails."

"They are."

"Then don't sweat it. It's not like we can change anything now."

"Well, I want to keep a sharp eye on those boats out here. Where are the binoculars?"

Monday, 6:30 am
Paul's residence, Baltimore, Md.

Andrea had searched the bedroom trying to find something to use as a tool, but so far, nothing. Her dad would be leaving soon and she had to stop him somehow. She'd thought about just breaking a window, but that would just bring him running with a belt. She thought about calling the police, but her dad wasn't wanted for anything, he was out on parole, and with everything that had been happening to her lately, they'd probably just laugh with Norman about how crazy she was before leaving her here. And then Norman would *really* be mad that she dared called the police.

She pulled out Steven's phone and stared at it a moment. There wasn't much power left and she had no way of recharging it. Well, it was worth trying again. Nick's phone went straight to voice mail so she didn't waste time leaving a message. She went to Conner next and luckily, he answered.

"Steven?"

"No, this is Andrea. Please listen to me, okay? Please? I don't have much time. My dad found my mom. He's going after her. He has me locked upstairs in this bedroom, but I've got to stop him. He's going to hurt her. Please, please help me get out of here. Just get me out, that's all. I'll stop him somehow, but please don't let him do this to her. He's going to be leaving soon and once he goes, I won't be able to stop him. Please, Conner, please. I don't know what else to do."

She listened to the silence and thought for a second that the phone had died. Then she heard Conner. "Hold on a sec."

Pacing in front of the window, she stared down at Chaos who by now had caught sight of her and was sitting on the lawn, staring up at her. Poor dog. No food or water for how long? It wouldn't occur to Paul or her father to actually think the animal might be suffering.

"Andrea? We'll be there in about twenty minutes, but how are you going to stop him?"

"If my mom knows I'm free, I can convince her to run again. But she won't as long as she thinks he has me and will continue to hurt me."

"So all you want is for us to escort you out of that house and then we can get back here, probably before anyone really misses us."

"Yes!"

"Okay, Rafe and I are on our way."

"Thank you, thank you."

Andrea tried once again to remember her mother's phone number. This was the problem with having numbers stored in a cell phone. You never actually get around to memorizing them. She needed her own cell phone but it was downstairs on the coffee table.

She walked over to the window and stared out. Then she saw her dad stroll out the front door. Chaos walked over to him, but Norman just kicked the dog. Andrea gasped and it was as if Norman actually heard her because he lifted his head, looking up at the window and waved at her.

"No!" She slapped at the glass. It was too late. He was leaving and would be long gone before Conner got here. Without a vehicle, she had no way of going after him. Think. Think. Maybe she could convince Conner to drop her off at her house so she could get her car! *Right*. She lived more than half an hour from here in the opposite direction.

Conner had made it clear that he couldn't waste a lot of time on this.

Sliding down the wall, she collapsed on the floor in a puddle of tears and self-pity. After all the years of hiding and looking over their shoulders, it was all for nothing. He'd found her mom and now her mom was going to get hurt for daring to divorce him, run from him, hide from him. He'd never let her go now. Never. Not until she was dead.

Chaos barked again. Andrea pulled herself up off the floor and looked down at him. He was upset now. He didn't understand why she wasn't letting him in or coming out to him. "I wish I could, boy. Just hold on. Help is coming."

Monday 6:45 am
En route to Paul's residence, Baltimore, Md

"Explain to me why we're doing this?" Rafe asked as he charged his tazer.

"We all thought Norman was going to be on that ship this morning. He wasn't. If we could have gotten in touch with Nick and Chamberland, and they knew Rotterbach was going after Andrea's mother, they would have told us to go help. It's going to be several more hours before Paul brings that shipment back. The ATF has the dock sealed up. We'd just be sitting on that boat, swabbing decks and walking planks."

Rafe chuckled. "Swabbing decks and walking planks? It's not a pirate ship, Conn."

Grinning, Conner hit the turn signal and slowed down for a turn. "You get my drift. We were close enough to the Lady to confirm the identity of the two men that boarded her and took her out. Job done. Besides, that constant motion under my feet was starting to get to me."

"So, you were bored and needed some action."

"Oh, like you were a tough nut to convince to come along. Admit it, you hated the idea of sitting on that boat pretending to be hard at work for the next five hours as much as I did."

"No argument from me on that one. If I had to scrape any more salt off that railing I was going to mutiny."

Conner made another turn and slowed down. "Okay, this is the street Nick wrote down, but I don't remember the house number."

"Nice of you to mention that now. We could be driving up and down this street all day."

Conner checked out every house on the left while Rafe did the same on the right. Half way down the block, Rafe said, "Stop. Look at that dog. Barking up at that window."

Conner pulled over to the curb, bending down low so that he could look up through the windshield. "That's Andrea at the window. Let's go."

Rafe ran across the yard to a spot just below the window. "Is he here?" he yelled up to her. She shook her head.

"We're good to go in. He's already left."

It took two kicks with Conner's massive legs to bust the front door and get into the house. They found the key to lock on Andrea's door hanging on a nail next to the door.

"Thank you!" she cried, grabbing Conner in a lung crushing hug. At least, for most people it would have hindered their breathing. Conner barely felt it.

"Okay, how long ago did he leave?"

"Maybe ten minutes." She swiped at her tears and then she saw the dog in the hall. "Chaos!" She dropped to her knees and the dog rushed to her, licking her face and wagging its tail furiously.

"Well, now we know why the dog was at the window." Rafe nudged Conner. "What are we going to do? If we just leave her here, it doesn't help her mother."

"You voting we go after this guy?"

"I'm voting to go rescue the mother."

"Same thing." Conner ran a hand over his bald head. "Problem is, we have no jurisdiction."

"He's on parole, right?" Andrea slowly stood up. "He's going to cross the state line to get to my mom. Doesn't that make him a fugitive?"

"Well, it doesn't make him a fugitive, but it does mean he'd be in violation of parole and that would give us some leeway. Let's go. He's got a head start on us." Conner raced down the stairs with Andrea.

"Wait!" Rafe called out as he ran down after him. "Where are we going?"

"Lancaster, Pennsylvania," Andrea called over her shoulder.

"Okay. That's better than Chicago."

Monday, 7:05 am
Task Force Headquarters, Baltimore

ATF Agent Chip Averton sauntered into the office, nodding to some of the task force members, sipping on his Starbucks. He hated being left out of the action, but he understood how important it was that no one in law enforcement suspected that anything was up. That meant sitting at his desk, fielding phone calls, pretending to be on the phone with Chamberland from time to time.

He would spend the next few hours attending meetings, keeping his ears open for any buzz that meant someone had caught on, and making note of who was there and who wasn't.

It was going to be a long, boring day. Opening a file folder, he tried to concentrate on actually reading it. Chamberland's phone rang and it took Chip a second to realize he needed to answer it. He punched the button to connect to Chamberland's line and picked it up. "Agent Chamberland's desk."

"Where is he?" It was the police chief.

"Out running down some leads, Sir."

"In my office. Now."

"Yes, Sir." Chip slowly set the receiver down. Uh-oh. This didn't sound good.

Leaving his coffee behind, he made his way upstairs. Knocking on the Chief's door, he waited a second and then eased the door open.

"Come in, come in."

Chip stepped in and closed the door behind him. "You wanted to see me, Sir?"

"Where is Chamberland?"

"I explained, Sir. He's out running down some leads."

"Then why isn't he answering his cell phone?"

"I can't say for sure, Sir. Could be he's out of cell range. Could be he has it turned off in case the ringing alert someone to his presence."

"Could be he's about to arrest one or more of my men," the Chief narrowed his eyes, glaring at Chip. "You better understand something, Agent. I don't care if you are the Feds, the Dallas Cowboys, or the entire Democratic Party. This is my department and these are my men. If one or more of them is involved in criminal activities, I want to know about it. I don't want to be blindsided by the press when all hell breaks loose and I'm left standing around wondering what happened." He stood up and walked around his desk.

"I don't like looking like a fool and I don't appreciate being made to look stupid, do you understand me, Agent?"

"Yes, Sir."

"So, I suggest you open that mouth of yours and say something other than, yes, sir."

"Sir, I'm not at liberty to speak." Chip met the Chief stare for stare, glare for glare.

"Then you better find the liberty."

Chip hesitated a moment and then decided to pass the ball. He pulled out his cell phone and called Benedict. "Sir, we have a problem."

Monday, 8:15 am
Lancaster, Pennsylvania

Conner slowed down behind a horse and buggy. Any other time and he'd enjoy the sight of endless corn fields, horses and carriages and bonnets and straw hats, but not today. Luckily, the horse and buggy went straight and Conner was able to turn left and pick up speed again.

Rafe was in the passenger seat, strapping on his Kevlar vest. Andrea was in the back seat, sitting in the middle and leaning forward between the front seats, giving Conner directions.

"How much further?" Rafe asked.

"Just a couple minutes." Andrea responded. "Left at this next light and then the first right. It's a gravel road and tucked between two farms is a blue mobile home with a white door. It's the only one around here, so you can't miss it."

"What is your father driving?" Conner asked as he made the left at the light.

"Paul's Taurus. It's Silver."

They all saw it before they saw the mobile home. Two police cars and an ambulance.

"No!" Andrea screamed, scooting across to the door. She tried to open it before Conner had stopped the SUV. She kept screaming and yanking on the car door, but Conner waited until he stopped the vehicle in front of the driveway before he unlocked the doors. Andrea half-stumbled, half-tumbled out of the SUV, then started running. Leaving the keys in the ignition, Conner pulled out his badge and exited with Rafe, following Andrea at a quick jog across the lawn.

A police officer grabbed Andrea by the waist, hauling her back as she tried to fight her way into the house. "Mom!" she screamed.

The dog started barking furiously and at one word from Andrea, sat down.

Another officer stepped out of the home and looked at first at Andrea and then at Conner and Rafe. He must have decided that Conner looked like the authority in the group because he came down off the porch and walked over to Conn.

"Lt. Weber, Lancaster County Police. And you are?"

"Matt Conner, Prodigal Bail and Recovery. This young woman's father is a parolee and she feared he was coming here to hurt her mother."

"She was right," the officer said, removing his cap and combing through brown and gray hair before replacing it. "Can you tell me the name of your parolee?"

So, the officer assumed that Prodigal had paper on Rotterbach. No point in correcting him. "Norman Rotterbach. Released last night from Hagerstown Correctional. How bad is the mother hurt?"

Andrea ceased struggling and stood silently waiting for the officer's answer.

"Oh, the woman is fine. Mr. Rotterbach, however, is dead."

Andrea sank to the ground. Rafe knelt down and wrapped an arm around her shoulder.

"What happened?" Conn asked.

Lt. Weber looked over his shoulder at the home. "He came busting through the front door with a baseball bat. She must have been expecting him because she shot him twice before he was more than about five feet through the door. She's fine. Shaken up, but that's to be expected."

"Can Andrea see her mother?"

"Don't see why not. She's out back on the deck." Weber nodded to one of the officers who stepped back to allow Andrea to go running around the home.

"If you'll excuse me," Weber nodded and strode off.

"Wow," Rafe muttered. "Not quite the ending we were expecting.

"No, it isn't, is it?" Conn nodded to the police officer on the porch and followed Andrea around to the rear of the home.

He found Andrea on the deck, kneeling at the feet of a tiny woman wearing a pale pink sweat suit and white sneakers. She was bent over Andrea, her arms wrapped around Andrea's shoulders. She didn't lift her head when Conner stepped up on the deck and glanced through the sliding glass doors where he had an unobstructed view of the living room where Rotterback was stretched out, face down and two techs were kneeling next to him, one taking pictures.

Rafe stepped up next to him. "What?"

"Nothing. Just thinking."

"About?"

Conner shook his head. Then he turned to Andrea's mother. "Will she be all right here with you? We have to get back."

The woman lifted her head, eyes red. He nearly stepped back when he saw her face. Her nose was bent from having been broken. Her jaw was crooked—also from being broken—and a scar ran from her temple to the corner of her mouth. There was no doubt this woman had been beaten on numerous occasions and from the dark, haunted look in her eyes, was still feeling the pain.

"She'll be all right."

Conn nodded. "Do you need anything?"

Andrea's mother shook her head slowly. "We'll be just fine."

Conner touched Rafe's arm and they walked back to their SUV. Rafe pulled off his vest and tossed it in the backseat. "You gonna tell me what was going on up there on the deck?"

"When?"

"She never even said thank you."

"You can't expect her to, Rafe. You saw her face. And that's probably not even half the story. She doesn't trust men and she won't rely on one. She definitely won't be beholding to one. She and Andrea will take care of each other."

Rafe buckled his seat belt as Conner started the engine and backed up to turn around. "I figured he'd come here and beat her. I didn't expect him to go busting through the front door with a baseball bat."

"I don't think he did."

"What?"

Conner stopped at the intersection and it took him a minute to remember which way to turn to go back. He reached over on the dash and turned on the GPS and programmed it to lead them home. "A baseball bat? It doesn't fly, Rafe."

"Why?"

"Where did he get it? Andrea never mentioned him leaving the house with a baseball bat and she would have. She was begging us all the way here to believe that her dad was a dangerous man and her mother's life was in danger. If he'd had a bat, she would have been telling us that every five miles the whole way."

Rafe fell silent, staring out the passenger window. "So you think the woman killed him and threw the bat down, telling the police that it was his?"

"That's my take on it. I could be wrong, but I don't think so. And she was too calm. Way too calm. She knew he was coming and she was resolved to do what she had to do to survive. He came through that door and she fired. Never thought twice about it."

"Well, I may have to repent for this, but that's for Weber and his team to figure out. Personally, I hope the woman gets some peace in her life. I'm certainly not going to be crying any tears for Rotterbach."

Conner glanced over at Rafe. "We need to call in and let everyone know that Rotterbach won't be showing up for his share of the take."

Chapter 23

Monday, 10:30 am
Out over the Chesapeake Bay

Marti raised her binoculars and scanned the water again. The Baltimore Lady was definitely slowing down. "Something's happening," she told Lisa.

Lisa lifted her binoculars and looked. "But there's no other ship nearby."

"Yet," Marti added, scanning the bay. She could see Chamberland's boat off in the distance, looking every bit the fishing vessel she was supposed to be—lines in the water, agents in flannel and baseball caps manning the poles.

"I see something," Lisa said, shifting in her seat. "Can you go around again, but this time, a little to the southeast."

The pilot complied, banking the plane softly. The morning sun bounced off the wing, momentarily blinding Marti. When it cleared, she tried to locate the Lady again. From that center point, she began to sweep to the south. On the third sweep, she picked up the sight of a yacht moving northeast. "The yacht?"

"Yeah. Look at it. It's heading straight for the Lady."

"We've got another problem," Marti stated, pulling away from the window. "They've got a spotter and they're locked on to us."

Lisa moved away from the window. "I saw that." She turned to the pilot. "Continue southeast, get us away from here without looking obvious about it."

He nodded.

Lisa grabbed her radio and called Chamberland. "We were spotted. We had to bug out for a while. Keep an eye on the yacht approaching. Over."

"Affirmative. Over."

Monday, 11:00 am
On the Chesapeake Bay

Chamberland ducked down into the galley. "You getting a good view?" he asked Nick.

"Perfect. I've counted five crates so far. They're taking them down in the hold of the Lady."

Chamberland sat down. "And it's all on tape?"

"Yes." Nick looked up from the camera. "What about Lisa and Marti?"

"They've moved north and will be waiting to follow him on the way back."

Nick stared at him for a long moment. "Okay, Chamberland. What are you not telling me?"

"Your men went after Rotterbach. He's dead."

"My men killed Rotterbach? No way."

Chamberland had to admire the loyalty that ran deep with these men. No question. No second thoughts. They just trusted each other to never fail one another. More like brothers than co-workers. "No. Rotterbach's ex-wife killed him when he broke into her house. Your men just happened to be a few minutes behind him with Andrea."

"Where are they now?"

"I'm not sure. They were on their way back to the harbor when they contacted Lisa." Chamberland knelt down and when Nick moved aside, looked through the lens. "They're leaving." He hurried back up on deck.

Nick continued to man the video camera until the Baltimore Lady turned and headed back up the Bay. He turned it off and followed Chamberland.

Up on deck, the men had stowed away the fishing rods and although they were mingling around on deck like a bunch of sports fishermen that just caught the big one, there was a tension that was hard to miss. Chamberland must have gone up to the wheel to get a better view because he was nowhere to be seen.

Looking out across the bay, Nick watched a tanker moving slow and low in the water in the middle of the shipping lane.

Suddenly the boat lurched, bucking like a bull under spurs. Nick grabbed a railing and looked up where Chamberland was climbing down. "Someone's in the water. One of the men on the Baltimore Lady was just shot and thrown overboard."

"Any idea who?"

"Too far away to be sure."

Nick leaned over the railing, trying to get see the body in the water. The Baltimore Lady had picked up speed, heading north toward the harbor. The way she was laying a wake behind her, whoever was behind the wheel was pushing her for all she was worth.

He saw the man in the water, floating face up in the water and he could just make out the dark stain on the chest. Nick propped a foot on the side of the boat and unlaced his boot.

"What are you doing?" Chamberland asked.

"Going in after him."

"Do you have any idea how cold that water is?"

"Just make sure I don't have to stay in very long." He untied the other boot and yanked them both off. Then he unzipped his coat and slipped it off. As they came alongside the body, Nick dived over the side.

The water wasn't just cold. It was wicked frigid and the moment his body went under, it stole his breath away. He hit the surface gasping and tried to ignore the waves coming down over his face as he swam over to the man. As he got within a few feet, he recognized Paul. He didn't know if the man was alive or not, but he had to try.

Grabbing Paul under the arm, he started to swim and drag back to Chamberland's boat which had come around and was now idling close by. Chamberland and two other men were leaning over the rail, ready to help and a fourth was tossing a preserver ring over to him.

Nick started to feel lethargic, heavy in the water and he couldn't feel his toes anymore. He grabbed at the ring three times before he finally caught hold of it. The men started pulling him in and he held on but it was getting harder every second. He knew what was happening. The water temperature was probably no more than forty degrees and hypothermia was setting in.

They reached the side of the boat and Nick slowly wrapped the ring and rope around Paul's body and the men started to haul him up over the side. Hands reached out for Nick but he couldn't lift his arms high enough.

He went under and came up sputtering. He looked Chamberland in the face, saw the concern, saw his mouth moving and knew he was yelling to him, but he couldn't hear anything. There was just this rushing sound like white noise in his ears and he slowly sank below the surface again.

Monday, 11:05 am
Baltimore Central Booking and Intake, Baltimore, Md.

Steven recoiled when Lance reached over to shake his hand. He didn't want anyone close to him. He felt as though he was dirty, smelly, disgusting. Picking up his personal belongings, he followed Lance through the doors to the hallway and through the front door.

Conn and Rafe was leaning against the SUV and when they saw him, pushed off and hurried over to him. Conn swooped him up in a big hug and swung him around. "Hey, Steven! You are now officially a man."

"Yeah. Great." He said when Conner put him down. "I desperately need a shower and food. Please."

"Coming right up," Conner responded circling the SUV to get behind the wheel.

Lance leaned in the window and patted Steven on the shoulder. "I have to get back to the office, but I'll be in touch."

"Thanks, Lance. Appreciate this."

"It'll be in my bill," he said with a wink.

Lance had shown up a little after nine with the Chief of Police and Ken Benedict. They went to an interview room and talked for nearly forty-five minutes. The Chief asked him question after question and Steven answered them all. Then they led him back to his cell. He thought was the end of it until Lance returned a little before eleven to tell him all charges had been dropped and Steven was free.

As Steven reached for the seat belt he saw his cell phone tucked in the seats. He pulled it out. "How did this get here?"

Rafe looked back, saw the phone and said, "Andrea must have left that there for you." He held out his hand. "Give it to me and I'll plug it in here and charge it."

"Where is she?" Steven handed Rafe his phone.

It only took twenty minutes for Conner to drive to Steven's house and on the way, Rafe filled him in on Rotterbach's murder.

"I'm glad she's okay. And her mother. I don't know why she didn't just do what I told her to do, but it is what it is."

When they arrived at Steven's, he led the way inside. "Where's Killer?"

"Marti came and got him. Right now he's with Jenna at the office. Now put a move on it. We have to get back to the harbor before that boat returns."

Steven took a long hot shower and then shaved. Feeling almost human again, he dressed in jeans, heavy sweatshirt, and his combat boots. He stared in the mirror on his way out of the bedroom and almost didn't recognize himself. It's not that anything in particular had changed. It was that *he* had changed.

Hours and hours of staring at a ceiling, listening to the cries and threats all around him, unable to sleep—all he could do was take his life apart and put it back together again. Andrea had been one messed up lady with a lot of issues, but she had stark clarity about some things. He hoped that Andrea and her mother would get counseling and find some peace in their lives finally.

There were times where Steven couldn't understand why God had walked him into this mess and other times when he thought he had it figured out and other times when it was all one big confusing mess.

But one thing finally managed to emerge from all the inner noise. And for the first time in a very long time, Steven felt as if he were finally on the right track. He knew what he had to do. And he knew what he was going to do.

"Ready to roll?" he asked Conner and Rafe as he passed them to the front door. They were both sprawled in chairs in front of his television. Rafe grabbed the remote and turned it off as they both came rushing after him.

"Man, what happened to you? We figured you'd be another half an hour at least." Conner pulled the door closed behind them.

"I'll explain later. This isn't the time."

Monday, 11:45 am
On the Bay

Nick sat in the galley and even though the owner of the boat had given him some heavy wool socks and Chamberland gave him a pair of black ATF sweats from his gear, he still felt so cold he in spite of the blanket wrapped around him, he was shivering.

The Coast Guard had sent in a chopper with a rescue basket to lift Paul out and take him to the nearest hospital. He'd been shot, but they felt that the only reason he held on to his life was being thrown in the water. The cold had slowed down Paul's heart rate and may have saved his life. They offered to take Nick to the hospital as well, but he refused. He was cold but he didn't need medical care.

Now they were speeding back toward the harbor, trying to catch up to the Baltimore Lady before she docked. They knew the team on the dock would prevent the shipment for disappearing before they got there, but there was always the slim possibility that it wasn't headed to Baltimore. There were other docks and harbors just as capable of handle a vessel the size of the Lady. Chamberland had Lisa and Marti looking for the Lady and once they had her, Nick could relax.

Until then, the Lady and the shipment were gone.

Chapter 24

Monday, 1:15 pm
Baltimore Harbor

Steven felt about ten thousand percent better than he had in days. Maybe months. His body was clean, his face was shaved, his stomach was full, and the sun was shining on his face. Okay, he wasn't exactly thrilled with the boat swaying beneath his feet, but it wasn't that big a deal.

"We're supposed to be cleaning this thing?" Steven asked as he looked around. It didn't look like it had seen soap and water in years.

"It's a fishing boat, Steven. Not a charter vessel or a cruise ship." Conner laughed as he looked around. "She has . . . character."

"She has rust and barnacles. Please tell me we aren't expected to clean those off."

"Nah. Mostly we're just supposed to look like we're cleaning when the Lady comes in." Rafe slapped him on the back. "Now aren't you sorry you didn't get to stay in that cell a few more hours?"

Steven braced himself on the railing and leaned over the side, staring down at the water below and then to the harbor before him. No, he wasn't sorry he wasn't still in his cell. He'd been a cell for years, he just hadn't known it. How was it that a person could fool themselves into thinking they were on the right path? Doing the right thing? Or that they were happy only to wake up one day and realize that they'd been sleepwalking?

In some respects, his life lately hadn't been much different than his mother's. She was lost in an Alzheimer's maze of old memories and illusions while he had been lost in a misguided maze of old expectations and obligations. And now that he knew what he'd been doing wrong, he had to figure out how to do it right.

"Ahoy, the Baltimore Lady approaching to starboard, maties." Rafe grabbed a mop and started pushing it around. Conner grabbed a rag and started going over the railing. Steven wasn't quite sure what to do, but he picked up a bucket and ducked behind a stack of crab traps.

The tension mounted and he couldn't help feeling it sweep him along. It seemed to take forever for the boat to pull up to dock and cut her engines. Steven saw the man at the wheel call out to Conner to help tie her to the dock and Conn ran to help.

But where was Paul?

And then everything started to go wrong. Steven looked up at the man coming down from the wheel and realized he knew this man. Had met him several times. He wasn't just a cop. He was Captain Summerfield.

And then Summerfield saw him and the recognition registered as shock on his face. He jumped off the boat and started running which surprised everyone. Steven took off after him, jumping from the boat to the dock in one easy movement. ATF agents stepped out from behind vehicles, crates, and cargo containers. Summerfield pulled out a gun and started shooting at the agents. A young woman stepped out of the hold of a ski boat, most likely curious about all the commotion. Summerfield jumped on board her boat and grabbed her, holding her in front of him as a shield.

"Don't come any closer!" he yelled in warning.

He backed up toward the wheel and ordered the woman to start the engines. With wide eyes and shaking hands, she complied. Then he looked up at Steven. "Untie her. Now."

Steven unwound the rope and tossed it into the boat. "You can't get away, Summerfield. It's over."

He shook his head. "I can't, Shepherd. You know what they'd do to me?" He stepped back and ordered the woman to throttle up and pull away from the dock.

Steven ran and jumped on board as it pulled away. Summerfield kept the gun aimed at Steven and the woman in front of him as she drove. Steven stood up and raised his hands. "I'm not even armed, Summerfield. But I can't let you hurt the woman. She doesn't deserve that."

"I'll let her go when I get where I need to go."

"And where do you expect to go? See that place up there? Didn't you notice that it's been shadowing you all day? And that boat over there. Didn't you notice it following you? Everything you did was under the watchful eye of the ATF. They knew everything all along. They set the trap and you stepped into it. There's no way out now."

Summerfield glanced up at the plane and then over at the boat. "They better keep their distance if they want you and this woman to live."

Steven slowly lowered his hands. When the boat lurched, he grabbed a rail and then slowly sat down on one of the benches running down the side. "And what do you expect to happen here today? That they're just going to let you sail off into the sunset? It's over. Put the gun down."

"I did everything I could to get them to believe you had killed Ryan."

"I know," Steven replied, trying to keep his voice even, soothing. "But in the end, the evidence just didn't add up. Too many inconsistencies. It raised enough questions that they had to keep digging."

"Only because Tony and Phil were idiots. If they'd just done what I told them to do in the first place, it would have been fine."

Steven shrugged. "We can't change the past now. All we can do is walk out the future. The way you're going now; it can't end well. You know that."

They were out in the middle of the bay now, a good mile or more from the harbor. The ski boat was capable of moving through the water far faster than the shipping vessels and Steven wasn't sure how anyone was going to get to them. It was all going to fall on him.

The woman was still shaking, her eyes darting from Summerfield's gun to his face to Steven. She was placing all her hopes on him and he wanted to let her know that his track record at saving people wasn't that good. She'd have better odds jumping into the water and swimming for shore.

"Make for Annapolis," Summerfield told her.

She nodded, keeping both hands on the wheel.

The Summerfield raised the gun at Steven. "Over."

"What?"

"Jump. Out. Now. Or I'll shoot you and throw you over."

Steven shook his head. "I won't last fifteen minutes in that water. It's too cold."

"Not my problem, Shepherd."

"Wait until we're a little closer to shore. Give me half a chance. We'll be pulling into Annapolis in a few minutes. I'll go over the side, you go on in and dock. No way I can swim to shore in time to stop you, but at least I have a shot at living another day."

Summerfield glanced over at the harbor coming into view. Steven needed every minute he could wrestle from the cop. The man was irrational now, watching all his plans, not to mention all that money, go up in flames. The shipment was lost to him. The ATF knew who he was. He had nothing to lose now and men with nothing to lose were very dangerous. You couldn't count on them to listen to reason.

"I was almost there. I suppose Norman has already been arrested."

"He's dead."

Summerfield stared at him for a moment and then laughed. "And so is his son. He thought he could kill me and toss me overboard. I showed him. I shot him and he fell into the water. I just left him there. Let the fish have at him."

"So Paul is dead. Just like everyone else involved in this, right? You got rid of them all one by one."

Summerfield almost seemed lethargic as he turned his gaze to Steven. His eyes were just dead pools of brown. No life. No passion. No fear. "It was getting too complicated. We just had one more big shipment. It was the biggest of them all and it would have set Norm and I up for life."

"How did you get involved with Rotterbach?"

"His son, Paul. I didn't know who he was the time. He found out about a woman I was seeing. She was young. He had pictures. I thought he was going to blackmail me for money, you know? But he had a proposition for me instead. Grease the wheels to get his father out early. Make sure everyone was looking the other way when the shipments came in and I got a third of the take. It was easy money."

Summerfield looked over at the harbor again. He waved the gun. "Time to go, Shepherd."

Steven looked over at the harbor of Annapolis. There were so many places that Summerfield could pull in and no one would see him. He could slip away and be gone before Steven even reached shore.

"Promise me you'll let the woman go. Don't take her with you. She doesn't deserve this."

"You expect me to make you a promise?" Summerfield snorted. "Get off this boat. Now."

Steven nodded as he stood up. "Good luck, Summerfield. You're going to need it."

"Not as much as you will."

Steven glanced over at the woman and then dived over the side of the boat.

Monday, 1:45 pm
Annapolis, Md

Rafe wanted to laugh when Conner grabbed the dashboard as Rafe took a corner too sharp and he would have if things weren't so serious.

"Killing us won't help." Conner growled.

"Don't worry about my driving. What is Steven saying now?"

Conner shook his head, pressing his cell phone against his ear a little harder as if it would help. "There's nothing at all. I think Steven went into the bay."

"Not good, not good. The Coast Guard better get there in time or I'll strip their hides."

Conner had been standing on the dock, watching Steven and Summerfield motor off into the bay when his cell phone rang. He almost didn't answer it but when he saw it was Steven's cell, he flipped it open. Smart Steven. It gave them an open line to everything that was being said on the boat. And as soon as they heard Annapolis mentioned, everyone had scrambled. One team had been left on the Baltimore Lady to keep the shipment secure while everyone else raced to Annapolis.

Nick was close enough to shore for Rafe to call him on his cell and let him know what had happened. They were still on the boat, moving at top speed toward Annapolis.

And it was Chamberland that said for Rafe to call the Coast Guard and have them secure the harbor.

The problem now was that there were so many places for him to pull in and get off that boat. The most likely spot was going to be Eastport, across from the Annapolis Naval Academy, but he could easily slip into Back Creek and pick any one of dozens of small marinas to hide in.

Rafe's phone rang as they came off the Randall Street roundabout and onto Compromise Street, heading for the 6th Street Bridge. "Yello."

"Rafe? It's Nick. Marti says she has Summerfield in view. He's heading for the marina near Spa Creek at the base of the 6th Street Bridge."

"Got it. We're minutes out."

"Minutes is about all you have."

"What about Steven?"

"A pleasure craft picked him up. You just get down there and get Summerfield. Is ATF still right behind you?"

Rafe glanced in the rearview mirror. Four black SUV's with lights blazing were behind him in addition to the one he was following. "Affirmative. Did Chamberland notify his lead where we're going?"

"Yes."

Rafe hung up as he went back to concentrating on keeping up with SUV in front of him. He wanted to yell at them to go faster, but he knew they were going as fast as they could through the traffic.

It seemed more like hours than minutes before they made it down to the marina. Now, where was Summerfield? SUV's parked helter-skelter all over the area and men in black were racing around, guns drawn, looking for Summerfield. Rafe stayed close to the man with the radio to their eyes in the skies.

It was Conner that spotted Summerfield, strolling down one of the docks, hands in his pockets, a baseball cap low over his face, trying to look like he belonged there. Tapping Rafe on the shoulder, he gave him a signal. Rafe glanced over and away, not drawing Summerfield's attention. They split off from the ATF and started moving toward Summerfield, hoping he didn't recognize them too soon.

Conner grabbed a fishing pole leaning against a railing and slung it over his shoulder. It wasn't a bad prop but Rafe wasn't sure it would help. Conner was a hard man to miss between his height, his bulk, and his bald head.

They were about twenty feet away from Summerfield when he spotted them. He sprinted off away from them. Conner tossed the fishing pole and took off after Summerfield with Rafe right on his heels. The sight of three men running drew the attention of the rest of the ATF agents and they moved to cut Summerfield off.

Summerfield darted off to the right and tried to disappear into a parking lot. Conner lunged, grabbing Summerfield by his collar. It brought the man up short. He swung out at Conner, but it was more like a butterfly swatting at a bear.

Conner flipped the man down face first onto the pavement and knelt down, pressing his knee into Summerfield's back.

Within minutes, ATF agents had Summerfield in cuffs.

Conner stepped back, letting the agents take Summerfield into custody. "We should check on that woman. Make sure she's okay," he told Rafe.

They walked back down the marina and found the woman sitting in her boat, arms wrapped around her waist, staring out across the water. Rafe took the lead, stepping down into the boat first. "Are you okay, Ma'am? He's been arrested and can't hurt you anymore."

She lifted her face and brushed back the hair from her face. The wind just tossed it back again. "I'll be fine. The man that went over. Did they find him? Did he make it?"

"He's fine. Another boat picked him up."

She reached over and picked up Steven's phone. She stared at it for a second and then held it out to Rafe. "Tell him thank you. From the bottom of my heart. I didn't realize what he was doing until he went over and I saw the phone tucked there in the seat. It gave me hope. I want him to know how much I appreciate that."

"I'll tell him. Are you sure you'll be okay?"

She gave him a watery smile. "I'll be fine."

Rafe nodded and stepped back to the dock.

"Excuse me."

Rafe looked back over at her. "Yes?"

"What was his name? The man that helped me. Who was he?"

"His name is Steven Shepherd. He's a bounty hunter with Prodigal Bail and Recovery."

Chapter 25

Monday, 4:10 pm
Prodigal Offices, Baltimore, Md

Steven picked at the cake Jenna had served when everyone had gathered back at the office. It was supposed to be the celebration at his release from Intake, but he didn't feel much like celebrating.

After his dunking in the cold bay waters, he'd gone home and taken another hot shower, changed clothes and headed back over to the offices to talk to Nick. Only to find that everyone was celebrating—the case was closed, Steven was free, Summerfield was in jail, and the shipment of guns and ammo had been confiscated by the ATF and headed for destruction. All was well with the world.

At least everyone thought so. Krystal came up behind him and wrapped her arms around his neck. "I'm so glad you're home, Uncle Steven. I knew they'd have to let you go."

"Thanks, sweetheart. It's good to be home."

She kissed his cheek and then hurried off for more cake.

Nick stood up and looked over at Jessica. She just smiled at him. He cleared his throat and everyone looked over at him. "I was going to wait on this but it seems like a good time for celebrations. I just want to let you all know that Jess and I are going to be parents again."

The room erupted into squeals from the girls and jokes from the men. Everyone was hugging and laughing. Steven hugged Jessica and congratulated Nick. Then he slipped out of the room. Stepping outside, he shoved his hands in his pockets.

"You want to talk?" Nick stepped out and zipped up his jacket.

"I'm not sure I know how yet."

"Oh, I don't know, how about, well, Nick, it's like this . . ."

Steven smiled and stared out across the parking lot. He missed his car. Wonder how long before he could get it released from the police? And then he had to get it fixed.

Nick dropped an arm across Steven's shoulders. "Is this about being in jail? I know it can be a real experience."

Steven shook his head. "Not exactly." He took a deep breath and then blew it out. "I'm quitting."

"Quitting what?"

"Quitting the company."

Nick stepped back and stared hard at him. "Explain that."

"I don't know if I can. I just know that I finally realized that this is not what I want to be doing with my life. I do it, but I don't enjoy it."

"Well, I could have told you that, little brother."

"Why didn't you?"

"Because even if this isn't what you're cut out for, you didn't seem to know what you wanted to do. You were always changing your majors in school. Always changing your mind about women. You just seem to be drifting around, trying to find something and I figured working here was better than no direction at all."

Steven sat down on the brick wall that lined the back steps. "I've been miserable. Well, maybe not miserable, but not happy."

"Okay, so what are you going to do?"

"I think I'm going to take my degrees and go into accounting and finance management. I'll find me an office somewhere, hang out my shingle and hope for the best."

Nick looked up toward the roof of the building. "Well, last time I checked, we have an empty office upstairs. Why don't you fix that up and hang up your shingle right outside the front door. And we can be your first clients. You can keep track of our books and file our taxes and do all that accounting stuff that Jenna and I dread doing."

"Seriously?"

"Seriously. Of course, eventually you'll have to pay rent, so you'll have to get yourself some good clients. We're not exactly in the low rent district around here."

Steven looked hard at Nick, trying to see some amusement in his face but it wasn't there. "You're really okay with this."

"I really am. Steven, all I've ever wanted is for you to be happy." Nick stepped closer and lightly punched Steven in the shoulder. "And frankly, I'm happy you don't want to be a bounty hunter. You really weren't that good at it."

They both laughed and then Steven reached over and slapped Nick on the back. "Thanks."

"Welcome. Now let's get back inside before the entire party moves out here."

When they returned to Nick's office, they found Chamberland there with two of his agents. Introductions were made all around, but Steven only heard one name that mattered. Lisa Somers.

She was tall, thin, and gorgeous with a spark in her eyes that held both intelligence and humor. Her voice was low and husky, almost as if it held secrets that he wanted to slowly discover. And he loved the way she made him feel like an overeager teenager.

He walked over to her and took her hand. "I think I'm in love."

She smiled. Then laughed. Then tucked her arm in his. "Well, I can't say I wasn't warned."

"What?" he asked, thoroughly confused and befuddled.

"Never mind. Why don't we just slip away and have a nice dinner somewhere?"

"Do you like seafood?"

"Adore it."

Steven led her out of the office, ignoring the gaping stares of everyone. Maybe he looked like a fool, but he felt great. "I know this little place run by a Greek couple and they do the most wonderful things with lobster and shrimp."

Lisa looked over at Chamberland. "Don't wait up for me."

Chapter 26

Tuesday, 5:30 am
Prodigal Offices, Baltimore

Marti cleared the history off her computer and then shut it down. Going through the files, she made sure that everything was clean before straightening her desk and grabbing her coat. She was almost to the door when she turned around and walked into Nick's office. She pulled out her keys and set them down next to his phone.

Outside, she folded herself in the waiting taxi. "Now to BWI, please."

"Yes, Ma'am."

There was an urge to cry but she didn't allow herself the luxury. The last time she left town, she hadn't cried either. But she'd only been seventeen then and anxious to get away from the pain. Little did she know that she'd only run headlong into more.

As they neared BWI airport, she watched the planes coming and going overhead. People off to visit relatives, businesspeople off to meetings, others off to vacations, conventions, adventures. Everyone rushing off to somewhere. Were any of them as anxious and as reluctant as she was?

"Which airline?" the driver asked.

"United."

He merely nodded and left her to her thoughts. She tried to tell herself it was the perfect time. Steven was out of jail, Nick and the team were back to taking care of fugitives, Chamberland was off on another ATF investigation, and she wasn't really needed.

Thoughts of Nick led to thoughts of Jessica. Another baby. What a shock that was. At the same time, she was thrilled for Nick and Jess. She wasn't sure how Krystal was going to react to a new baby in the house, but she'd probably love it. Especially if it was a boy—a Shepherd male she could boss around.

Marti was still smiling when she realized the driver had stopped. She checked the meter and pulled out her wallet. After paying the fare, she climbed out of the taxi and stood by patiently as the driver pulled her one carry-on bag out of the trunk.

"Thanks," she said when he pulled out the handle and handed it to her.

Wheeling it through the airport, heading for security, she second-guessed herself again. Why couldn't she just settle in her mind that she'd go to Winston-Salem, settle things and then return? Why did she feel as if she were running away again? Why did coming back feel like one of those *maybe one day* things?

She was standing in line for security when she looked up and realized Nick was standing there scowling, arms folded across his chest.

"What are you doing here?" she asked, trying not to feel like a kid that just got caught sneaking out the window on a school night.

"Where are you going, Marti?"

"I have some business to take care of."

"Your business is family business, Marti. When are you going to realize that?"

The man in front of her moved forward. She stepped up. If only the line could move a little faster.

"Go home, Nick."

"Just tell me why, Marti. That's all I ask. Do you hate all of us that much?"

"I don't hate any of you, Nick. I love you. And Steven. And Krys. And don't tell her I said this, but I even like Jessica. This isn't about any of you. It's about me."

Nick stared at her a minute. "You're breaking our hearts, Sis. Don't you understand that?"

"I'm not trying to break anyone's heart. I have something I need to do. It's important to me. It's always been important to me. I warned you when I came back that I could leave again at a moment's notice. Well, the time has come. I have to go. I should have been gone days ago, but I couldn't leave until I knew Steven was out of jail and cleared of all charges."

The man in front of her looked over his shoulder at her, obviously more interested in their conversation than in minding his own business. "We're not talking to you," Marti snapped. The man turned away.

Nick moved in a little closer. "Where are you going? Can you at least tell me that much?"

She stared down at the floor and then slowly looked up at him. "North Carolina, okay? And don't ask me anything else. And don't you and the guys come charging down there looking for me, either."

"As long as I know you're okay, I won't come after you," Nick assured her. "Can't you at least call in every couple of days just to say you're fine? Leave a message on my answering machine. Send a telegram. I don't care what you do, but don't just disappear again."

She could agree to anything and everything and then not to any of it, but Nick would know if she were lying to him. He almost seemed to have some kind of radar when it came to her. "I'll call, okay?"

"How long do you think this business of yours will take?" he asked, settling in beside her and clearly not leaving until he was forced to at the security gate.

"I honestly don't know, Nick."

"Do you have enough money with you? Your cell phone?"

"Yes, Mother."

Nick's lips twitched as he fought not to smile. "You have your ATM card, right? I'll make sure Jenna deposits your paycheck in your account every Friday."

"I won't be working, so I won't be earning a paycheck," she reminded him.

"You own one-third of this business, Marti. You'll have money in your account every Friday."

She could see the Transit Authority guard checking I.D's and boarding passes coming up. She fished through her wallet and pulled out her driver's license. "You can't go any further, Nick."

He surprised her by sweeping her up in a hug and held her for a long moment. Then slowly he released her and that's when she saw the glaze in his eyes. No way. Nick Shepherd crying? Is the world coming to an end? And that brought out tears of her own. "I'll be back, ya big pain."

"Promise me, Marti."

"I'll be back, Nick. I don't know when. But I'll be back. Until then, take care of everyone for me. And don't let Steven marry Lisa next week. I think she's perfect for him, but make him wait."

Nick laughed as he wiped the moisture from his eyes. "I'm not sure Lisa is all that anxious to get involved with him."

"She fell as hard for him as he did for her. Trust me. I'm a woman. I know these things."

The man in front of her handed over his boarding pass to the guard. Marti looked up at her brother. "I love you."

"I love you, too, squirt. Don't make me hunt you down. You know what us bounty hunters always say."

Marti reached up and kissed him on the cheek. "You can run, but you can't hide."

Last Will and Testament for

Rosswell Shepherd

To my daughter, Martina Marie Shepherd: Your mother will leave you all that woman stuff—the crystal and silver and such, but I want to leave you something special. My only girl. My little princess. I didn't always understand or even do right by you, but I loved you. For you, I leave my coin collection that you might understand that the past is always with us, but it doesn't have to own us; I leave my grandmother's prayer book that you might always know where true peace comes from;

And I leave you one-third of Prodigal Fugitive Recovery Agency—use that incredible intelligence and wisdom to help everyone you love and even those you don't. Don't let your heart guide you to chase too many windmills and remember always that family is the foundation for all that you build in your life.

I hope you enjoyed Steven's story and if you haven't had a chance to read Nick's story yet, you can check out ***Shepherd's Fall*** at Amazon.com.

In the meantime, stay tuned for Marti's story- ***Shepherd's Chase*** coming December of 2015

And if you liked ***Shepherd's Run***, I hope you will go back to Amazon.com and leave a nice review.

You can find out more about all my suspense novels on my website:

www.WandaDyson.com

Abduction

Obsession

Intimidation

Retribution

The Restoration

Judgment Day

Made in the USA
Lexington, KY
15 February 2017